Keep in contact with Jessica:

jessicasorensensblog.blogspot.co.uk
Facebook/Jessica Sorensen
@jessFallenStar

Acclaim for
Jessica Sorensen's Mesmerizing Books

Nova and Quinton: No Regrets

"Totally consumed me…heart-wrenching…[Sorensen] is masterful when it comes to dealing with the hard issues life throws your way." —LiteratiBookReviews.com

"Torn, twisted, and beautiful are the best words I can use to describe this story. Jessica Sorensen has taken her talent on a new level with this one." —LittleReadRidingHood.com

"[*Nova and Quinton*] just dug into my heart…This book was more than entertainment for me; it was a lesson in life…Five stars and highly recommended!"

—TheBoyfriendBookmark.com

"This series goes down as one of my all-time favorites…It was definitely heartbreaking to read some parts, but oh so worth it… I can't recommend this enough." —TheBookHookup.com

Saving Quinton

"This story pulls at so many emotions and is written so well… I would recommend this to anyone looking for a gut-wrenching yet very realistic book full of hope and second chances."

—DarkFaerieTales.com

"*Saving Quinton* addresses intensely personal issues that will hook right into the reader's heart. As emotions take a toll, this book will have you cheering on its characters."

—UndertheCoversBookBlog.com

Breaking Nova

"*Breaking Nova* touches the heart and squeezes the most powerful emotions from your body...one of those books that pushes you to the limits and makes you feel things you never thought you would feel for characters."   —UndertheCoversBookBlog.com

"Four stars! I am committed to this series."

—SweptAwayByRomance.com

"*Breaking Nova* is one of those books that just sticks with you. I was thinking about it when I wasn't reading it, wondering what was going to happen with Nova...an all-consuming, heartbreaking story."   —BooksLiveForever.com

"Heartbreaking, soul-shattering, touching, and unforgettable...Jessica Sorenson is an amazingly talented author."

—ABookishEscape.com

The Destiny of Violet & Luke

"Gripping and heartbreaking...You will be hooked, and you won't be able to not come back."   —ReviewingRomance.com

"Sorensen's intense and realistic stories never cease to amaze me and entice my interest. She is an incredible writer as she captures the raw imperfections of the beautiful and the damned."

—TheCelebrityCafe.com

The Redemption of Callie & Kayden

"Extremely emotional and touching...It made me want to cry, and jump for joy."

—Blkosiner.blogspot.com

"I couldn't put it down. This was just as dark, beautiful, and compelling as the first [book]...Nothing short of amazing... Never have I read such emotional characters where everything that has happened to them seems so real."

—OhMyShelves.com

"A love story that will overflow your heart with hope. This series is not to be missed."

—UndertheCoversBookblog.com

The Coincidence of Callie & Kayden

"Another great story of passion, love, hope, and themes of salvation."

—BookishTemptations.com

"Romantic, suspenseful, and well written—this is a story you won't want to put down."

—*RT Book Reviews*

The Temptation of Lila and Ethan

"Sorensen has true talent to capture your attention with each word written. She is creatively talented... Through the mist of demons that consume the characters' souls, she manages to find beauty in their broken lives."

—TheCelebrityCafe.com

"An emotional, romantic, and really great contemporary romance... Lila and Ethan's story is emotionally raw, devastating, and heart wrenching."

—AlwaysYAatHeart.com

The Ever After of Ella and Micha

"This is a perfect conclusion to their story... I think Micha Scott may just be my number one book boyfriend!"

—ReviewingRomance.com

The Forever of Ella and Micha

"Breathtaking, bittersweet, and intense... Fans of *Beautiful Disaster* will love the series."

—CaffeinatedBookReviewer.com

"Powerful, sexy, emotional, and with a great message, this series is one of the best stories I've read so far."

—BookishTemptations.com

The Secret of Ella and Micha

"A beautiful love story…complicated yet gorgeous characters…I am excited to read more of her books."

—SerendipityReviews.co.uk

"A really great love story. There is something epic about it… If you haven't jumped on this new adult bandwagon, then you need to get with the program. I can see every bit of why this story has swept the nation."

—TheSweetBookShelf.com

"Absolutely loved it…This story broke my heart…I can't wait to get my hands on the next installment."

—Maryinhb.blogspot.com

"Wonderful…delightful…a powerful story of love…will make your heart swoon."

—BookswithBite.net

Nova and Quinton:
No Regrets

Also by Jessica Sorensen

The Secret of Ella and Micha

The Forever of Ella and Micha

The Temptation of Lila and Ethan

The Ever After of Ella and Micha

Lila and Ethan: Forever and Always

The Coincidence of Callie & Kayden

The Redemption of Callie & Kayden

The Destiny of Violet & Luke

Breaking Nova

Delilah: The Making of Red

Saving Quinton

Tristan: Finding Hope

Nova and Quinton: No Regrets

JESSICA SORENSEN

sphere

SPHERE

First published in Great Britain in 2015 by Sphere

Copyright © Jessica Sorensen 2014
Excerpt from *Breaking Nova* copyright © Jessica Sorensen 2013

1 3 5 7 9 10 8 6 4 2

A CIP catalogue record for this book
is available from the British Library.

ISBN 978-0-7515-5537-0

Printed and bound in Great Britain by Clays Ltd, St Ives plc

Papers used by Sphere are from well-managed forests
and other responsible sources.

MIX
Paper from
responsible sources
FSC
www.fsc.org FSC® C104740

Sphere
An imprint of
Little, Brown Book Group
100 Victoria Embankment
London EC4Y 0DY

An Hachette UK Company
www.hachette.co.uk

www.littlebrown.co.uk

For everyone who suffered loss and learned
how to live again.

Acknowledgments

A huge thanks to my agent, Erica Silverman, and my editor, Amy Pierpont. I'm forever grateful for all your help and input.

To my family, thank you for supporting me and my dream. You guys have been wonderful.

And to everyone who reads this book, an endless number of thank-yous.

Nova and Quinton: No Regrets

Prologue

December 28, the day of the funeral

Nova

It's a strange feeling, getting ready to watch someone get put under the ground into their final resting place. I've been to enough funerals to know that my senses always become hyper-aware of everything going on around me: the touch of the wind seems stronger, the sun a little more blinding, the smell of the leaves, grass, and fresh dirt overpowering. It's like my mind is reaching out and trying to grasp each aspect of the moment, when part of me wants nothing more than to forget.

I'm actually at the church earlier than I'm supposed to be and I don't even know why, other than that sitting home for a second longer just didn't seem possible. So I left the house without telling anyone and got in my cherry-red Chevy Nova, the car my dad left to me when he died, and drove it to the church where my dad's and Landon's funeral took place. And

1

in just a bit, I'll say good-bye to another person I once knew and will never see again.

Now that I'm here, staring at the brick building with a white tower pointing to the sky, I'm not sure what I should do. I'm three hours early to a funeral, which might say a lot about me. A lot of people would likely show up late, wanting to avoid death for as long as possible, but I've become so familiar with it it's unsettling.

After sitting in the car for about ten minutes, watching snowflakes fall from the sky and frost the grass and the wind-shield, I decide to take video instead. I didn't bring the fancy camera my mom gave me, but the one on my phone works and honestly I use that one a lot more because it's handy for sporadic recording, which seems to be my specialty.

I blow out a deep breath as I sit back in the seat, aim the camera at myself, and hit record. I have the screen flipped to me and my image immediately pops up. I look tired. The bags under my eyes are pretty obvious, even though I've tried to cover them up with makeup, and my brown hair wasn't being cooperative so I ended up pulling it up into a ponytail. I'm wearing a black dress and earrings and the contrast with my fair skin makes me look pallid.

"It's amazing how everything can seem so perfect one moment and then suddenly it's not. How quickly perfection can evaporate…how rare it is." I pause, gathering my thoughts. "I've seen a lot of death. More than the normal person, probably. I watched my father's life vanish in front of me within minutes. Found my boyfriend's body right after he took his own life. Too early. Too suddenly. Both of them. I never had time to prepare myself and I thought it was the worst feeling in the world. I always wondered how different it would be, if it ever happened again. If maybe the third or fourth time around, I wouldn't hurt so badly. If it'd be easier letting someone go now that I've had so much practice." I tuck a fallen strand of my bangs behind my ear and swallow the lump in my throat. "And maybe it has gotten easier...but it still hurts. I still shed tears...it's still agonizing...painful..." I trail off as a few tears slip from my eyes and roll down my cheeks. "Even now, just thinking about some of the stuff I saw...I should have stopped it...should have done things differently..." I trail off, staring at the window. "But I didn't... and now they're gone forever."

Chapter One

Two months ago...

October 30, day one in the real world

Quinton

I write until my hand hurts. Until my head is numb. It's the only outlet I have at the moment. My attempt at a replacement for the drugs I've done for years. But most days it can't fill even a small part of the void I feel inside me since I stopped pumping my body with poison, slowly killing myself. But there are a few times when it briefly instills a small amount of silence inside me, makes taking one breath, one step, one heartbeat, just a bit more bearable. And so I write, just to feel those few and far-between moments of peace.

Sometimes I feel like I've been reborn. Not in a religious way. But in the sense that it feels like part of me has died and I'm learning once again to live with the new,

5

remaining parts of me. Some of which I don't like, parts that are ugly, broken, misshapen, and don't seem to quite fit right inside me. But my therapist and drug counselor are both trying to build me back up to a person that the pieces can fit into again.

I still don't know if it's possible. If I can live with a clear head, feel the sting of every emotion, the weight of my guilt, the heaviness of each breath, the way my heart beats steadily inside my chest. I'm trying, though, and I guess that's a start. I just hope the start can turn into more, but I'm not so sure yet.

"Quinton, are you ready?" Davis Mason, the supervisor of the Belvue Rehab Facility, enters my room, rapping on the doorframe.

I glance up from my notebook and nod, releasing a nervous breath trapped inside my chest. Today is the day that I'm going back into the real world, to live with my dad, no walls around me, no restrictions. It scares the shit out of me, to be out there, free to do whatever I want, without anyone watching me, guiding me. I'll be making decisions myself and I'm not sure if I'm ready for that.

"As ready as I'll ever be, I guess," I say, shutting my notebook and tossing it into my packed bag on the floor beside my feet. I aim to appear collected on the outside, but on the inside my heart is hammering about a million miles a minute, along with my thoughts. *I can't believe this is happening. I can't believe*

I'm going out into the real world. Shit, I don't think I can do this. I can't. I want to stay here.

"You're going to do awesome," Davis assures me. "And you know if you need anyone to talk to, I'm totally here and we've got you set up with that sobriety support group and your dad got you a really good therapist to replace Charles."

When I first met Davis, I thought he was a patient at the drug facility, with his laid-back attitude and the casual plaid shirts and jeans he always wears, but it turned out he was the counselor that I'd be spending two months with during my recovery here. He's a pretty cool and oddly enough was once an addict, too, so he gets some of my struggles. Not all of them, though.

I get to my feet and pick up my bag. "I hope you're right."

"I'm always right about these things," he jokes, giving me an encouraging pat on the back as I head past him and out the door. "I can always tell the ones who are going to make it." He places two fingers to his temple. "I have a sixth sense for it."

I don't understand his optimism. I'd think he was this way with everyone, but he's not. I overheard him once talking to one of the nurses, saying he was worried about one of the guys leaving. But he seems sure I'm going to be okay and keeps telling everyone that. I'm not, though. I'm going to fall. I know it. Can feel it. See it. I'm terrified. I have no idea what's going to happen to me. In the next minute. The next step. The next moment. I'm feeling so many things it's hard to even think straight.

I swing the handle of my duffel bag over my shoulder and walk down the hall with Davis following behind. I say good-bye to a few people I met while I was here and actually developed friendships with. There's not a whole lot—it's hard to make friends when you have to focus so much on yourself.

After the brief farewells, I head to Charles's office, which is right beside the front section of the facility. Every time I'm in this part of the building, I get a peek at the outside world, the cars on the highway, the pine trees, the grass, the sky, the clouds. It always makes me want to lock the door and stay behind it for the rest of my life, because behind that door I feel safe. Protected from myself and all the scary things out there. Like the last two months. And now I'm about to go into the wild.

"Quinton, come on in." Charles waves me in when he notices me lingering in the doorway, staring at the exit door just to my right.

I tear my attention away from it and step into his office, a narrow room with a couple of wooden chairs, a desk, and scenic paintings on the walls. It's plain, with minimal distractions, which might be on purpose to force whoever is in here to focus on nothing but himself. I've had a few meltdowns in this room, a lot of them stemming from when Charles urged me to pour my heart and soul out about the accident and express how I felt about the deaths of Lexi and Ryder. I haven't talked about everything yet, but I'm sure I'll get there. One day. But for now I'm taking things one step at a time. Day by day.

8

"So today's the big day," he says, standing up from the chair behind his desk. He's a short man with a bad comb-over and wears a lot of suits with elbow patches. But he's nice and gets things in a way most people don't. I'm not sure if it's because of his PhD hanging on the wall or because maybe he's been through some rough shit. If he has, he never shared it with me. "This is about you," he always said whenever I tried to turn the conversation around on him. "And what you've been through." I hated him for it. Still do a little bit, because he opened a lot of fucking doors I thought I'd bolted shut. Stuff poured out of me and is still continuing to stream out of me, like a leaky faucet, one I can't get to turn off, but now I'm not sure I want to.

"Yeah, I guess so." I move to the center of the room and stand behind one of the chairs, gripping the back to hold myself up because my legs feel like two wet noodles.

He offers me a smile. "I know you're a little worried about how things are going to be out there, but I assure you that as long as you stick to everything we talked about, you're going to be okay. Just keep going to meetings and keep writing." He strolls around the desk and stops in front of me. "And keep working on talking to your father."

"I'll try to," I say with apprehension. "But it's a two-way street, so…" My father has visited a few times, and Charles mediated for us. *Rocky* would be one of the words to describe the time we spent talking. That and *awkward* and *uneasy*. But it helped break the ice enough that it's not completely and utterly terrible to know that I'm going to be living under the same roof with him again. Just terrible, maybe.

Charles puts a hand on my shoulder and looks me straight in the eye. "Don't try. Do." He always says this whenever someone shows doubt. *Do. Do. Do.*

"Okay, I'll talk to him," I say, but just because I will, doesn't mean my father is going to reciprocate. I barely know him anymore. No, scratch *anymore.* I've never known him, really, and it feels like I'm moving in with a stranger. *But I can get through this. I am strong.* I tell myself this over and over again.

"Good." Charles gives my shoulder a squeeze and then releases me. "And remember, I'm always here if you need someone to talk to." He takes a step back toward his desk. "You have my card with my number, right?"

I pat my pocket. "Yeah."

"Good. Call me if you ever need anything from me." He smiles. "And take care, Quinton."

"Thanks. You, too." I turn for the door, my chest squeezing tighter with every step I take. By the time I exit into the hallway, I'm on the verge of hyperventilating. But I keep moving. Breathing. Walking. Until I get into the lounge area near the doorway, where my father's waiting for me in one of the chairs in the corner of the room. He has his head tipped down and his glasses on as he reads the newspaper that's on his lap. He's wearing slacks and a nice shirt, probably the same clothes he wears to the office every day. He must have had to leave early to pick me up and I wonder how he feels about that, whether he's irritated like he always used to be with me or glad that I'm finally getting out. I guess that could be something we talk about in the car.

I don't say anything as I cross the room toward him. Sensing my presence, he glances up right as I stop in front of him.

He blinks a few times like I've surprised him with my appearance. "Oh, I didn't even see you walk out," he says, setting the newspaper aside on the table beside the chair. He glances at the clock on the wall as he rises to his feet. "Are you ready to go?"

I nod with my thumb hitched through the handle of my duffel bag. "Yeah, I think so."

"Okay then." He pats the sides of his legs awkwardly, glancing around the room like he thinks someone's going to come out and take me off his hands. Realizing that nothing is going to happen, that it's just him and me, he gives me a small smile, but it's forced. Then he heads for the door and I reluctantly follow. Ten steps later, I'm free. Just like that. It feels like it happens so fast. Faster than I can handle. One minute I'm saying good-bye and the next I'm walking out the door into the outside world and fresh air. There are no more walls to protect me, no people around me who get what I'm going through.

I just exist.

The first thing I notice is how bright it is. Not hot, but

11

bright. The grass has also browned, along with the leaves on the trees. It's managed to turn from summer to fall during my two-month stay here and somehow I didn't even notice. I've been outside and everything, but not outside with freedom. It makes things feel different. Me feel different. Nervous. Unsteady. Like I'm about to fall down.

"Quinton, are you okay?" my father asks, assessing me as he removes his glasses, like that'll help him see what's going on inside my head or something. "You look like you're going to be sick."

"I'm fine." I squint at the general brightness of being outdoors. "It just feels a little weird being outside."

He offers me another tight smile, then looks away and starts toward the parking lot at the side of the building. I trail behind him, grasping the handle of my bag slung over my shoulder, the wind grazing my cheeks, and I note how unnatural it feels. Just like the cars driving up and down the highway that seem way too loud. Everything seems extremely intense, even the fresh air that fills my lungs.

Finally, after what feels like an eternity, I make it to the car and get my seat belt secured over my shoulder. It grows quiet as my father turns on the ignition and the engine rumbles to life. Then we're driving up the gravel path toward the highway, leaving the rehab center behind in the distance, the place that for the last couple of months protected me from the world and the pain linked to it.

I stay quiet for most of the drive home and my dad seems

pretty at ease with that at first, but then abruptly he starts slamming me with simple questions like if the heat is up enough or too much, and am I hungry, because he can stop and get me something to eat if I need him to.

I shake my head, picking at a hole in the knee of my jeans. "Dad, I promise I'm okay. You don't need to keep checking on me."

"Yeah, but…" He struggles for what to say as he grips the steering wheel, his knuckles whitening. "But you always said you were okay in the past but then after talking to you with Charles… it just seems like you needed to talk to me but you didn't."

He's probably thinking about how I told him, during one of our sessions, that I felt sort of responsible for my mother's death because he never seemed to want to have anything to do with me. He was shocked by my revelation and I was equally shocked that he didn't realize that's how I felt—at how differently we saw things.

"But I promise I'm okay right now." I ball my hands more tightly into fists the closer we get to the house. Deep breaths. Deep breaths. *I can do this. The scary part is over, right? I'm sober now.* "I just ate before we left and I'm warm, not hot or cold. Everything's good. I'm good." Which I am, for the most part.

He nods, satisfied, as he concentrates on the road. "Well, let me know if you need anything."

"Okay, I will." I direct my attention to the side window

and watch the landscape blur by, gradually changing from trees to a field, then ultimately to houses as we pass through the outskirts of the city. Before I know it, we're entering my old neighborhood made up of cul-de-sacs and modest homes. It's where everything started, where everything changed, where I grew up and where I decided I was going to slowly kill myself with drugs. Each house I've passed a thousand times on foot, on bike, in the car, yet the surroundings feel so foreign to me and I feel so off-balance. The feeling only intensifies when we pass one of the houses I used to buy drugs from. I start wondering if they still deal or if that's changed. What if they do? What if I have drugs right on hand? Right there? Just blocks away from where I'm living? Can I handle it? I'm not sure. I'm not sure of anything at the moment, because I can't see five minutes into the future.

My adrenaline starts pumping relentlessly and no matter how hard I try to get my heart to settle down, I can't. It only beats faster when we pull into the driveway of my two-story home with blue shutters and white siding. I've been in this house more times than anywhere else in the world, yet it feels like I've never been here before. I'm not even sure that it ever really was my home, though, more simply a roof over my head. I'm not sure about anything anymore. Where I belong. What I should feel. Who I am.

Reborn.

But what am I going to be reborn into?

"Welcome home," my dad says, again with a taut smile. He parks the car in front of the shut garage and silences the engine.

"Thanks." I return his forced smile, hoping we're not going to pretend that everything is okay to each other all the time because it's going to drive me crazy.

He takes the keys out of the ignition while I get my bag out of the backseat, then we get out of the car and walk up the path to the front door, where he unlocks it and we step into the foyer. It hits me like a bag of bricks, slamming against my chest and knocking the wind out of me. This is bad. So bad. I needed more preparation for this. The memories, swirling in torturous circles inside my head. The good ones. The bad ones. The ones connected to my childhood. Lexi. It's too much and I want to run out the door and track down one of my old pothead friends, see if they're still into drugs, and if I can get something—anything—to take away the emotions swirling around inside me.

Need.

Want.

Need.

Now.

I suck in a sharp breath and then turn for the stairs, telling myself to be stronger than this. "I'm going to go unpack," I say as I head up the stairs.

"Okay." My dad drops the keys down on the table by the

front door, below a picture hanging on the wall of my mother and him on their wedding day. He looks happy in it, an emotion I've rarely seen from him. "Do you want anything in particular for dinner?"

"Anything sounds good." I remember how many days I could go without eating dinner when I was fueling my body with crystal and smack. Getting healthy was actually part of my recovery over the last two months. Exercising. Eating. Thinking healthy. I actually chose to get some tests done just to see how bad my health was, if I'd done any permanent damage to my body with the use of needles. Like HIV or hepatitis. Everything came up negative and I guess I'm grateful for it now, but at the time I felt upset because disease seemed like the easy ticket out of the hellhole I was in coming off heroin and meth. I'd hoped that maybe I'd have something deadly and it'd kill me. Then I wouldn't have to face the world and my future. My guilt. The decision between going back to a world full of drugs and living.

When I reach the top of the stairs, I veer down the hallway, walking to the end of it to my room. I enter gradually, knowing that when I get in there a lot of stuff I've been running from is going to emerge. I thought about asking my dad to clean everything out for me: the photos, my drawings, anything related to the past. But my therapist said it might be good for me to do it because it could be the start of giving myself closure. I hope he's right. I hope he's right about a lot of things, otherwise I'm going to break apart.

I hold on to the doorknob for probably about ten minutes before I get the courage to turn it and open the door. As I enter and step over the threshold, I want to run away. I'd forgotten how many pictures I had of Lexi on the walls. Not just ones I drew. Actually photos of her laughing, smiling, hugging me. The ones I'm in with her, I look so happy, so different, so free. So unfamiliar. Less scarred. I don't even know who that person is anymore or if I'll ever be him again.

There are also a few pictures of my mother, ones my grandmother gave me before she passed away. Some of them were taken when my dad and mom first married, and I even have one from when she was pregnant with me, her last few months alive before she'd pass away bringing me into this world. The only pictures of her and me together. She looks a lot like me: brown hair and the same brown eyes. I was told a lot by my grandmother that we shared the same smile, but I haven't smiled for real in ages so I'm not sure if it still looks like hers.

I manage to get a smile on my mouth as I look at a photo of her giving an exaggerated grin to the camera. It makes me feel kind of happy, which makes me sad that I'm supposed to take them down. It's what I've been taught over the last few months, let go of the past. But I need just a few more minutes with them.

After I take each one in, breathing through the immense amount of emotional pain crushing me, I drop my bag onto the floor and wander over to a stack of sketches on my dresser.

I lost my most recent drawings when the apartment burned down, and this is pretty much all that's left. I'm not sure if that's good or bad. One thing's for sure, I'm glad I don't have any of my self-portraits. In fact, I hope I never have to see myself look the way I did two months ago. I remember when I first looked in the mirror right after I got to rehab. Skeletal. The walking dead. That's what I looked like.

There's a mirror on the wall to the side of me and I step up to it. I look so different now, my skin has more color to it, my brown eyes aren't bloodshot or dazed. My cheeks are filled out instead of sunken in, my arms are lean, my whole body more in shape. My brown hair is cropped short and my face is shaven. I look alive instead of like a ghost. I look like someone I used to know and am afraid to be again. I look like Quinton.

I swallow hard and turn away from my reflection and back toward my sketches. I fan through a few of the top ones, which turn out to be of Lexi. I remember how much I used to draw her, even after she died. But during the last few months of tumbling toward rock bottom, I started drawing someone else. A person I haven't seen in two months or talked to. Nova Reed. I haven't talked to her since I got on a plane to go to rehab. I wrote her a few times, but then never sent the letters, too afraid to tell her everything I have to say, too terrified to express emotions I'm pretty sure I'm not ready to deal with just yet. She tried to call me a few times at the facility, but I couldn't bring myself to talk to her. A month ago she wrote me a letter and it's in the back of my notebook, waiting to be opened. I'm not sure I'll ever be able to do it. Face her. Be forced to let her go if that's what she wants. I wouldn't blame her if she did. After everything that I put her through—having to visit me in that shithole I called home, my mood swings, the drug dealers threatening her.

Blowing out a heavy sigh, I get my notebook and a pencil out of my bag, then flop down on the bed. I open the notebook up to a clean sheet of paper and decide which I want to do more, write or draw. They're both therapeutic, although I'm way better at drawing. After some debating, I put the pencil to the paper and start drawing. I know where it's headed the moment I form the first line. I lost all my drawings of Nova when the apartment burned down. Not a single one remains. It's like the memory of her is gone. But I don't want it to be gone—I don't want *her* to be gone. I want to remember her. How good she was to me. How she made me feel alive, even when I fought it. How I'm pretty sure I love her, but I'm still trying to figure that out for sure, just like I'm trying to figure out everything else, like where I belong in this world and if I belong in this world. Everyone keeps telling me yes—that I belong here. That what happened in the accident wasn't my fault. That yes, I was driving too fast, but the other car was, too, and took the turn too wide. And that Lexi shouldn't have been hanging out the window. And I want to believe that's true, that perhaps it wasn't my fault entirely. That's the difference between now and a couple of months ago, but it's hard to

let go of something I've been clutching for the last two years—
my guilt. I need to find a reason to let it go and to make life
worth living in such a way that I don't have to dope my body
up just to make it through the day.

I need something to live for, but at the moment I'm not
sure what the hell that is or if it even exists.

Chapter Two

Nova

"I sometimes sit in the quad and watch the people walk by. It probably sounds creepy but it's not. I'm just observing. Human nature. What people do. How they act. But it's more than that. If I look close enough, I can sometimes tell when someone is going through something painful. Maybe a breakup. Perhaps they just lost their job. Or maybe they've lost a loved one. Perhaps they're suffering in silence, lost in a sea of questions, of what-ifs. Pain. Loss. Remorse." I shift in the bench that's centered in the quad yard as my back starts to hurt. I've been sitting out here for hours, recording myself, watching the people walk by. What I really want to do is run out there and stop each one. Ask them their story. Listen. Hear it. If they need consoling, I could do it. In fact, that's what I want to do. Be able to help people. I just wish I could somehow figure out a way to do it through filming.

"Death. It's around more than people realize. Because no one ever wants to talk about it or hear about it. It's too sad. Too

21

painful. Too hard. The list of reasons is endless." The wind gusts up from behind me, causing leaves to circle around my head and strands of my hair to veil my face. The fall air gets chilly in Idaho during this time of year and I forgot to bring my jacket.

Shivering, I get to my feet and collect my bag. After putting my camera away, I start back to the apartment, picking up the pace when I realize how late it is and that I should have been home already. Today is actually a very big and important day. Not because I have a calculus test or had to turn in one of my mini video clips for my film class. Nope. Today is important because Quinton was released from the drug facility. It's not information I learned directly from him. Sadly, I haven't even spoken to him since the day he got on the plane with his father and headed back to Seattle to get help. But I have other sources to get me information. Tristan sources, to be exact.

Tristan is Quinton's cousin and he just happens to be my roommate. They talk occasionally on the phone and I think he hears stuff from his parents, but that's mainly negative stuff, since Tristan's parents still blame Quinton for the car accident that killed their daughter, Ryder. It's a messed-up situation, but I don't think it's ever going to change. Tristan agrees. He told me once that he doesn't believe his parents will ever let their blame go, that they have to hold on to it in order to live each day, no matter how fucked up it is. But thankfully, Tristan is a good guy and tries to make up for it by being Quinton's friend and forgiving him.

Forgiveness. If only more people could do it. Then maybe there'd be less pain in the world.

When I walk into the house, it smells of vanilla, the scent flowing from a candle burning on the kitchen countertop. There's a stack of magazines by the front door, along with the mail. And Tristan is sitting on the sofa, staring at his phone as if it's the enemy.

"Hey," I say, dropping my bag to the floor. "Are you ready to call him?"

"I feel like a narc," Tristan gripes as I plop down on the sofa beside him.

I give him a friendly pat on his leg. "But I assure you, you're not."

He narrows his eyes at me, pretending he's mad, but I know him enough now to know he's not. Just a little annoyed. "But I sort of am, seeing as how I'm calling him, but only so I can get information for you."

"But you want to know, too," I remind him, grabbing a handful of Skittles out of the candy bowl on the coffee table. "What he's going to do—if he's okay. If he needs anything now that he's out."

"Yeah, but I'm not even sure he'll talk to me since he barely would in rehab," he says as I pour the Skittles into my mouth.

I stop chewing and pull a pouty face and clasp my hands in front of me. "Pretty please."

He shakes his head and then swipes his finger across the screen. "Fine, but I'm only doing this because you let me live

23

here and because your pouty faces are ridiculously hard to say no to."

"You don't owe me for living here," I say reassuringly. "And you pay rent, so this apartment is as much yours as it is mine."

"But you take care of me," he says as he pushes buttons on his phone. "And keep me out of trouble."

"And you're such a good boy about it." I pat his head like he's a dog, although he's much cuter than a dog. His blond hair, blue eyes, and smile make him seem like he belongs in a boy band, all perfect and charming. But his past is dark. Haunted. Full of mistakes and addiction, something he struggles with every day.

"I'm not a dog, Nova." He gives me a dirty look for the head pat and then gets up from the sofa with the phone pressed to his ear, rounding the coffee table and heading toward the hallway.

"Hey, where are you going?" I call out after him, slanting over the arm of the chair and peering down the hallway at him.

"To talk in private," he says, disappearing into his room. "Because your excessive staring is driving me crazy." Seconds later, his bedroom door shuts.

I sit back and retrieve my cell phone from my pocket. I've been making recordings of myself for a year and a half now and it's sort of become a habit whenever I've got a lot of clutter in my head, like I do right now. For me it's like writing in a diary, even though I also use some of the stuff for film class. Although it didn't originally start out like that. I first started doing it during a rough time in my life, about a year after my boyfriend Landon killed himself. He'd made a recording right before he did it and for some reason making recordings myself made me feel closer to him. Eventually I learned to let it go—the need to still connect with him.

I sit up straight on the sofa and press the button that flips the screen at myself, and my image pops up on the screen. My long brown hair runs to my shoulders and my green eyes stare back at me. My skin has a healthy glow to it and freckles dot my nose. I'm not the most beautiful girl in the world, but I look decent when I'm sober and my system is clean, which it has been for a year now.

After I get the right angle, I clear my throat and start recording. "Tristan can be so serious sometimes, at least when he's doing stuff he doesn't want to do. Not at all the same person I knew two months ago or even two years ago. He's been sober for over three months now and living with me and Lea, my best friend for over a year. It's good that he's more serious though because it seems to be keeping him out of trouble. He goes to work at the coffee shop a mile away from the house and attends the university and stays away from parties. I can tell there's times when he'd rather be out doing something fun than sitting in the house eating pizza with Lea and me, but he always stays, which to me means at the moment everything is okay, at least I hope it is. And I hope it is for Quinton. I wish I knew. Something…anything about him, but he won't talk to me and never wrote me back when I sent him a letter a month ago. I'm not sure if he's mad at me, but Tristan assures me he's not. That he probably feels guilty over putting me through what he did, but I don't want that for him. He has enough guilt as it is and I'm okay now. I really am. Healthy. Happy. And moving forward."

I click off the camera, and then I get up and start doing the dishes as a way to keep myself busy. Part of me wants to revert to my habit of counting because I'm anxious right now, but the urge is nowhere near what it used to be. In fact, it's been sort of silent for the last couple of months. I think maybe that's because I've managed to stay so busy with school, my job at a photography studio, and of course my band.

Yeah, I'm in a band called Ashes & Dust. Jaxon, Lea's ex-boyfriend, is the singer, the bassist's name is Spalding and the guitarist is Nikko. I'm the only chick and Lea always makes jokes about how lucky I am, but it's awkward because things with Jaxon and her didn't end well. Sometimes things even get uncomfortable between Jaxon and me, whenever Lea's name is mentioned. Still, it's awesome that I get to play my drums and I wish I could do it all the time. Life would be so much less complicated if I could.

Tristan is still in his room when I get the dishwasher loaded and I can hear him talking through the door. I think about putting my ear up and listening, but it makes me feel bad, so I go into the living room and crank up the stereo, putting on some Papa Roach. Then I start to rock out, dancing around. I'd play my drums but I'm not allowed to anymore, ever since the neighbors complained about the noise. So sadly I have to dance to vent and I pretty much suck at dancing.

I'm whipping my long brown hair around and really shaking my ass as I belt out the lyrics when suddenly I hear a cough from behind me. I immediately stop dancing and try to ignore the rush of heat I feel on my cheeks as I go over and turn the music down.

I smooth my hair and wipe the sweat from my forehead before I turn around and face Tristan. "So what'd he say?" I ask, breathless.

He crosses his arms and arches a brow at me, trying not to smile. "Nice dance moves."

I take an embarrassed bow and it gets him to relax. "Thank you." I straighten back up. "Now tell me what he said. Is he okay? Good? Bad? What?"

"Come sit down." He nods at the leather sofa and I walk over and have a seat. He sits down beside me, seeming slightly nervous as he fiddles with the bottom button on his shirt. "He's doing okay," he says.

"And." I motion my hand, needing him to give me more details. "Did he seem, I don't know, in need of help?"

He sighs, sweeping his fingers through the locks of his blond hair. "I think he sounded pretty okay. He's staying with his dad and he says they're talking and everything, which they never used to do. He's supposed to start going to a therapist next week and to a sobriety support group, which is good in my opinion. A support group helped me a lot when I got out of rehab. He told me he'll probably stay in Seattle for a while and try to find a job there." He pauses, watching my reaction, like he thinks I'm about to break apart.

"Oh." I should sound happier than I do—should be more happy for him. And I am, but for some stupid reason I was hoping for...I don't know...that I could see him again. "That all sounds great, I guess."

"Then why do you sound so sad?" he questions, searching my eyes for the truth.

I lift my shoulders and shrug. "I'm happy for him. Just sad that I can't see him."

"You could always call him...in fact, I told him you might."

I swallow the lump of nerves that has shoved its way up my throat. "And what'd he say?"

"He said you could." He looks like he wants to retract the statement as soon as he says it. "Well, I mean, he sounded nervous about it and everything, but I think that's more because he feels guilty about what happened to you while you were down in Vegas, which he shouldn't." He stares down at his hands. "That shit that happened with the drug dealers... that was my fault."

I remain silent, not just because of what Tristan told me about Quinton but also because of Tristan's guilt. Even though it was his fault—what happened with the drug dealers and them threatening me and beating up Quinton—it still doesn't mean he needs to feel guilty about it. "You don't need to feel bad for that, Tristan." I slouch back in the sofa and cross my arms over my chest. Everyone's always blaming themselves for stuff, including me, and I'm sick and tired of it. I just want us to let go of stuff. Move on. "I get that your mind wasn't in the right place when all that stuff happened."

He glances over at me. "You're too forgiving sometimes."

"And you're too sad sometimes," I retort. It gets quiet and I can feel us both moving toward a depressing slump. Before we can get there, I rise to my feet and extend my hand to him. "Come on. Let's go do something fun."

He cocks a brow. "Like what?"

I shrug with my hand still extended. "I don't know. We could go see a movie, maybe? Or rent one, pick up some pizza, and come back here and watch it."

"No documentaries," he says quickly, taking my hand, and I help him to his feet. "I know you love them and everything, but I can't take another one." He lets go of my hand and clutches his head with a joking smile. "They give me a boredom headache."

"Oh, poor baby." I roll my eyes, then walk toward the door, collecting my purse from the table, but when Tristan doesn't follow me, I turn around. "What's wrong?"

He dithers in the middle of the living room, massaging the back of his neck tensely. "Aren't you going to call him?"

I slide the handle of my purse over my shoulder, nerves bubbling inside me at the idea of actually getting on the phone and hearing Quinton's voice. God, I want to hear it so much, but it's scary at the same time, because I want him, yet I don't think he wants me—at least he isn't ready for whatever it is between us. "I was thinking that I would do it tomorrow… after I figured out what to say." I pause as he shuffles over to me, trying to figure out what on earth I'm supposed to say to Quinton, especially if he's read the letter. "What do you think I should say to him?"

The corners of his lips quirk as he stops in front of me. "'Hi.'"

I gently pinch his arm. "Come on. I'm being serious. I have no clue where to begin."

He considers my question intently, his expression twisted in deep thought, then he abruptly relaxes. "Just be yourself, Nova." He swings his arm around my shoulder and steers me to the front door. "You have this way about you that makes it easy for people to feel like they can talk to you and I know Quinton feels that way, too, since, besides me, you're the only person he really talked to through all that shit."

"Thanks," I say, but I get a little uncomfortable with his touch—always do. Tristan and I have a weird history full of awkward conversations. He's always sort of flirted with me and once, right after my boyfriend committed suicide, I got really drunk and made out with him. Then I ran away crying and tried to slit my wrist open.

I wasn't exactly trying to kill myself when I did it. It was just a really low time in my life, perhaps the lowest I've ever been, and I was confused. But I'm better now—stronger. I don't

30

get drunk and make out with random guys and I even have a tattoo right below that scar—*never forget*—to remind me never to forget any of the stuff that's happened. Good or bad. It's a part of me and sometimes I think it's made me stronger.

Tristan and I leave our apartment and I lock the door behind us. We live in an indoor complex that has an elevator, but it's so ancient and slow that most of the time we take the stairs. As we're making our way down, I try not to count them, but I'm finding it hard. I need a distraction from my thoughts of Quinton and the complication building between Tristan and me, so I get out my phone to call Lea to see if she's in for a movie-and-pizza night. Hopefully she is. That way Tristan and I won't be alone.

"Hey, it's me," I say after she answers, then stupidly add, "Nova."

"No duh." She laughs. "You're such a dork."

"Gee, thanks," I reply sarcastically. "That means a lot coming from the girl who colored on her face with a permanent marker the other day."

"I was trying to have school spirit," she explains defensively. "How the hell was I supposed to know the damn 'Go Broncos' wouldn't wipe off my face afterward?"

"Um, by the fact that the marker said 'Sharpie' on it." I stop at the bottom of the stairway. "And 'permanent.'"

"Ha ha," she says as Tristan opens the door for me and I step out into the sunlight beaming down from the crystal-blue sky. "You're such a smartass."

"So are you." I head up the sidewalk toward the carport with Tristan lollygagging behind me, messing around with his lighter.

"I know, and I love that I'm rubbing off on you."

"Me, too." I rummage through my purse for the keys to my car. "Anyway, so Tristan and I are heading to get some pizza and a movie, then we're going to bring it back home. Are you down for a pizza/movie night?"

"Can't," she says hurriedly. "I have plans."

"Plans with who?" I halt at the edge of the carport in front of my car. Tristan stops with me, observing me with curiosity. "I know you're secretly dating," I say to Lea. "So fess up."

"I am not," she replies, feigning offense.

"You are, too," I retort. "It's why you've been hanging out at all the football games."

"Hey, I like football," she argues. "I even turned on ESPN once."

"On accident," I remind her. "You were channel surfing and then stopped on it because you thought the reporter was hot."

"Hey, if I say I like football, then I like football."

"No you don't. In fact, you told me once that it was a pointless sport that only existed because guys have this need to prove that they're tougher than each other."

"Hey, not all guys." Tristan hops off the curb and underneath the shade of the carport that runs around the entire complex. Then he rounds the front of my car to the passenger

32

side and opens the door. "In fact, I don't mind being wimpy at all."

"Sure you don't," I tease, going to the driver's side. "That's why you tried to pick a fight with that guy in the campus yard the other day."

"I did that because he slapped your ass," he says, ducking into the car, and I open my door and get inside, too. We slam the doors and then I rev up the engine. "I normally try to avoid fights."

"He slapped my ass accidentally," I protest, buckling my seat belt.

"Sure, keep telling yourself that," he says with an eye roll as he guides his seat belt over his shoulder.

"Um, hello," Lea says through the receiver. "I'm still here, you know."

"Sorry, we were just arguing," I tell her, putting on my sunglasses.

"Yeah, I heard." She uses that tone that has been getting under my skin for the last few weeks, the one that implies that she thinks Tristan likes me. Normally I'd call her out on it, but not with him right next to me.

"So are you in or out for movie night?" I change the subject.

"I already told you I'm busy."

"Fine. Go on your date, then."

"It's not a date." She attempts to sound irritated but I can hear the smile in her voice.

"If you say so." It's slightly humid inside the car so I crank the air up a notch. "But just so you know, I'm going to wait up all night to see who drops you off."

"Fine by me," she says, but I can tell she doesn't believe me.

"Have fun on your *date*," I say sarcastically, getting ready to hang up.

"You, too," she replies with hilarity. "On your date."

I shake my head, but laugh and then say good-bye. After we hang up, I toss the phone into my bag. I wonder if Tristan could hear any of that. It doesn't seem like he could as he squints out the window at Stan, our twenty-five-year-old neighbor, dragging a keg toward the entrance of the apartment complex.

"Looks like Stan's having a party," he notes, and I hate the interest in his tone.

"Isn't he always?" I put the shifter in reverse and pull down the visor. The sun is starting to descend and it's so blinding I can barely see, even with my sunglasses on. That's how sunsets are in Idaho, though. Because of the shallow hills and non-existent buildings, there's not much to block out the light, so the sky turns into one big orange-and-pink reflection at dusk.

"Maybe we should go," he suggests, watching Stan struggle to keep the entrance door open so he can drag the keg inside. Tristan glances at me with an unreadable expression. "It could be fun."

I'm starting to press on the gas to back up, but quickly tap on the brakes, stopping the car. "Tristan, I don't think that's such a good idea. You're still in a really vulnerable place in your life. I mean, I remember what happened when I tried weed four months after I stopped doing drugs…and you did really hard stuff…I know your sponsor would agree with me…" I stop rambling because he looks like he's about to laugh at me, his lips pressed tightly together, his blue eyes sparkling. "Why are you looking at me like that?"

His smile breaks through. "I was just fucking with you, Nova." Laughter escapes his lips as he reaches for the cigarettes in his pocket. "I wouldn't go to a party. I care about my recovery enough not to fuck up right now."

I narrow my eyes at him. "That wasn't funny."

He keeps on smiling as he puts the end of the cigarette between his lips and lights up. "It kinda was."

I shake my head, rolling down my window as smoke laces the air. "It's not funny to make me worry like that."

"Hey." He leans across the seat, sticking the hand holding the cigarette out to the side and cupping my face with his free hand, startling me with his unexpected, almost intimate, touch. "I'm sorry. You're right. It's not funny to make you worry about that, but it's always good to know you care about me."

I sigh. "I care about everyone, which makes my life too stressful sometimes."

"I know." He smoothes his finger across my cheekbone and I try not to flinch, despite the fact that I want to. I wonder what these touches mean and worry that one day things are going to get out of hand and confrontation is going to be inevitable. I hate confrontation. I really, really do. "Which makes you such a good person."

I plaster on a smile, because I have to. He's in a fragile state—I know that. And he relies on me a lot. If we weren't friends, I have no idea what would happen with him. Whether he'd be able to take care of himself or slip back into old habits, and I don't want to find out.

I casually turn my head toward the windshield, pretending that the only reason is that I'm going to back up the car. "You're so weird sometimes…" I crank the wheel to the left and finish backing out of the spot. "Always complimenting me."

"*I'm* weird." He gapes at me, pointing at himself. "You're the one who always says goofy things."

"I do not," I protest, even though it's true. I do say goofy things sometimes, when I get nervous.

"You do, too," he insists as I straighten up the wheel and drive out of the parking lot. "Like that one time you told me some random fact about a raccoon."

"I do that when I'm nervous."

"Still, it's goofy."

"It's not that goofy. It just means I have a colorful personality."

"A colorful, goofy personality." He takes a drag on his cigarette and then starts hacking as he blows out the smoke. He hurries to roll the window down, coughing as he spits.

"You're so gross." I pull a disgusted face. "Seriously."

"Hey, I have a cold," he says defensively as he slumps back in the seat with his arm resting on the sill so most of the smoke goes out the window. "I can't help it."

"You've had that cold for a couple of weeks now. Maybe it's time to go get it checked out." I turn out on the main road that goes straight through the center of town. It's bordered by trees and, since it's fall, the leaves have fallen onto the street and sidewalks. It's a beautiful sight and fall is one of my favorite times of the year.

"Okay, Mom." He rolls his eyes as he takes another drag.

"Or maybe stop smoking," I say. "You know those things can kill you, right?"

"You know, you're sounding sort of preachy." He ashes his cigarette out the window, grinning amusedly. "But that's okay. I know you only do it because you're secretly in love with me."

I give him a blank stare, working hard to restrain a smile because the big goofy grin on his face looks so silly. "You're such a dork."

"Good. I can be the dork and you can be the goof and we can complete each other."

I can't help it. I burst out laughing. "Okay, easy there, Jerry Maguire."

His face contorts with perplexity. "Who the hell's Jerry Maguire?"

My laughter shifts to shock. "Are you kidding me?"

He shakes his head. "No, who is the guy?"

"It's not a guy... well, it is, but what you just said... it's from the movie *Jerry Maguire*..." I trail off as his confusion deepens. "Never mind. But may I point out the fact that you weren't quoting the movie makes you saying that ten times cheesier."

Grinning, he raises his balled fist in the air, like he's celebrating. "Yeah, now I'm a dork and cheesy. That makes us even more compatible."

I can't help but smile again, despite the fact that I think he might be hitting on me, because it's funny. And I need funny right now. Need happy, otherwise I'll start focusing on the worry. Focusing on Quinton and if he's okay.

We continue to talk for the rest of the drive to the pizza place, about goofiness and being dorks. Eventually the topic shifts to school, like how many classes he's going to sign up for next semester. By the end of the drive, he's telling me again that I act like his mom. Well, not his mom, per se, because he rarely talks to her, something I don't understand because he hasn't opened up to me about it yet. But by the time we get back to our apartment, we've veered off the arguing and started chatting about the movie we rented, *Anchorman*, which he insists is hilarious and can't believe I haven't watched yet.

"For someone who's so into movies, you're seriously movie-deprived," he says as he sets the pizza box down on the coffee table.

I put the DVD beside the television, then go into the kitchen to grab a soda. "I've seen a lot of movies. Just not this particular one."

"Yeah, right. I've heard you say a ton of movies that you haven't seen that a lot of normal people have." He drops down on the sofa, kicks his shoes off, and puts his feet up.

I open the fridge door. "Well, I think we already established that I'm not a normal person." I grab a can of Dr Pepper for me and a Mountain Dew for him before I bump the door shut with my hip. Then I toss him the Mountain Dew. "Besides, I've seen a lot of movies you haven't."

He catches the soda. "Like what?" he questions.

I pop the tab and the soda fizzles, then I take a sip as I head for the sofa. "I don't know." I sit down beside him, thinking of a good answer. "How about *Fight Club*. I know you haven't seen that."

He taps the top of the can before popping the tab. "Yeah, because it's old."

"It's not that old," I argue as he leans forward and opens the pizza box. "It was made in the nineties and we were born in the nineties."

He takes a slurp of his soda, then puts the can down on the coffee table and gets a slice of pizza. "So maybe we're old."

"Maybe we are," I say. "Sometimes I feel older than I am."

"Me, too," he admits, picking a pepper off the pizza and discarding it into the box. "I think that comes with life experiences, though."

He's right. I think we've both been through so much that sometimes we both feel older than we are. It's probably that way for Quinton, too, and it makes me want him here with me, so I can cuddle up on the sofa with him and know that he's okay.

It becomes quiet as I get lost in my thoughts, and finally I set my soda down and get up to put the DVD in. Once the previews start, I return to the couch and start eating. Tristan and I chat again about being old until the movie comes on, then grow quiet.

The further into the movie we get, the closer he scoots toward me on the sofa to the point where I feel like I'm on a date. I begin questioning if I should get up and move. But I don't want to hurt his feelings, especially when he's in such a vulnerable place. Just like Quinton, who I wish were here with me. Quinton, who's so far away, but I want him right here. I want to touch him. See if he's okay. Be with him more than maybe I should—will ever be, maybe.

The longer the night goes on, the more my thoughts drift to Quinton. What he's doing. Thinking. How the last two months have been for him. I want to talk to him, but I'm afraid of all the unsaid stuff I know there's going to be between us. I just hope we can say it, otherwise things will be like they were in the past, when he wouldn't talk to me. It was the same thing with Landon. When we were dating, I thought I knew him. I thought we had a good relationship. I thought I was going to spend the rest of my life with him. But there was so much unsaid between us and in the end it never did get said.

"So what do you think so far?" Tristan interrupts my

40

thoughts as he inches closer to me so that the side of his leg is pressed up against mine.

I strain a smile, stiffening as his breath touches my cheek. "It's good. Really funny." But I'm barely paying attention.

He slides his arm across the back of the sofa and behind me. I catch a whiff of soap mixed with cigarette smoke. "See, I told you you'd like it."

I make my lips curve into an even bigger smile and either he doesn't notice I'm faking being happy or he doesn't say anything. He returns his attention to the movie, his eyes locked on the screen as he gets another slice of pizza. I start to become hyper-aware of him and his movements, how tired he looks, the bags under his eyes. I think he's tired and I start to debate whether I should say I'm exhausted as an excuse to get out of the growing discomfort of the situation. It'd be so easy to go back to my room, but at the same time I know my being here helps Tristan stay out of trouble. So I stay put and attempt to concentrate on the movie the best I can.

"What are we doing here?" I ask Quinton as I stand on the edge of a cliff, staring out at the land before us. Rolling hills that go on for miles and miles, until they connect with the horizon.

"We're getting some peace and quiet," he says, and I can feel his honey-brown eyes on me so I turn and look at him.

He looks healthier than the last time I saw him, more muscular, his eyes brighter, his hair cropped short like the first time I met him. He's not wearing a shirt, the defined scar on his chest visible, along with the tattoos on his arm: Lexi, Ryder, and No One. Even though I know both the scar and the tattoos are related to the accident, I only know from the stuff I've put together on my own. Quinton's never really told me anything himself about what happened that night, and I wonder if he ever will.

"What?" he asks, his brow arching, and I realize I've been silently staring at him.

I shake my head, still unable to take my eyes off him. "It's nothing," I say. "I was just wondering…" I trail off. "Never mind."

He reaches out and touches his palm to my cheek. "It's not nothing, Nova. So please just tell me…I want to know…I want to know everything you're thinking."

It's such an honest request that it takes me a moment to respond.

"I was just thinking about your tattoos and scars and what they mean." As soon as it leaves my lips, I know I've said the wrong thing.

I can see his muscles wind tight, his fingers fold into his palms, his scruffy jaw go taut. I want to retract what I said, but it's too late and suddenly he's stepping away from me.

"Don't go," I call out, reaching for him, but my feet won't move. "Please, I didn't mean it."

He shakes his head, his skin paling, his muscles shriveling until he looks like a skeleton. His eyes sink in and his cheekbones become more distinct. When his body is finished shifting, he looks just like the Quinton I last saw, the one who lost his body to heroin. The one who gave up on life. The one who wanted to die because he hated himself.

"I'm sorry," he says, which isn't what I was expecting.

"For what?" I question, lowering my hand to my side.

"For this." He starts running toward the cliff like he's going to jump.

"No!" I scream as he springs onto his toes, leaping toward the edge.

I'm finally able to move my feet and run for him, but it's too late. He flies through the air and when he starts to drop, he's falling off the cliff toward the rocky bottom . . .

My eyes shoot open and I gasp for air. It takes me a second to get my bearings, but when I finally do, I realize that I was dreaming and that I'm not on a cliff, watching Quinton fall, but lying on my side, cuddled up with Tristan on the couch with our legs tangled. My eyes widen as I realize this and I hurry and wiggle out of his arms. I end up rolling off the sofa and falling face-first onto the floor. I quickly sit up, worried he's going to wake up and wonder what the heck's going on. I can't see him because night has settled, the living room nearly pitch-black except for the light flowing through the window and from the television screen, which has gone blue, the movie long over. But I can hear the soft sound of his breathing, which hopefully means he's asleep.

I get to my feet and shake off the lingering terror of the dream as I tiptoe into my room. I close the door behind me and take my phone from my pocket. I want to call Quinton, but even thinking about it with the phone in my hand is terrifying. Besides, what if he's asleep or something?

It's ten o'clock and that makes it nine o'clock in Seattle, so it doesn't seem likely. Still, I dither for about ten minutes, organizing my CD collection while I carry the phone around in my hand, my OCD habits kicking in with my nerves. Finally, after realizing that I'm just going to have to rip off the Band-Aid and get it over with, I flop down on my bed and dial Quinton's dad's home phone number, which Tristan gave me.

I rest my head on the pillow and stare up at the ceiling as I listen to the phone ring, trying to figure out what to say. I need to be careful with my words—make sure I don't say anything that will upset him or put pressure on him. But what is the right thing to say? I'm not sure, especially since I have tons of questions sitting on my tongue, like what's been going on? Are you okay? Do you miss me? Ever want to see me again?

"Hello." A man picks up after four rings, sounding tired.

"Um...is Quinton there?" I ask, worried I've woken up his dad or something.

"Who is this?" he questions with an edge in his voice.

I hesitate. Does he even know who I am? "Um...Nova Reed."

He pauses. "Nova Reed, Carry Reed's daughter, right?" I'd almost forgotten that he knows my mother because she's the one who convinced him to go look for his son when Tristan and I lost track of Quinton when he was living on the streets in Vegas.

I relax a little. "Yeah, that's the one," I say, trying to keep a light tone. "I know it's late and everything, but I was wondering if I could talk to him."

He remains silent and I worry that maybe Quinton told him he didn't want to talk to me. Perhaps he told Tristan I could call only because he felt pressured and then changed his mind.

But then his dad says, "Let me go see if he's awake."

"Okay, thanks." I chew on my fingernails as I wait. I can hear the sound of footsteps and then a door opening. There's music playing in the background. "Cover Me" by Candlebox. I absent-mindedly get up from my bed and turn my iPod in the dock to the same song, quietly enough that he won't hear it, but loudly enough that I can. It makes me feel connected to him in a strange way, but then again, my emotions are greatly connected to music, so this would probably be the case under any circumstances.

The music on the other end gets quieter as I go back over to my bed. His dad says something, there's a reply, then his dad says, "Nova Reed."

Silence, except for the lyrics of Candlebox. I hold my breath as I lie down on the bed again, fearing his dad's going to get back on the phone and say Quinton doesn't want to talk to me. Instead there's a thud followed by a rustle. A door clicks shut and then I hear soft breathing from the other end.

"Hello," Quinton utters quietly, like he's afraid to speak.

I get tongue-tied, trying to figure out what to say, and then Tristan's and my earlier conversation pops into my head and I sputter, "Hi." I roll my eyes and shake my head at myself.

There's a pause and I scrunch my nose up, waiting for his response, wanting to smack myself on the head for not thinking of something more epic to say after not talking to him for months.

"Hi," he finally replies, and I detect a hint of humor in his tone. "It's . . . it's good to hear your voice."

Not the reaction I was expecting, but I'll take it. "It's good to hear your voice, too."

"I'm sorry for not talking to you sooner," he says uneasily. "I just . . . well, I felt like an ass because of the shit I put you through."

"You're not an ass." I twist a strand of my hair around my finger. "And you didn't put me through anything. Everything that happened was my own choice because I chose to stay and try to help you. You didn't make me. In fact, you tried to tell me I shouldn't be there about a thousand times."

"I treated you like shit," he says. "And honestly, the really messed-up part is I can't even remember everything because I was so high a lot of the time."

46

"That might be a good thing," I reply. "Then it's like we have a clean slate."

"Clean slates don't exist," he mutters. There's a long pause and considering how moody he's been in the past, I half expect him to get angry with me, but thankfully he sounds calm when he speaks again. "But maybe we could try to create a new one."

I perk up. "A happier one?"

"Yeah, maybe...and we can write everything down in bright-colored chalk and everything." There's playfulness in his tone that I've never heard before and it makes me laugh and feel giddy inside, tummy butterflies and everything.

"We are still speaking metaphorically, right?" I ask. "Or are we really planning on getting a slate and writing everything we do?"

"We don't have to write. I can draw everything," he jokes, but hidden in his light-humored tone is nervousness.

"We can do that." I unsteadily play along, working to keep my footing in the conversation because this brighter, lighter Quinton is new territory for me. From the day I met him, he's been sad. It's actually what drew me to him to begin with. The sadness in his honey-brown eyes reminded me so much of Landon. "But when are we going to start on this new slate together...or I guess what I'm trying to say is, when am I going to see you again?"

The line gets quiet and I think he might have hung up on me. But then I listen really closely and I can still hear the music in the background and the sound of his breathing.

"I can't go anywhere yet," he eventually says. "Not because I don't want to, but because I need to get my life on track here before I start doing other things."

"So you're going to stay in Seattle, then?" I ask, trying to conceal my disappointment but failing miserably.

"I kind of have to," he tells me with a bit of remorse. "I have a therapist all set up and sobriety meetings…and my dad…well, he's trying to work on our relationship and I think…well, I hope it'll help with stuff. At least I'm hoping it does."

By *stuff*, I think he means his guilt, which was the fuel driving his desire to use drugs, judging from the bits of information I picked up during my time in Vegas this summer.

"How are you doing with stuff?" I ask with caution.

"Honestly, I have my good and bad moments…I haven't been sober in about two years and it's sort of weird having a clear head. I really don't know what to do with myself."

"I'm sure you'll figure it out. In fact, I know you will."

"Maybe, but it seems really fucking hard whenever I think about it," he says truthfully. "And I've only been out for a day."

"Yeah, but it'll get easier." I sit up and rest my head against my headboard, stretching my legs out and crossing them. "You think a lot more now, right? I mean, your head's not so foggy."

"Yeah, and sometimes I really hate my thoughts," he admits. "And it makes me want to…" he trails off, but I know what he was going to say. Do drugs.

48

"Well, I think you can do it," I say, aiming to be motivating. "I think you're strong and you're going to keep your clear head."

"You're always so optimistic and caring," he says, sounding confused by his own words. "I've missed that . . . missed you."

A small smile touches my lips and my head gets all foggy, but in a good, what-the-hell-am-I-feeling way. "I want to see you." Crap, how can I slip up twice in one conversation? "I didn't mean to say that. Wait, I mean, I do want to see you, but I just didn't want to put pressure on you." I bite my lip to shut myself up. "God, I'm so sorry. I went into this phone conversation not wanting to put any pressure on you and I'm totally doing that already." I sink my teeth down harder on my lip until I draw blood, because it's the only way to get myself to stop rambling.

"Nova, relax," he says. "I'm not some breakable object that's going to shatter at any moment. You don't have to be so careful around me."

"I know, but at the same time, at least from what Tristan told me, when you first get out of rehab, it's really hard and you're really fragile."

He chuckles under his breath. "Did he actually use the word 'fragile'? Because it makes him sound really girly."

"He actually did," I say, feeling a little more at ease. "But it's not really his fault. He's been living with two girls for the last couple of months and I think we've been rubbing off on him. In fact, my friend Lea convinced him to let her paint his fingernails once. Granted, it was the color black, but still. I think he's one step away from letting us put makeup on him."

Quinton laughs harder and I feel very proud of myself. I was terrified of this conversation and it's been okay so far— well, minus my two slipups about wanting to see him. I do have a feeling that he hasn't read my letter yet because if he had, there could very easily be some tremendous awkwardness between us.

"Thanks. I really needed that," Quinton tells me after his laughter dies down. "I haven't laughed in a while."

"Anytime," I say, my pride increasing. "I can keep going if you want me to. Tell you all of Tristan's little secrets that only happen behind the walls of our apartment." He grows quiet again and I wonder if I said something wrong. "Are you okay?"

"Yeah, I'm fine. It's just that it's weird…you two living together."

"Us three live together," I remind him, kind of thrown off by the hint of jealousy in his voice.

"Yeah, I know, but still…" He trails off. "Never mind. It doesn't matter. I shouldn't even be getting onto the subject of this anyway."

The subject of what? Tristan and me living together? I'm not 100 percent sure what he's trying to get at, but I let it go, deciding it'd be stupid to push him. "So what is the weather like over there?"

It takes him a second to answer. "Cloudy and windy. How's the weather over in Idaho?"

"Dry and sunny." I scoot back down on the bed and roll to my side to face the frosted window. "Although it's a little cold."

"Yeah, it's the same way here, too." He wavers. "Nova, we don't have to talk about mundane things like the weather. Like I said, I'm not fragile."

I'm not sure where to go from here. We've been through so much together, yet at the same time I don't really know him, not the sober version, anyway. "So what do you want to talk about?"

"How about you and me," he says, his voice cracking. "And what we are."

His bluntness makes me stutter. "I-I'm not sure how to answer that. I mean, I don't really know the answer."

"Neither do I and I'm not sure how we can figure that out or . . . or if we should." He pauses. "God, I just replayed what I said in my head and I didn't mean for that to come out the way that it did. What I meant was that right now, I kinda am still trying to fix myself and I don't want you to feel obligated to wait around for me to get better."

My heart slams excruciatingly against my rib cage. "You read my letter, didn't you?"

"No . . . why? Did you say something like that in your letter?"

"No," I say quickly. "And you don't even have to read it if you don't want to. Or maybe you threw it away already."

"I still have it," he tells me reluctantly. "I was just too afraid to read it, afraid of what you said. Afraid it might mean too much."

51

"You should probably just burn it. I sometimes ramble when I write, like when I talk, and I don't know how you're going to take the stuff I said."

"I don't want to burn it. And besides, I've always liked your rambling. It can actually be insightful sometimes."

"You say that now," I tell him, forcing a teasing tone. "But try living with it."

He's silent for a moment and I have no idea what he's thinking. Whether he thinks I'm crazy? Amusing? I remember that when I was younger I wished I could have mind reading powers, and I'm starting to wish that again so I could crack his head open and see what on earth he's thinking.

"Nova, I'm going to read the letter," he says. "I just want to make sure I can handle whatever's in there."

"I wish I could answer that for you," I say. "But I don't know what you're expecting. Really, it's just my feelings. About you and me." Feelings I can still barely admit to myself. I was actually surprised at what came out of me. How much I care for him and how much I see him when I look into the future.

"Then I'm not sure I'm ready yet." There's an ache in his voice. "If it's rejection, then I'm worried it'll break me and if it's the opposite . . . if you want me as more than a friend, then I'm not sure I'm ready for that, either. Because honestly, I'm really weak right now and even taking care of myself feels really hard."

I get what he's saying a little too well. It took me over a year to watch Landon's video after he committed suicide, because I worried whatever was on there was going to shatter me into pieces. When I did finally watch it, though, I didn't shatter. In fact, I started picking up the pieces of my life, but only because I was ready to.

"Then wait to read it until you're ready," I tell him. "And for now, I'm okay with just being your friend." It feels like such a huge lie when I say it and actually kind of hurts my heart a bit.

"I would love that," he says, unwinding. "So tell me something friendly."

I snort a laugh. "What does that even mean?"

"I don't know." He sounds amused. "Tell me something you'd tell Lea or Tristan."

"Um, well, I watched *Anchorman* for the first time tonight." God, I'm so lame.

"And what'd you think of it?"

"I fell asleep," I admit. "But only because I was tired to begin with."

"Yeah, but it's not for everyone," he explains. "Although I know Tristan loves it."

"Yeah, he's the one who made me watch it," I divulge. "He acted like I was crazy because I never had."

He pauses again. "I'm jealous of him," he confesses. "And I only said that because my therapist has been pushing me to talk aloud about stuff that's bothering me...and it's bothering me...that you and Tristan get to spend so much time together."

"It's not like that," I promise. "We're just friends and roommates."

"I know, but I just wanted you to know that it's making me feel…jealous," he says hesitantly. "Although, if something did happen between you two, I'd understand."

"We're not going to get together. Trust me," I say, thinking about what happened back on the sofa and how much I would rather it had been Quinton than Tristan. "And besides, we fight all the time."

"Really? You two never did before."

"Yeah, we did. And he can be kind of cranky…I think he sometimes has a hard time adjusting to the boredom."

"I can see that," he states with understanding. "I'm already getting sick of staring at my walls and I've only been out for a day, but talking to you helps."

"Well, I can talk your ear off."

He laughs. "Please do."

I smile at the beauty in his laughter. "What do you want me to talk about?"

"You."

"What do you want me to tell you about me?"

"Everything…I want to know everything about you, Nova like the car." Amusement laces his tone as he says the nickname he gave to me pretty much the first day we met.

My smile takes up my entire face. Not because of his comment but because it's the first real moment I think Quinton and I have had without drugs and anxiety filling in the blanks in our conversation. And so I do the only thing I can do. I start talking. In fact, I talk well into the early hours of the next day. And for a moment everything feels perfect, but I have a hard time believing it's going to stay because it never seems to. Things just always sort of happen. Life always just sort of happens. And no matter what I do, I can never keep the bad out completely, despite how much I want to.

55

Chapter Three

November 17, day nineteen in the real world

Quinton

Jesus, time moves slow. Really, really slow. Especially when all I can think about is everything that's happened. I knew I had a rough road ahead of me, but this is ridiculous. Everything is pissing me off today. The rain. The clouds in the sky. My therapist. It's our sixth meeting and I'm starting to realize he's a pushy bastard. Nothing like Charles at the rehab center, who always let me do things on my own terms. Greg, my new therapist, seems to take the opposite approach, like if I don't start talking as soon as possible, then I'll never get better or "learn to deal with my feelings," as he puts it. Plus, after a suggestion he made to my dad, I've started helping around our community. Doing things like volunteering at the homeless shelter and visiting the elderly to keep me busy, like that's the key to keeping me out of

56

trouble. It's not like I hate doing it. In fact, at times it's nice because it makes me feel like I'm attempting to create something good to make up for all the bad I've put in this world. I just feel weird being out and about with people, who I swear can see what's hiding under my skin. The invisible scars that make up my past and the things I've done.

Add that to the fact that I'm living in my old bedroom in my old home with my father, and I'm feeling a little unbalanced right now, like I'm walking on a tightrope and am about to fall. On one side lies a fall to that rock bottom I'm so familiar with and on the other is the fall that just ends it all. Both seem like easy choices, yet I keep making myself attempt to balance and walk forward, especially when life keeps throwing me challenges. Like the other day when I was in the grocery store and I saw Lexi's mom. She didn't see me, thankfully, otherwise I might have slipped up in my sobriety. She's verbalized in the past how she feels about me and she has every right to feel that way. One day, though, I wish I could just tell her I'm sorry and that I hope maybe she can forgive me. The same with Ryder's parents. I want them to know that I think about them all the time. That I hate that I'm the one who lived. That I'm trying to make up for it the best I can.

Despite the fact that life is complex, writing seems to help a lot, actually. So here I am writing and in

just a few minutes I'll go to a job interview for a painting job. Not an artist painting job, but a construction
painting job, which isn't ideal, but the hours are flexible
and right now I have no more than a high school education so my job options are limited. Nova thinks I should
go back to school, but I'm not sure I can handle that
right now. Still, it's nice listening to her ramble about
the plus sides of getting a college education. The girl really
could have a job as a motivational speaker if she wanted
to, with all the positivity she sends out. I like her positivity, just like I like having her as a friend. I like everything about her and I wish I could tell her that. How
much she means to me. But that'd be opening a door I
know I'm not ready to open, which is why I haven't read
her letter, even though I'm dying to. In fact, I stare at it
every day.

Even though there's good stuff going on in my life, I
still have frequent nightmares about the accident. I keep
seeing Lexi die over and over again. Then myself. When I
wake up, it feels like I'm back in the place of death again.
That's actually another thing Greg's been pushing me to
talk about. My death. He thinks for some fucking reason
that some of my emotional problems and obsession with
dying are connected to the fact that I already died. He
even asked me how I felt when I died, what I saw, how I
felt when I came back. I told him to fuck off, though, so
he dropped it.

It made me angry that he opened the door and I was even more angry at myself for still not being able to talk about stuff like that. I still have such a very long way to go, everyone keeps telling me, like I don't get it. I know I do. I think about it all the time, how long it might take me to get some sort of balance in my life. But the fact that I can envision that long away has to mean something, right? Has to mean there might be some sort of hope for me other than relapse, a word I became very familiar with in rehab. A lot of the people were in there because of relapse and I can't help but think about it. How easy it'd be just to do it again. Get lost. Stop thinking about jobs. And therapy. Stop dreaming of Lexi and death. But it's also hard because I have a few people now pushing me in the opposite direction.

Still, I can't help but be hyper-aware of all the places I know I could get drugs from. Like Marcus down the street, who's still dealing, from what I heard. Or my old friend Dan, one of the guys I first got high with. I ran into him the other day at the grocery store while I was picking up some milk for my dad. He looked ripped out of his mind and it made me sort of envious. He even asked me if I still did it and I almost wanted to say yes, because I knew where that path would lead me. But instead I found myself saying no and a few minutes later I was standing in the checkout line, such a simplistic, boring thing, which allowed too many thoughts to slip into my *mind. Like how close the lake is to the grocery store, the one where the accident took place. The one where I died and came back to life. The one where two lives were lost.*

"Are you about ready to go?" my dad asks as he knocks on my doorway before strolling into my bedroom, interrupting my writing.

I stop moving the pen across the paper and glance up from the notebook. He's dressed in a polo shirt and slacks, instead of his usual button-down shirt and tie, but that's because he took today off from work.

"What time is it?" I ask as I set the notebook and pen aside on my bed.

He glances at his watch. "A quarter to two. It's a little bit early, but I figured we could stop and get a bite to eat and maybe talk or something." He scratches the back of his head, seeming uncomfortable.

"Sure." I get up from my bed and grab my jacket off the back of my computer chair, then we head out of my room.

As usual, neither of us talks as we get into the car and drive down the road. The entire journey there's nothing but silence, but I'm familiar with it. In fact, it's become really comfortable. Things only start to drift toward unfamiliar territory when my dad pulls up to a restaurant instead of a fast food drive-through. Sit-in dining has never been his thing. In fact, I can't even remember a time when he took me to a restaurant.

"Are we eating here?" I ask as he parks the car in an empty space toward the back section of the parking lot, near a grassy knoll.

He turns off the car and stares at the restaurant, which is decked out in Thanksgiving decor: orange lights trimming the rain gutter and pictures of turkeys painted on the windows. "I thought we could get something good to eat for a change. I know I've been a crappy cook for the last few weeks. I'm just too used to cooking for one, I guess."

"Trust me, I've eaten better in the last few weeks than I did for the entire summer." As soon as I say it, I want to retract it. I never know how honest to be with my dad. How much he wants to know about the stuff I did—how much I want him to know. It's not like we ever had that great a relationship anyway and honestly, I thought he hated me because of the accident. And maybe he does. Maybe he just feels obligated to help me because I'm his flesh and blood. I'm not really sure. I asked Charles about it once about three weeks into my recovery and he said I should talk to my dad about my feelings, but I don't think I'm ready to go there yet, not knowing whether I can handle it or whether he can.

"Still, it'd be good to get a nice meal." He doesn't say anything else, getting out of the car and shutting the door.

I get out, too, and then we walk across the parking lot and enter the restaurant. We're greeted by a blond hostess wearing a pair of teal vintage glasses, and I immediately smile at the sight of them. I think she thinks I'm checking her out because she gets this really big grin on her face and starts coiling a strand of her hair around her finger as she chats about the food and guides us to the table.

I'm only smiling, though, because yesterday Nova asked me if she should get glasses. She said the eye doctor recommended them for when she was reading and working on the computer. She said she hated the idea and that it would probably make her look dorkier than she was. When I disagreed with her and told her she could totally rock the look, she laughed and said she should just get a vintage pair with a little chain that hooked around them, like women wore in the 1950s.

"What are you smiling about?" my dad wonders as we take a seat at the corner booth.

"Nothing." I glance up at the hostess, who's still grinning at me as she sets our menus down on the table in front of us.

"Is there anything else I can do for you?" she asks, glancing at my father, and then her eyes land on me and fill with expectancy.

My dad starts to shake his head as I say, "Yeah, can I take a picture of your glasses?"

My dad gives me a befuddled look from across the table, like I've lost my mind, but the hostess seems flattered.

"Absolutely," she says, and then she flashes me a big grin as I raise the cell phone I bought three days after my dad was an hour late picking me up from therapy and couldn't get ahold of me to tell me he'd be delayed.

I snap the shot of the glasses, then thank her before she saunters away, looking really pleased with herself.

"What was that about?" my dad asks, as I try to crop the picture and zoom in on the glasses as much as I can. "Do you like that girl or something?"

I shake my head as I attach the picture to a text message addressed to Nova. "No, Nova and I were just talking about glasses the other night and she mentioned getting some like that girl had." I type: **these would look good on u. They match your eyes**. I move my finger to hit send, but then stop myself, wondering if maybe I'm being a little too flirty with her. We're supposed to be just friends. It's a good thing, too. Everyone says I need to take it easy. No stressful situations, and relationships are stressful, especially when my feelings for Nova are so intense.

But it's just a text message.

Dammit, I'm so confused at my life choices, from where the hell I'm supposed to go from here to sending a simple fucking text message. Things used to be so much simpler. Or maybe I was just oblivious.

Finally I just hit send and let it be, telling myself to stop over-analyzing everything. But even as I put my phone away, thousands of thoughts race through my mind, like what it means that I can be sitting here and picking out glasses for Nova, when ten miles away Lexi is buried under the ground in a cemetery up on the hillside near her neighborhood. And if I drive about fifteen miles to the east, I'll arrive at the place where her life ended. *But you need to let it go. Heal. Accept what is. Stuff happened to you. Bad stuff. But it doesn't mean you don't deserve to live.* That's what Charles used to tell me in rehab and I try to remind myself over and over again. But I fall into a slump and by the time my phone buzzes in my pocket, I don't want to look at it, so I hit ignore and order my food when the waitress comes to take our orders. She brings us waters and when she leaves, my dad starts chatting about his job to me. I zone off, wondering how I went from okay to down in the time it took to text a picture.

"So what do you think?" my dad asks as he unfolds the napkin that's around the utensils.

I tear my attention away from my thoughts and focus on him. "About what?"

His forehead creases as he places his napkin on his lap. "About moving to Virginia."

"Why would we move to Virginia?" I ask, and then take a sip of my water.

"Because my company wants to transfer me?" His puzzlement deepens. "I just told you this a minute ago. That my boss wants to put me up for the transfer."

Great. Apparently I zoned off and missed something really important. I'm finding it very hard to breathe and there's no way I can wrap my mind around the abrupt change he's throwing out there. Move. I can't move. Not when I just got here. Not when I'm just starting to get my life back on track.

64

"What would you do?" I ask, battling to keep my emotions under control, otherwise I know I'm going to flip out. "Sell the house or just keep it until we moved back?"

"I'd sell it," he says, stirring the straw in his glass of water. "It's a permanent transfer. The pay is great. And Virginia seems interesting and it's close to the ocean and a few art institutions."

"So's Seattle." I frown as I feel the familiar constricting sensation inside my chest. I'm not sure if I can move—go anywhere, when everything is so unstable as it is. I need to stay here. Need to keep doing what I'm doing. I need to do more. Everything might not be great, but it's okay. And I haven't had okay in a long time. "And I don't think you should sell the house."

"Why not?" he asks. "You've barely lived here in the last couple of years."

"Because it's Mom's house." I'm not even sure where the hell the thought came from. It's not like I've had a sentimental attachment to it before. Well, maybe I did before... the accident. But the last couple of years I've felt detached from everything. Maybe that's where the feeling's coming from— now that I'm sober maybe I'm heading back toward the old Quinton who existed at seventeen, before the accident, before he died. But would that mean I'm letting go enough of my pain and guilt to get there? *Shit*. No, I can't.

Pity fills my dad's eyes. "Quinton, I know that, but still...

I don't quite understand your attachment." He rakes his hands through his hair, at a loss about what to do or say next. "It's not like you have memories of your mom in that house, and you haven't even been living there for a year and a half."

This is the thing about my dad. He comes off as a douche a lot, but I'm not sure if he's aware of it or not. I haven't figured it out yet—haven't figured him out yet. And that's why I tell myself to try to calm down, but this forced, major, life-changing question is making my thoughts go into overdrive. I'm not ready for this.

"Could you just think about it?" he asks. "I think a change might be really good for you."

"I think I've had enough change to last a lifetime," I say as I scoot to the edge of the booth and rise to my feet. I can't take it anymore. This sitting-and-listening thing. I need to get the hell out of here. Go somewhere else and cool down before I explode.

I dash for the door as my dad turns in his seat and calls out, "Where are you going?"

"I need some air," I call out over my shoulder as I wind around the tables. I keep walking, not looking anywhere but at the floor until I get outside. Then I immediately light up a cigarette and feel the nicotine soak into my body and saturate my lungs, but it barely reduces the anxiety clawing at my throat. I take puff after puff as I pace in front of the car. I draw my hood over my head when it starts to rain, but I don't go inside. I just keep pacing, like somehow these small movements will help me outrun the cravings and need. Everyone keeps telling me it'll get easier. That if I just work through moments like these, things will settle back down. But at the moment it feels like everyone's been lying to me and it makes me want to lie to them.

It makes me want to break my promise to myself to try to stay clean.

But I can't.

No. I need to be stronger than that.

But I'm not strong.

I'm weak.

Give up.

Stay strong.

By the time my dad walks outside, carrying two to-go boxes, my mind feels like it's about to rupture over what I should do. The rain has stopped, the ground is covered with puddles, and my jacket is soaking wet. I'm cold, but I hardly notice because my thoughts are still centered on one thing that I know would make this whole moving thing easier. Just one hit, and I wouldn't have to deal with the erratic thoughts inside my head.

My dad doesn't help the situation when he gets into the car without saying a word, so I start obsessing about that as well as I climb in. After he starts the engine and cranks the heat, the warm air makes my chilled skin sting. The slight pain is distracting, though, and I'm grateful for it, like I'm grateful that I'm headed to my therapist so hopefully I can get a grip on this madness spiraling inside my head.

I buckle my seat belt and wait for him to back up, but instead he stares out the windshield dotted with raindrops.

"This wasn't how things were supposed to go," he says, shaking his head. "This was never the plan."

I suck it up the best I can. "Look, I'm sorry I walked out on lunch…there was just a lot of stuff going on inside my head."

"I'm not talking about lunch." He glances at me and for a fleeting moment, I think he's going to cry. "I'm talking about your life." He slumps back in the seat, staring ahead with his hands on top of the steering wheel. "You know, your mother and I once had a talk about what we'd do if something happened to the other one. She was pregnant with you and I remember she told me that if she could make sure one thing happened if she was gone, it'd be that you were always happy." His hands clench into tight fists. "She only asked one thing of me and I couldn't even do that for her."

I want to tell him he's wrong, but we'd both know that was a lie. He knows I'm not happy, that I haven't been in a long time. "Dad, I'm fine," I manage to say, despite how thick the lie is in my throat. "I know things have been super shitty, but I'm trying to make them better and you're here, so…" I shrug, unsure how to finish the sentence.

"I kicked you out," he mumbles, more to himself than to me. "I kicked you out because I knew you were doing drugs and I didn't want to deal with it."

I want to ask him if that's the only reason he kicked me out, because sometimes I wonder if he did it because he couldn't stand looking at me. If I reminded him too much of my mother or maybe it had to do with the fact that I'm responsible for two people leaving this world early. I should just ask him, but honestly I don't want to hear the answer. Whatever the reason was, it doesn't matter anymore.

"I'm sorry for what I put you through," I say for the first time since I came back to Seattle. "I know it had to be hard."

He looks at me with his brows dipped together. I think he might be about to tell me something important because of the intense look on his face, but then all he says is, "I'm glad you're home." Then he puts the car in drive and pulls out of the parking space.

"I'm glad to be home," I reply, but I'm not quite sure it's the truth. I still feel so out of place, like I'm living a dream that I'm not sure I'm a part of.

A small smile touches his lips as he starts the drive to my therapist's office. "Am I dropping you off at Mrs. Bellington's after therapy?" he asks.

"Yeah, I told her I'd stop by for like a half an hour." Mrs. Bellington is one of the elderly people I visit. She's seventy and actually not too bad to spend time with. She always has fresh-baked cookies and these stories about when she was younger and worked as an artist. She also always has soap operas on whenever I'm over there and while I'm not a fan, she likes to give me recaps in a very animated way and it's kind of entertaining.

After about five more minutes go by, I start to relax enough that I dare take out my phone and read Nova's message.

Nova: Who is that???

Me: A waitress at this restaurant my dad and I were eating at.

I start to put my phone back into my pocket when a text comes through.

Nova: I like the glasses. I think I'll get a pair. In fact, I think I'll even go all out and get a poodle skirt to go with it.

Me: And saddle shoes.

Nova: And a beehive hairdo.

Me: Sounds sexy.

Shit. Why do I always have to cross the "just friends" line? And why do I seem to care less and less each time I do? This isn't how things are supposed to be. I'm supposed to be suffering. Paying for what I did, not flirting with a girl I'm pretty sure I fell in love with over the summer, even in my drugged-out daze, although I haven't told her that yet.

Nova: Okay, you talked me into it, but you have to wear a leather jacket, slick your hair back, and roll up the bottoms of your tight jeans so we can match.

Me: It sounds like you're trying to make me look like a character from Grease, which btw was made in the 1970s not 1950s.

Nova: Lol, I think my era mishap was totally just

overshadowed by the fact that you know when the movie Grease came out.

Me: Hey, there's nothing wrong with knowing what year an old movie came out.

Nova: An old movie that has a bunch of singing and dancing. Tell me, do you know the lyrics and dance moves too?

Me: You're freaking hilarious today. You know that?

Nova: I do know that. In fact, I'm thinking about entering a stand-up comedian contest that's going on at this pub later tonight. Jokes about you and tight pants will be the highlight of my bit ;)

I'm about to type back when I realize the car has come to a stop. When I look up, we're parked in front of the therapist's office, an undersize brick building centered between a second-hand shop and a diner on the more worn-out side of town. That doesn't mean it's the bad side. Just older.

Me: Gotta go. Just made it to my therapist's.

Nova: K. R u calling me tonight?

Me: Of course.

I type it without even thinking, and as I put my phone into my pocket, I begin analyzing that fact way too much. How comfortable we've gotten in just a few weeks. I need to stop what's going on between us, but how do I end something I want so fucking badly? But maybe that's my punishment. Maybe I'm supposed to want her like that so I can suffer through not having her.

"Was that Nova you were texting?" my dad asks as I reach for the door handle.

I nod. "Yeah, why?"

"It's nothing." He shrugs. "I just notice you smile a lot when you're texting."

My face twists in puzzlement as I recap the last few minutes, but honestly I was in some sort of Nova zone and can't remember much of anything. I do realize how much lighter I feel at the moment. But the feeling dissipates as I get out of the car, which makes me hope today is a decent day in therapy so I can continue on this "high." Turns out the world wants to play opposite-of-what-Quinton-wants, because therapy not only sucks but opens up a hell of a lot of emotional shit I didn't feel like dealing with today.

It starts off when I begin talking about how I don't want to move to Virginia, but staying in Seattle on my own seems like it'd end up a huge problem. When Greg asks me why, I tell him it's because I think I'll get into too much trouble on my own and I don't want things to change when I'm just getting my life back together.

"Things are going to change no matter what you do, Quinton. That's life," he says in the monotone he always uses when he's forcing me to talk about something that's emotionally draining.

"But what if I can't handle them changing?" I ask. "Because just the idea of something as simple as moving makes me feel like my head's going to explode."

"You'll get there," he reassures me. "It'll just take time."

"But what if I don't want to get there?" I say, staring at the clock on the wall, the hands moving around and around. Time always moving no matter what I do. "Dealing with the future seems so hard."

"You will, but it'll take some time and effort on your part," he says, scooting his chair closer to his desk. "Tell me, have you worked on taking down those photos and pictures on your wall yet, like we've been talking about doing?"

"No, and I'm not ready to," I say coldly, gripping the handles of the chair. "So stop pushing it."

"Why do you think you're not ready?" he inquires, crossing his arms on his neatly organized desk. He's always calm, just like he's always wearing a wrinkle-free suit without a tie. I can tell he's a man of routine, which makes me wonder how the hell he's supposed to help me with my erratic instability, because he probably doesn't understand it.

"I don't think it. I know I'm not." I slump back in the chair and fold my arms, fighting the overpowering urge to reach for my cigarettes and light up right here in the office. "Every time I go to do it, I feel like I'm going to freak out and lose it...I feel like I'm letting go of stuff I shouldn't be letting go of." Like Lexi. My mom. My anguish and self-torture.

"I know it's hard." He reaches for the pen and notebook in the file cabinet just behind his desk. "And I'm not saying you have to take them all down. But I worry that the reason you're keeping them up there is to remind you of the past, which is hindering you from completely working on moving forward and healing yourself."

I want to get angry with him, but he's only saying the truth. "You know what, you're right," I say straightforwardly. "That's why I'm holding on to them, but even thinking about taking down the photos and sketches—letting go—makes me want to do drugs again. If I had drugs in my system, then I'd easily be able to take them down or at least feel better about it."

"Why, though?" he asks with attentiveness. "Why would doing drugs make you feel better about taking pictures on the wall down?"

"Because I wouldn't have to feel the things I know are coming when I pull the pictures down."

"Feel what exactly?"

"The guilt."

"Over what?"

I narrow my eyes at him because I've talked to him enough about this that he knows what I'd feel guilty about. "You know what."

"You're right. I do." He jots something down in his notebook. "But I'd like you to say it aloud. Verbally express what's going on inside your head."

My jaw sets tight. "I'd feel guilty about the fucking accident and that I killed people," I say through gritted teeth. "There. Are you happy? I said it."

He shakes his head. "What I'd like to know is, what about the accident do you feel guilty about, exactly?"

74

I shake my head, fearing the emotions that will prickle at the surface. "You know the answer to that." I dig my fingers into my palms and stab hard, trying to override the emotional pain with physical pain. "So quit asking."

He sets the pen down and overlaps his fingers on his desk. "No, I don't, Quinton. Because every time we get to the accident you never fully say how you feel about stuff. You always tiptoe around it and run away from it. Something that drugs help you do, which is why you always want to go back to that every time you have to deal with the hard stuff."

"The hard stuff." I give him a cold, hard stare as I scratch my arm where the tattoos mark my skin: *Lexi, Ryder, No One*. All the people who died that night, *No One* being myself. I remember that when I got it, the tattoo artist looked at me like I was a nut job, but I didn't care. I didn't care about anything but making sure I hurt myself more and more because it was the only way I could distract myself from the pain and the guilt. "Do you know how much talking about the hard stuff hurts and makes me feel like shit? How hard it is to breathe whenever I have to talk about the hard stuff...about the accident...about the deaths...dying?" My voice is sharp because he's digging up memories I don't want to deal with. "Jesus, it's not like anyone else would act differently. Causing people's deaths...I'm sure no one else would want to talk about it."

He considers what I said and then reaches for his pen again. He scribbles something down on the corner of a piece of paper and tears it off. "I want you to attend a group meeting," he says, stretching his arm across the desk to hand me the piece of paper.

"I already do that every Tuesday and Thursday night." My tone is clipped as I snatch the piece of paper from his fingers.

"Yeah, but this is a different kind of support group. It's not a sobriety group like the one you've been going to. This is one that'll help you deal with your guilt over the accident," he explains. "Many of the people who go have been through similar experiences. Both with the accident and with the drugs afterward."

I glance down at the piece of paper, which has a phone number and an address on it. "People go to this because they've caused car accidents and caused people to . . . die?"

He wavers contemplatively. "Well, not all of the instances were driving accidents, but I think it'd be good for you to talk to people who've gone through something similar to you and have experienced your form of guilt."

My fingers wrap around the piece of paper in my hand. "What stuff have they gone through, then?"

"Well, the founder of the group, Wilson Ferrison, ran a red light while he was on the phone," he says sadly. "It killed an older couple. He got into drugs for a lot of years . . . he's actually a friend of mine, so I saw firsthand how bad it got for him. But he does a lot of community service now and spends time talking to people about what happened, trying to not only prevent things like it from happening, but to help people who've experienced similar things and are left trying to cope with the guilt."

I put the piece of paper into my pocket, taking what he said in, but it's hard to process. "Should I call first or just go?" I ask, getting to my feet.

"Call first and tell them who you are. I'll give Wilson a call and let him know," he says, putting the notes he took through-out today's session into my folder. "Just please make sure you do call. I really think it's important for you to know that you're not alone."

Not alone. Such a foreign concept to me, and I'm not even sure how to respond. When I died and came back, I felt sort of like a ghost that no one wanted to talk to, because I was the reminder to everyone of the horrible thing that happened. So I did the world a favor and did everything I could not to exist. Over the last few years the world has felt really big and empty, but now he's saying that's not the case and that there are people out there who will understand what I'm going through, under-stand what it's like to live life with a void in your heart, put there by pain.

"Fine, I'll call," I finally say, and a tiny bit of the weight on my shoulders chips off and falls to the ground.

"Good," he says, and then he shakes my hand, some-thing he does after every meeting. "And work on taking down those pictures. Like I said, it doesn't have to be all of them. But only leave enough up that you're not overwhelmed by the past."

77

I don't respond to that comment and leave his office with my thoughts jumbled inside my head. For the briefest second, I wonder if talking to someone who gets what I'm going through could possibly help. What if I *am* helpable? I don't know how I feel about that. I'm not sure how I feel about anything, but maybe I'm on the right track to finding out.

Chapter Four

November 29, day thirty-one in the real world

Nova

"Life is strange. Life is complicated. Life is messy. Watch the news. Read headlines. Go help out at suicide hotlines. You'll hear stories. Heartbreaking stories. I've heard my fair share and lived a few of them myself." I'm sitting in the living room on the sofa with my legs crisscrossed, passing time filming while I try to figure out what to do for the rest of the night. "Today my film professor, Professor McGell, was talking about the heartbreak in the world after he showed us an interview clip with a woman who lost her husband to suicide…a clip that made me think of Landon and Quinton…" I trail off, remembering how much the woman cried in the video and how I wished I could tell her that everything would eventually be okay again.

After staring into empty space for a while, I concentrate on the camera again. "My professor said he wants to do something that could show what people are going through, not just when they lose someone to suicide but to other kinds of death, drugs, abuse. He said he was starting up a program that would be committed to making a documentary about the aftermath of surviving. He said he would have more information on it at the start of the next year. That it would require travel. Part of me wants to join. Take off and do what I've always wanted to do. Film stuff that matters. But it's a four-month program where I'd be on the road, in different countries. I'd have to leave everything behind... I'm not sure I can walk away and just leave everyone behind when they need me." I shift my legs out from under me and lower my feet onto the floor. "How can I just walk away when Tristan and Quinton are still healing? Leave Lea behind? My mom? Walk away from school for a semester? It just seems too... I don't know... impulsive, selfish, risky." I seal my lips shut, not wanting to say the words tickling at the tip of my tongue, but I ultimately let them slip out. "But I really want to do it. So much."

I leave my recording at that and put the camera down on the coffee table, figuring out what to do next. Classes are coming to an end and I don't have a lot of homework left to do. Most of my free time is spent texting and talking to Quinton and Tristan. I'm glad, though, because I'm getting to know Quinton better. And with Tristan, I figure as long as he's here talking to me all the time, then I know for sure that he's not going to parties and getting into trouble.

After thinking about what I really want to do for the night, I end up getting my cell phone out and texting Quinton.

Me: I saw something really interesting today.

Quinton: Let me guess. A purple dog.

Me: What kind of response is that???

Quinton: With you, it seems like a reasonable response.

Me: Hardy-fucking-har, u r soooo hilarious.

Quinton: I think that might be the first time I've ever heard you use the word fucking. It seems...unnatural.

Me: Fuck. Fuck. Fuck. Is that more natural now?

Quinton: No. Now it's just making me think of fuck and you.

I pause, staring down at the screen, wondering if he meant that as dirty as it reads. He's usually so careful with his comments, making sure to never get too flirty. It's completely sidetracked me from telling him about the filming project. But maybe it's better I don't say anything about it to him, so I don't either set something off or worry him that I'm going to leave. Although I'm not that confident in our relation... friendship...whatever it is, that I know for sure he'd even care if I took off for a while.

Quinton: Sorry. I didn't mean for that to come out that way. It sounded really dirty, didn't it?

Me: No, it's okay. And I figured u didn't mean it.

I'm glad you said it. That's what I really wish I could type. But I don't because I'm not brave enough, nor do I think Quinton is ready for anything like that.

Me: Off the subject, but how have things been going with that Wilson guy and those meetings?

Quinton: Okay, I guess. It's nice to hear someone talk about stuff that I've been through. I haven't really talked to him much personally, but I think I might want to one day.

Me: You should. Talking to Lea helped me deal with Landon's death a lot, since she'd been through something similar with her father.

Quinton: Can I ask you a really weird question?

Me: You can always ask me anything.

Quinton: I just don't want to make you uncomfortable…it's about Landon…

Me: I'm fine. In fact, I sometimes like talking about him because then I know I'm not forgetting him.

Quinton: U think it's important not to forget, even if remembering is hard?

Me: I think remembering is important but you need to get to a place where it's not so hard to remember and maybe even therapeutic.

Quinton: Yeah, I guess that sort of makes sense…I'm going to ask you that weird question now…please don't hate me, but I really just want to understand something.

Me: I never could hate you, so ask away.

Quinton: Yeah, we'll see…do you, I don't know, ever feel guilty about Landon's death?

I pause. I once told him I did, but I guess he was too high

to remember. I also remember that he didn't really want to hear it, which makes me wonder how much he's changing if he wants to hear it now.

Me: Yeah, I used to. Not really anymore. I mean, I do have days when I overthink it and I feel shitty all over again, but it's not as hard as it was when it first happened. Back then, I nearly went crazy thinking about all the things I could have done to save him...it was really bad that summer I spent getting high. And honestly, I kind of felt that guilt again this summer...it's part of the reason why I wanted to help you so much...to make up for not helping Landon.

I push send, but when he doesn't respond right away, I think maybe I shared a little too much—I'm never sure with him. But then my phone beeps.

Quinton: And how do you feel now? I mean, do u still feel the need to save people?

I can't help but think about the film project again. While it wouldn't necessarily be saving anyone, it could help people realize that they're not alone in this world, which I feel is important. I remember when Landon died and how no one seemed to really talk about it and I felt really alone, confused, and just plain lost. But perhaps if I'd had Lea earlier on, I wouldn't have fallen so fast and so hard.

Me: Yeah, but not in the helpless obsession sense. I still volunteer at the helpline sometimes and that helps. Plus, you're okay so that makes me sort of happy.

Quinton: I want to stay okay, but sometimes it's hard, you know. Especially when I really start thinking about stuff.

Me: I know it can get really difficult sometimes, but I know you can do it.

Quinton: Why, though? Why have you always had so much faith in me when you barely know me?

Me: I think I know you more than you think I do. And I think that you're going to be okay because you're working on being okay. If you were still running away from the problem, then I'd feel different.

Quinton: I hope you're right.

Me: I'm always right and the sooner you realize that the easier things will be. J/k ;)

Quinton: You're so goofy sometimes.

Me: Thanks :)

Quinton: It's actually one of my favorite things about you.

I smile to myself as I type.

Me: Want to know one of my favorite things about you?

It takes him a moment to respond.

Quinton: Sure.

Me: That you're a good, strong person.

Quinton: Are you sure u know who you're talking to?

Me: Yeah, the person who was good to me when I was in such a vulnerable place. The person who managed to pull himself away from a life of addiction. That takes strength, my friend.

Quinton: It takes weakness to get to that place to begin with. To walk away from my life like that. Give up everything instead of being strong and actually just facing my problems. I wish I could be stronger and face them now. And I wish I hadn't given up everything.

Me: You'll get there. It'll just take time. Facing the hard stuff is...well, hard. And as for giving everything up, you can still get it back. You just have to know what you want and work toward getting it.

Quinton: But I'm not sure what I want exactly. I know I like helping people and everything. It keeps me busy and makes me feel like I'm giving stuff back. But other than that, I don't know what I want to do. Draw and paint, yeah, but that's not a whole hell of a lot.

Me: Sure it is. U just have to do it.

Quinton: I don't even know what to draw anymore. All my sketches and paintings over the last couple of years have been trippy. I want to draw things that mean something. I want to draw things that I can put passion into. Like life. Happiness. Sadness. Pain. I want to draw stuff that's important to me...I want to draw you, too. And not from how I see you in my head. I want to draw you in front of me. Every line. Every inch of you.

Before I have time to react to the text, another one comes in.

Quinton: I'm sorry if that last text made u uncomfortable. I'm blaming it on the fact that Greg made me share way too much today and broke me down I think.

I take a deep breath, thinking about what it would be like for him to draw me like he described. I remember when Landon first sketched me: halfway through it, he kissed me for the first time. It was magical at the time and it's heartbreaking to remember it now, but I wouldn't want to forget how it felt for anything.

Me: I want u to draw me like that. In fact, I'm going to hold u to it and make u do it the next time I see u.

Jesus Christ. Did I seriously just text that? Wow. I can't even breathe.

Quinton: I wish I could do it right now…see you right now…touch u right now.

My heart pitter-patters inside my chest and I have to suck in a huge breath when I realize I've been holding it. My initial response is to skirt around the conversation because of where it's heading. But then I realize that it's been a long time coming so I just go for it.

Me: I wish I could see you and touch you, too…I wish you were touching me. In fact, I think about it all the time.

My hands shake as I hit send.

Quinton: Nova you're killing me right now. I swear to God. Now I've got pictures inside my head of us touching each other.

I shut my eyes and bite my lip as images appear inside my mind as well. How it felt when he ran his hands across my body. How his tongue tasted. How his tongue felt. How his fingers felt when they were in me. God, it's been a long time.

Me: Good, because I do, too…do u remember that kiss we shared right after we got off the roller coaster last summer? It was our last kiss.

It takes him a moment to answer and I grow worried that maybe it was the wrong question to ask.

Quinton: I do. I should have never kissed u when I was like that.

Me: And I probably shouldn't have kissed u when I knew u were like that, but at the same time, I'm glad u did. It made me realize a lot of stuff…how I feel about you. And how much I want to kiss u, over and over again.

Another pause and I start to feel stupid for being so forward. But then a message comes through.

Quinton: Nova, I don't want to sound like a jerk, but I don't think I can take much more of this kind of talk with u. It makes me want to do things I'm not ready for. I'm seriously one step away from getting on a plane and flying over there so I can kiss u again—do a hell of a lot more than kiss. But I don't think I'm ready for that just yet.

I restrain a grin. He said *yet*. Which means he's thinking about us in the future sense. That has to be good, right? Part of me believes so, but the other part has to wonder how long is too long. What if the waiting goes on for years?

I shake the thought from my head, not ready to go there just yet. Not ready to give up hope yet.

Me: Okay, we can talk about something else. Anything u want.

Quinton: How about something to cool me off and settle me the fuck down. You've got me all riled up.

Me: Popsicles. Snowflakes. Icicles. Does that help?

Quinton: Lol, you are so crazy and I love it.

Me: Good. I'm glad because not a lot of people get me.

Quinton: I doubt that at all. Everyone loves u. I'm sure of it.

I want to ask him if he loves me, too, but I'm not even sure I'm ready for the answer, let alone if he's ready to give me one. Even though I've let go of Landon for the most part, it still feels strange to think about loving someone again, but alarmingly exciting.

Quinton: I actually have a problem I'm trying to figure out. And since you're a problem solver I thought u could maybe help.

Me: Of course. What's up?

Quinton: Well, my dad's moving to Virginia.

Me: What? Why?

Quinton: It's for work. And he wants me to go but I don't want to go.

Me: I think if u don't want to go with him, then don't go. You've been through enough already and I think u should be focusing on getting better.

Quinton: But I worry about living by myself. Too much freedom for one thing.

Me: U could get a roommate. It's hard to get into trouble when u have people watching u all the time. Like Lea. She'd kick my ass if I did anything.

Quinton: Yeah, but how would I know I was getting a good one? One that would help me stay out of trouble instead of get into trouble, because sometimes it's hard to tell with people.

Me: I could come screen them for u. Break them down and discover all their secrets.

Quinton: I don't think u would have to break them down. Knowing u, u would just start talking to them and they'd open up to u. U have that way about u.

Me: Everyone keeps saying that, but I don't get why.

Quinton: U need to give yourself more credit. I've said more to u about the accident than I've told most people.

Me: U didn't tell me much. In fact, u were furious when I told u the stuff I knew about the accident that I read on the Internet.

Quinton: I know.

There's a long pause and the longer it goes on the more I think I might have lost him.

Me: R u there?

Quinton: Yeah... I was just trying to remember what I said to u... some of the stuff that went on in Vegas is a little hazy.

Me: I could tell u if u want me to, but honestly I figure what's in the past is in the past.

Quinton: I wish it were that easy. That the things that happened in the past would just sort of fade away, but they don't. I'm realizing that everything that happened...it's going to stay with me forever.

Me: Although the memories won't ever fade completely, they will eventually fade. I promise. And one day you'll even be able to talk about what happened.

Quinton: I hope so. I want to be able to talk about it. Explain to u everything so that maybe you'll understand how I ended up in that place. I don't want u to always think of me like how I was in Vegas. Or even during that summer in Maple Grove. I want u to know the person that I sort of gave u a glimpse of while we were dancing in the gas station parking lot.

Me: U remember that???

Quinton: Yeah, that's actually one of the clearer memories I have.

Me: Good. It was a good memory.

Quinton: Yeah but I was high. I feel like I should do a redo for u.

Me: U always could.

Quinton: Maybe one day.

Me: Yay :)

Me: And just so u know, I never thought of u as anything other than a person who had something really crappy happen to them that was completely out of their hands and you were just trying to find a way to survive through it. You're not a bad person. U just made some mistakes but only because u were hurting.

Quinton: I don't completely agree with u. Some of the stuff I did was because I was selfish. I didn't want to stay in this world and live with the consequences of what I did.

Me: I wish I could hug u right now.

Quinton: God, I wish that, too.

My phone grows silent as I try to figure out what to type next. What I want to do is put in all caps THAT'S IT. I HAVE TO COME SEE U. But he texts me before I get a chance.

Quinton: Can I say one more thing and then we can change the subject, because I'm seriously one step away from falling apart again.

Me: Sure.

But I'm kind of bummed out, because things were just getting really good.

Quinton: I think if every person had a Nova Reed in this world, then life would be a little sunnier. Now change the subject quickly before I can't handle this anymore.

Not knowing what else to type, I send out a panic text.

Me: I think Lea might be having an affair with a professor.

Quinton: Nice subject change... why a professor?

91

Me: She's too secretive, which makes me think she's doing something forbidden.

Quinton: U should follow her one day and see where she goes ;)

Me: Sounds like a great idea. I could put on my detective coat and my vintage glasses and shadow her every move **taps fingers together**

Quinton: You're a genius. She'll never suspect anything.

I'm smiling as the front door to the house opens. I glance up from the phone as Tristan walks through the front door with bags of groceries in his hands. He's hacking so hard, I swear a hairball is going to fly out of his mouth.

"A little help please," he coughs, dropping the bags in the foyer as he struggles to breathe.

Me: Gotta go. Tristan needs help carrying groceries in.

Quinton: Tell him that's the man's job.

Me: I would but he's been sick.

Quinton: Okay, call ya tonight?

Me: Aren't u sick of me yet?

Quinton: No way. Never.

Me: Okay, talk to ya later :)

I set my phone down and get up from the sofa to go over to the foyer and help Tristan pick up the spilled groceries. "I still think you should get that cough checked out," I tell him as I bend over to pick up a can of soup that rolled out of one of the bags.

He leans against the wall, covering his mouth with his hand, and hacks into it. "It's just a cough," he says, but he looks pallid.

"Yeah, but you've had it for over a month now." I put the soup can down on the counter and then start carrying the bags into the kitchen. "Coughs don't normally stick around for a month."

"I'm fine," he insists after his coughing settles. He rolls up the sleeves of his hoodie and bends over to pick up the remaining bag, but then quickly puts his hand against the wall to brace himself, like he's dizzy and about to fall over.

"Jesus, are you okay?" I ask, rushing over to him.

He nods, wiping his forehead with the back of his hand, and suddenly I notice how damp his skin is. "Yeah, I think I just need to get some rest. It's been nothing but school and work nonstop for the last couple of weeks and I'm feeling drained."

"Go lay down and I'll make you some soup," I tell him, and he gladly obliges, letting go of the wall and trudging toward his room.

I go into the kitchen with the bags of groceries. There are cupboards on both sides and enough room between them for one person, barely, and I end up banging some of the bags on the edges of the counter. One snags on the handle of a drawer and rips open. Items fall out and scatter all over the floor. A two-liter of soda ends up exploding. Cursing, I pick up the spraying bottle and put it into the sink, then grab some paper towels and start cleaning up the floor. After I wipe it up, then mop away the stickiness, I've started to unpack the groceries when my phone rings. I hurry over to the coffee table and pick it up, confused by the unknown number on the screen. I reluctantly answer it as I make my way back over to the kitchen.

"Hello," I say, taking cans of soup from a bag.

"Hey." A woman's voice comes through from the other end that sounds familiar, yet I can't place it. "Is this Nova... um...Reed?"

"Yeah." I stack a soup can in the cupboard and then turn around and lean against the counter. "Who is this?"

"It's Nichelle Pierce, Delilah's mom." She pauses like she's waiting for me to say something to her.

I'm not sure what to say, though. She's the one who called me and I've met the woman maybe three or four times, when Delilah and I would have to go to her house to get something, back when we were seniors in high school and still lived at home. For the most part, though, Delilah hated going to her house, because she said her mother made her feel insignificant.

"I don't really know how to say this," she finally says, sounding annoyed. "So I'm just going to come out and say it...Delilah's missing."

I'm not surprised at all, considering what went on with Quinton, who was roommates with Delilah before, and how we couldn't find him for months. "Have you checked around Vegas, by chance?"

"Yeah, I have, but I haven't found any sign of her…" She clears her throat. "Look, I'm really worried about her and I didn't know who else to call, since I don't know any of her other friends. Have you heard from her at all or do you know where she might be?"

"I haven't," I tell her, wondering if I should tell her about the last time I saw Delilah in Vegas. What a mess she was. How crazy her boyfriend Dylan was acting. How her life was full of drugs and drug deals gone bad. "Not since about June."

"Did she say anything about going anywhere at all when you saw her?" she asks. "The last time I talked to her was about a year or so ago and all I know is she was going to Vegas to live her life or whatever."

"Honestly, I didn't talk to her very much when I saw her," I say, and then I cautiously add, "She was a little…out of it, though, and her boyfriend seemed pretty…strange."

"Strange how?"

"I don't know…" I hope she's not going to take what I say next badly. Sometimes parents have issues with hearing that their child's gotten into drugs. "They were both into drugs and I think Dylan was a little violent with her."

"That doesn't surprise me," she says with zero shock in her voice. "He always did seem to fly off the handle over the stupidest things."

I shake my head, irritated that she doesn't seem to care about her own daughter. Delilah and I might not have left our friendship on a good note, but there was a point when we were close and she helped me through some hard times in her own crazy way.

"That's all I know about her," I tell Nichelle. "Well, that and the apartment she was living in with Tristan and Quinton burned down, but I don't think anyone was hurt."

"I didn't know that." She seems mildly shocked. "Do you happen to know the address of the place she was staying at . . . the one that burned down?"

"I don't remember it, but if you give me a minute I can maybe find out." I walk out of the kitchen and head for Tristan's room.

"Yeah, okay. Thanks."

"No problem." I move the phone away from my ear and cover it with my hand as I nudge Tristan's ajar door open with my elbow and step inside.

He's curled up in his bed with a blanket over him, his head nuzzled into his pillow. I can hear him breathing softly as I walk over to his bedside and I'm fairly sure he's asleep. I feel bad for waking him, but he's the only person, besides Quinton, I can think to get the address from.

"Tristan," I say softly. He doesn't stir, so I tap him on the shoulder with my finger. "Hey, I have a question for you."

He rolls over to his back as his eyelids flutter open and he blinks around dazedly. "What are you doing in here?" he asks in a hoarse voice.

"I need the address to your old apartment in Vegas."

96

He yawns, stretching his arms above his head, his eyes reddened with exhaustion. "Why?"

I lift my hand with the phone in it. "Delilah's mom is looking for her and wants to know the address."

He noticeably tenses. "Well, the place burned down, so . . ." He shrugs, rubbing his eyes. "Does it really even matter what the address is when the place isn't even there anymore?"

I nod, watching him closely. "Yeah, it does, so what's the address?"

He rolls his bloodshot eyes, like I'm being ridiculous. "Five five five Mapletonville Drive," he mumbles, then rolls over so he's facing the wall and his back is turned toward me. "I'm going back to sleep now. I feel like shit."

I remember when he first told me the place had burned down, how it seemed like he'd left out some of the details of what happened. Now I'm really starting to question if there's more to it. I think when he's feeling better I'll have to press him to tell me, but for now I let him rest because he looks terrible.

I walk out of his room and close the door behind me. I can't help but speculate about if something bad did happen to Delilah when the apartment burned down. If maybe Dylan did something to her. But what would that say about me? Since I just left her in that place, knowing how he treated her?

I can't stop thinking about it as I walk back into the kitchen, telling Delilah's mother the address Tristan gave me.

"Thanks," she says when I finish.

"You're welcome," I reply, returning to putting the groceries away. "Can you let me know what happens? When you find her?"

"Sure." She doesn't sound like she's going to, though, and I hang up feeling irritated.

The irritation only builds as I make Tristan some soup, my thoughts stuck on Delilah and where she is, what she's doing, if she's okay. I should have pressed her more when I was down there. Should have told someone about how Dylan was treating her.

Dammit, is there ever going to be a time in my life when I don't regret the decisions of my past? I'm starting to think no and that regret is just a part of life and I can't get hung up on it. Still, by the time I take Tristan his soup, my old counting habit is surfacing with my stress and all I want to do is count all the noodles in Tristan's soup and all the specks of brown in the tan carpet.

When I enter his room, Tristan is lying on his bed, gazing up at the ceiling with his arms tucked under his head, and the lamp on. "Eat this," I tell him as I make my way over to the bed, balancing the steaming bowl in my hand.

He turns his head toward me and frowns at the bowl. "I'm too tired to eat," he gripes. "And I'm not even hungry."

"God, you're like a little kid." I set the soup down on the nightstand beside his bed. He shoots me a dirty look and I return it. "And if the soup's not gone by the time I come back, you're going to be in big trouble." I wave my finger at him sternly.

That gets him to laugh a little bit. "Fine." He sits up, reaches for the bowl, and stares at the soup in it.

"It's good. I promise."

"I'm sure it is." He picks up the spoon and starts absent-mindedly stirring the soup. "So why's Delilah's mom suddenly looking for her?"

"Who knows?" I shrug. "From my understanding, she's always been a shitty mom to Delilah."

"Yeah, I got that, too, but then again, aren't a lot of mothers?" He glares at his soup like it's the enemy and pokes one of the noodles with the spoon.

"I like my mom," I state, sitting down on the edge of the mattress and crossing my legs. "She's always been good to me."

"You're one of the lucky ones, then." He peers up from his soup, his blue eyes appearing gray in the low lighting of the room. "Do I really have to eat this?"

I nod sternly. "Yeah. All of it, too."

He sticks out his tongue, but takes a bite anyway. I leave him to it and spend the next few hours cleaning, because it keeps my thoughts focused on eliminating mildew in the shower and crumbs on the carpet, and I even get a few loads of laundry done. I'm folding up the clothes in my bedroom, making stacks on the bed, when my phone starts ringing again. After the call I got from Delilah's mom, I'm hesitant to answer it, since I'm not sure I want to deal with any more drama for the night.

But it's Quinton and that's definitely a call I don't want to miss. "Hey," I say, positioning the phone between my cheek and my shoulder so I can continue to fold the clothes and put them into orderly piles on my bed. "I'm glad you called."

"I said I would." He sounds okay, which gives me a strange sense of peace inside. "I would never stand you up on one of our phone dates."

"Yeah, but we texted so long on the phone, I thought you'd be sick of me by now."

"I don't think I'll ever be sick of you," he says. "In fact, I think we made it pretty clear how not sick of you I was. How I-want-to-touch-you-so-badly-I-can't-stand-it not sick of you I am." There's an extended pause. "Jesus, that sounded cheesy, didn't it?" he says, sounding disappointed in himself.

"A little." I smile, but it's almost agonizing as I think about Delilah and where she is. "But I liked it. It makes me feel like I'm getting to know the real you."

He chuckles. "You know what? I can kind of remember being cheesy at one point in my life."

His happiness makes my sadness vanish. "I'm so glad you called tonight." I put a pair of boxer shorts on top of the pajama stack on my bed.

"Why? Is something wrong?" he asks worriedly. "You seemed okay earlier when we were texting, but you sound a little sad now."

100

I pause with the folding, regretting that I even brought it up. The last thing he needs is to hear any of my problems when he's got so much on his plate. "No, I'm fine. Nothing major's going on. Just school stuff."

"Want to talk about it?"

"Not really." I feel bad for lying to him, but at the same time I know it's the best thing. "Let's talk about something happy."

"I'm probably the wrong person for that," he says with honesty, his mood deflating. "You might want to try Tristan or Lea."

"Tristan's pretty sick right now, so he's not feeling that happy, either." I put a folded-up shirt on top of the pile. "Besides, hearing your laugh is already making me feel better."

"Yeah, but you're the one who made me happy enough to laugh. I was a little bummed out before I called."

"How come?" I pick up two socks and pair them, adding them to the pile of socks.

"I don't want to gripe about my problems when you're having a bad day," he says.

"Please, tell me," I beg, going over to my closet and getting a few hangers out. "In fact, it'll make me feel better to listen."

"You're too easy to please, but if that's what you want, then…" He sighs heavyheartedly. "It's nothing major, but remember earlier how we were talking about moving? Well, I was sort of hoping my dad would change his mind, but when he got home tonight he told me that he listed the house with a Realtor, and he had boxes for us to pack our stuff in. And I think he might be excited about it or something."

"Did you ever tell him that you definitely didn't want to go with him?" I collect a stack of jeans in my arms and turn for the dresser.

"Sort of... I mean, I said I'd think about it, but I know I won't move," he says gloomily. "And I don't want him to sell the house... it's the only real thing I have left of my mother."

I stop in front of the dresser, wanting to cry for him. It hurt a lot to lose my father, but at least I got to spend twelve years with him. Quinton's mother died giving birth to him and he never got to know her.

"I understand that completely," I say, opening the dresser drawer. "Even though it took me forever to drive it, I could never imagine getting rid of my father's car."

"Did you..." He struggles for words. "Did you ever get that dent fixed that Donny... that... drug dealer put in the fender?"

I'm actually surprised he remembers that, seeing as how he was so out of it when it happened. "Yeah, you can't even tell it happened anymore." I place the stack of jeans in the drawer, then walk back over to the bed.

"Yeah, but it did. And it's my fault it did... I'm sorry, Nova." He sounds like he's choking up. "For everything... all that shit that went down in Vegas."

I pick up a hanger and a shirt. "You don't need to be sorry

for anything. I told you that and I mean it. What happened in the past is in the past. We're moving forward now. Remember, a clean slate."

"You sound just like my therapist," he states as I put the shirt on the hanger. "He keeps pushing me to let go of the past and take down my pictures hanging up in my room...but I don't want to forget everything. In fact, I need to remember, otherwise it'll make it easier for me to go back...if I forget all the bad stuff that happened."

I get what he's saying, but I still wish he didn't feel so bad about some of those things. Besides, they weren't all bad. Like the couple of kisses we shared, the dance. The few talks we had a year and a half ago during the summer we spent together when we first met, getting high and going to a concert. And the couple we had this last summer in Vegas. Those moments were genuine. "I think it's okay to hold on to the past just a little, but at the same time I know I always feel better when I'm moving forward and letting go. As for the pictures, I actually had all Landon's boxed up for a long time. I finally took them out and put them in an album, which I look through every once in a while."

"And it doesn't hurt to look through them now?" he asks.

I go to the closet and hang the shirt up. "Not really. In fact it feels good to remember some of the stuff, because there were some really good moments."

He's quiet for a while. "Still, it feels like everything's going to fall apart the moment I take them down from the wall. Even

103

in Vegas, I had sketches lying around. I just can't imagine not having them around me to remind me of...everything."

"You'll get there," I promise, returning to my bed. "I know you will."

"I sure hope so, otherwise I'm going to have a nagging therapist to answer to every other day." His tense tone relaxes a smidgen. "Although things could be a lot worse. I could be living in that shitty apartment again in Vegas."

"You regret that, then?" I'm so glad to hear him say it. "Being in that place?"

"You know what, in the beginning when I was coming down I didn't," he says with honesty. "But now, yes. I don't want to go back to that place again. I think it was a good thing when it burned down...of course I wouldn't be saying that if anyone got hurt, but some of the stuff that went on there was really fucking bad."

His comment suddenly reminds me of Delilah. "Speaking of that, can I ask you a question?" My voice carries caution as I slide the remaining clothes to the side and sit down on the bed. "Warning, it's kind of an intense question."

"I don't care," he says. "I want to help you with whatever it is."

I hope I'm not crossing a line by asking. "Were you around when the apartment burned down?"

He doesn't answer immediately. "Yeah, why?" he finally asks with wariness.

"Well, Delilah's mom called me today, asking if I knew

where she was, which was weird since she never cared where Delilah was all during the few years that I knew her." I flop down on the bed on my stomach. "She said she was missing and I just want—need to know if she's okay. And I was wondering if maybe you knew."

"If Delilah is okay?"

"Yeah, or maybe where she could be, possibly."

Silence takes over the line and my heart squeezes inside my chest with the fear that maybe he does know something and it's really, really bad.

"I don't really remember much." He eventually speaks with hesitation. "Other than the fire was started intentionally and…" He swallows hard. "A gunshot was heard right before it happened."

"Gunshot?" My eyes widen and I cover my mouth as I start to breathe loudly.

"Yeah, and it came from…God, this is so hard to talk about." He gradually exhales. "It came from our old apartment."

I'm shocked. Appalled. Terrified. Sickened. Many different things that are so overwhelming I'm suddenly sick to my stomach.

I lower my hand from my mouth. "You think Dylan shot her?" I don't even know why I say it, other than that I can't forget how strange and creepy he was acting and how Delilah had signs of abuse on her.

"I'm not sure, since I was living downstairs with…

someone at the time, but it could have been a lot of things. Anything from a drug deal to the simple fact that maybe Dylan's gun went off. But no one was found in the remains of the fire, so no one was hurt," he says, his voice cracking at the end. "And even though I hate to say it, I honestly wouldn't be surprised if Delilah was living on the streets somewhere high or . . . even working as a prostitute."

I suck back the tears threatening to spill out as I rest my cheek against my bed. "Dylan had a gun?" My voice is just a whisper.

"Yeah, at least he did right before I moved out," he says. "But I don't really think he'd do anything with it. I think he just had it to make himself seem tougher than he was." He doesn't sound that convincing, though, and I'm not even sure he believes himself.

I realize how much we've been talking about death for the last few minutes and how that's probably not the best thing for him. No matter how much I want to get answers, the last thing I ever want to do is make him hurt more than he already does.

"This conversation has really gotten dark, hasn't it?" I ask and I take his silence as agreement. "Let's talk about something else."

"Like what?" He sounds depressed, which pretty much matches how I feel.

But I can handle being sad. It's him I'm worried about. So

I try to think of something cheerful to say, but I'm having a hard time. "How about work? How's that going?"

"Okay, I guess," he replies, and I can tell by his deflated tone that I failed in thinking of a better topic. "I mean, it's painting houses, so it's not too complicated, and the hours are flexible, so that's good."

"But you don't like doing it?"

"Not really," he admits. "It's not really my thing."

"What is your thing?" I ask, really wanting to know what he thinks about the future, because he rarely ever talks about it. "You said earlier that you wanted to paint and draw. Is that what you want to do? Be an artist?"

"Maybe. Although if I did, I'd have to accept that I'd more than likely be poor for the rest of my life and that I'd also probably have to have a side job."

"Does it really matter, though? If you're doing something you love?"

"I guess not, but being poor would sort of suck, at least that's what Lexi always used to say."

The lengthiest pause passes between us at the mention of Lexi. He never, *ever* talks about her. I can tell that it was completely accidental and that he probably wants to take it back. Dammit, this conversation is really turning into a depression-fest. I need to find a way to salvage it somehow.

"Do you think you'll ever go back to school?" I ask, trying to casually skip over the topic.

"I already told you, maybe one day." His voice is uneven and I can tell he's on the verge of crying. "I mean, I used to think about it a lot, but I don't know... it'd be really real, you know."

"But sometimes real is good." I pause as I hear the front door open. Moments later my door opens and Lea sticks her head in. A week ago she cut her hair to her chin and she always wears it down now. It looks good, but right now it's wet, like she's been swimming in the indoor pool at our apartment complex. But she's dressed in jeans and a long-sleeved shirt, not really swimming attire, since usually she just goes in her swimming suit.

"Hey," she says, looking flushed as she steps inside my room. "I brought some takeout from that Italian restaurant if you want some. It's in the kitchen." Lea's been hanging out at this restaurant down on the corner of Bralford and Main a lot and is always bringing home food with her. I wonder if it has to do with whomever she's dating.

"Hey, can you hang on a second?" I ask Quinton.

"Yeah, sure." He almost sounds relieved to have a break from talking.

"Thanks." I move the phone away from my mouth, roll onto my back, and say to Lea, "Sure, but can I ask you something?"

Her expression fills with wariness. "Yeah, as long as it's not more accusations about me secretly dating some guy."

"It's not." I sit up on the bed and swing my legs over the edge, putting my feet onto the floor. "I just want to know why your hair's wet."

She shrugs nonchalantly, combing her fingers through her hair. "I don't know. Maybe it was raining."

I glance at the window, noting the glass is dry, and so is the grass down below. "It doesn't look like it's rained." I return my attention to her. "And how do you not know if it was raining when you just walked in from outside?"

"I don't know why you're so surprised. I'm a pretty oblivious person." She glances at the phone in my hand. "Who are you talking to?"

"Quinton."

"Well, I'll leave you alone, then." Her lips curve into a smile; she's pleased she has an easy escape from my excessive questioning.

"Don't think this conversation is over," I call out as she exits the room with a skip to her walk. "I'm going to find out what you're keeping from—"

She shuts the door, cutting me off, and I put the phone back to my ear, dumbfounded. "Sorry about that," I say. "But she's definitely acting weird."

"Yeah, I definitely think it's detective time," he says, his mood seeming to lift ever so slightly. "Go grab that pencil and paper and follow her."

"I wish I would have followed her earlier," I tell him. "She just came home with her hair drenched and she says she has no idea why."

"Maybe she went swimming?" he suggests. "That seems logical, doesn't it?"

"Yeah, maybe." I lie back down on my bed and prop my feet up on the wall. "But she didn't have her bathing suit on. And besides, if she had gone swimming, wouldn't she have just said so?"

"Maybe she doesn't want you to know." He pauses, considering the possibilities. "Because she's dating her swimming instructor and she doesn't think you'll approve of him. Or maybe you are right. Maybe she's having an affair with a professor and the only place they can meet is in the swimming pool after hours where they can have sex in the water."

I suddenly get a picture of the time Quinton and I almost had sex in the water. I was confused at the time and was glad he backed out, but now...well, thinking about having sex with him in general gets my skin burning and makes my stomach somersault.

But I try my best to pretend the word "sex" coming out of his mouth doesn't have any effect on me. "You sound so scandalous. Has that older lady that you've been helping out been making you watch soap operas again?"

"Yeah, sometimes. Why? Is it starting to show?"

"Yeah, kind of," I reply. "How is Mrs. Bellington doing?"

"Good. Although her family put her in a nursing home the other day clear across town so it's really hard for me to visit her," he says, then pauses. "You know, she kind of reminds me of you."

"A seventy-year-old woman reminds you of me." I frown, taken aback a little. "Wow, I feel kind of stupid right now."

"Don't be," he says. "It's a compliment. And besides, she reminds me of you because of some of the stories she's told me about when she was younger."

I relax a little. "Like what?"

"Like how she spent time in the Peace Corps."

"I've never been in the Peace Corps, though."

"Yeah, but I could easily see you being a volunteer, going around, trying to help the world," he says, his mood lightening. "Spreading Nova peace everywhere."

"Is that really how you see me?" I wonder, feeling a little uncomfortable with how much he actually might *see* me—more than Landon, maybe. "As a do-gooder?"

"In the best way possible." His tone is much more upbeat than it was a few minutes ago. "You're a good person, Nova Reed. Too good to be talking to me, probably, but I don't want to stop you."

"No way," I argue defensively. "You're perfect for me." I shake my head at my cheesiness. I'm one step away from Jerry Maguiring it like Tristan did the other day. "Sorry, I didn't mean for that to come out the way it sounded."

"It's okay. You can call it payback for me being cheesy earlier, but I think I'm just a little on emotional overload between this phone chat and our text conversation earlier. You're giving me a high dose of the feel-goods and I'm starting to get really nervous about how I'm feeling right now. It's freaking the shit out of me." He stops talking and if I listen really closely I can hear the scratching of a pencil across paper.

I wonder if he's drawing and, if he is, what he's drawing a picture of. "So would you mind if we call it a night and go to the song?"

We started the song thing a week ago, when Quinton asked me for some good ones to listen to. Instead of telling him, I turned some on for him. Every night since then, I've picked out a song and we've listened to it together before I hang up.

Honestly, I'm not really ready to stop talking, but if that's what he needs then I'll give it to him. So I get up from my bed and go over to my dresser to turn on my iPod. "Sounds good, but what kind of one do you want for tonight? Happy? Sad? Angsty?"

"How about a mellow, relaxing one?" he requests. "Because I think I need to chillax a little."

"Hmm..." I consider my options, then scroll to one that I hope will relax him. "Okay, you ready?" I ask with my finger hovering over the play button.

"Yep, hit me with your best shot." He laughs at his own joke, since the other night I picked "Hit Me with Your Best Shot" by Pat Benatar.

"Hey, no recapping the previous night's song choice." I press play. Moments later, Pink Floyd's "Wish You Were Here" comes on. I crank up the volume and stay near the speakers so he can hear it.

He's quiet, absorbing the guitar solo until it gets to the lyrics, then he finally says, "Excellent choice, although I've heard it before."

"Yeah, I figured, but is that a bad thing?"

"Nah. In fact, I like that I have. Usually you're so music-superior over me, but now I feel like we're equals."

"That's because I've taught you well, young grasshopper," I joke, turning up the volume a notch.

"Did you seriously just quote *Kung Fu*?" He's stunned.

"Yeah, so what? I'm cool like that." I plop down on my bed on my back, bouncing a little before settling and returning my feet to the wall and tapping them to the beat of the music.

"You know what? You seriously might be the coolest person I've ever met, Nova Reed."

"And vice versa, Quinton Carter." I lean over and pick up my drumsticks from my nightstand. Then I start drumming them on my legs to the beat as we listen to the song together.

When it gets to the chorus, he tells me, "This song makes me think of you."

I stop tapping the drumsticks and set them aside. "How so?"

"I don't know…the lyrics just make me want to see you."

I rotate to my side, trying not to grin. "That's secretly why I picked it. So that you'd want me to come out there and see you."

"I don't think I'm ready for that." He seems irritated with himself. "I'm sorry, Nova. I wish I was, but I'm afraid. Not just of how it'll feel or if I'll be able to handle it, but of what

113

it'll mean for us. And what we've got now is so great at the moment. I just don't want to ruin that."

It stings a little, but I let it go, because he's only being honest. "That's okay. We'll see each other one day, right?"

"Yeah, one day." But he doesn't sound that committed, which seems somewhat strange. I mean, we've been spending all this time on the phone, and it felt like we were headed somewhere, but maybe this is how he plans on things being. Maybe he can only talk to me when there's a few-hundred-mile barrier between us.

We don't really say much after that and when the song's over, we say good-bye and hang up. It's about eleven o'clock, not extremely late, but at the same time, all I want to do is go to bed.

After getting into my pajamas, I decide that before I go to sleep I'll make a recording. I do it lying on my back, with the camera above me, the good one my mom gave me, because the clarity is always better. Plus, it's right there on my nightstand.

After I hit record, leaving the iPod on so there's music in the background, I sort of just lie there for a while. I wonder, if anyone actually watches this, if they'll think I'm nuts. Probably. But maybe that could be my point. Maybe one day I'll put every video I've ever made together and title it *Diary of an Erratic, Over-Thinking, Do-Gooder Madwoman*. Definitely not a life-changing video.

I summon a deep breath and pull myself together before I speak to the camera. "You know, a while ago I kept having that dream about Quinton jumping off the cliff. I think it was my subconscious letting out its fear of him falling back into drugs again. The dream stopped, thankfully, after I started talking to him regularly, and I can hear the clearness in his voice— the soberness. But now I've started having these weird dreams where he's standing on one side of a long stretch of land and I'm on the other and we're just waving to each other. When I first started having it, I wondered if it was a representation of us reuniting soon, but now I'm starting to speculate if it really just means that we're going to remain long-distance friends forever. If maybe we'll never move forward in our relationship." I press my lips together, gathering my thoughts. "You know, when I first met Quinton, I was in a strange place. One filled with confusion and memories of Landon. Stuck in the past and I didn't know what I wanted for my future. Then there was this summer where all of my thoughts were consumed by the urge to save Quinton . . . which I didn't really do, but he's getting better and that was the whole point of going to Vegas. Now I really don't have too much to think about other than if Quinton's doing well, so I can feel my future out there, flashing before me, like a stupid neon sign that's reminding me that I'm going to have to go somewhere with my life. And I'm not talking about career-wise. I've already got sort of a map for that with college and my part-time job at the photography

115

shop. And while it's in no way what I want to do with the rest of my life, I know that I want to do one of two things. One, make a career of helping people, like I hope I'm doing when I help at the suicide hotline, or two, do something in film, which is why I've been taking film classes…although I wish I could just get the balls to take a break and go help with the documentary…"

I daze off momentarily, thinking about how many people I know who have stories to tell. Then I blink back at the camera. "But anyway, that's not the point of this recording. The point is that I'm headed somewhere with my career, but when it comes to relationships, I'm not headed anywhere. I haven't gone out on a date since the end of my sophomore year. I'm twenty, veering toward twenty-one, and I'm still a virgin, which is just plain weird. I almost got there with Landon once, but I waited too long and then he was gone. And then I was going to let Quinton take my virginity when I was high out of my mind, but he was too good of a guy to take advantage of me." I recollect the time in the lake, when he nearly slipped inside me, but then backed out and left me there. It was the moment the memory I'd been suppressing finally broke through. The moment I remembered finding Landon hanging from his ceiling by a noose.

"But I think the really strange thing is that I don't even think about dating. I've been asked out a couple of times this year but declined. I used to do this because I was still hanging on to my love for Landon, but now…well, I think it's because my feelings are caught up in someone else...and sometimes I have to wonder if I'm in love with Quinton, but I'm not sure where that's going to get me since I'm pretty sure he doesn't love me back. Yeah, I know he cares for me, but love...I'm not sure. And what really scares me is, what if he never does?"

Chapter Five

December 9, day forty-one in the real world

Quinton

My support group's okay, I guess. For the most part, I just sit by myself in the back and listen to everyone talk. Although Wilson, the guy who's in charge of the meetings, has cornered me a few times and asked me to share my story. I told him I wasn't ready, though. That I've only been out for a month—well, forty-one days to be exact—and I'm not ready to share what's going on inside me yet, not even with myself, let alone a whole roomful of people. He told me he gets it and I actually believe that he does, considering what he's been through. What's surprising to me is how normal he seems, despite what happened. Like right now. I'm listening to him talk about the accident and his guilt over it and it's the strangest thing to me because, for starters, he can talk about it sober. And also because he doesn't look like he's going to break down.

"You know, I remember right after, I was sitting in the

hospital, getting a few cuts stitched up, which was pretty much the only thing I had from the accident." He sounds calm, but I can see it in his eyes, the remorse, existing, yet it's not eating away at him, like it feels like it's doing with me. "And I kept thinking, why me? Why did I survive?" He adjusts his tie, something he always does whenever he's speaking. I think he might even wear the tie for the sole purpose of having it to fidget with. "Why couldn't I have been the one to die in the car accident instead of the other way around?" He pauses there, loosening the tie as he glances around at the ten to twelve people sitting in the fold-up chairs, staring at him. All different ages, heights, weights. Male. Female. So different, yet we all share the same thing. Guilt.

He starts to pace the room, taking short, slow strides, even though his legs are long, like he wants to take his time. He's thirty-five years old and told me the other day that the accident happened almost ten years ago. Ten years on March seventeenth, to be exact, which is his birthday. I thought it was totally fucked up when he told me that, that something like that happened on his birthday, and he replied that it would be fucked up no matter what day it happened on.

He suddenly stops pacing and faces the group. His choked-up demeanor has changed into one of what looks like anger. "For the longest time I kept asking myself, why me? And there were a lot of people who were asking the same thing, especially the children and the grandchildren of the people I killed when I ran the red light. They blamed me—still do.

119

And I don't blame them. It's my fault. I know that, and for the longest time I thought I had to suffer for it. Pay for what I did." He crosses his arms, the anger switching to passion. "And you know what, I should...pay for it, but not by having a pity party for myself." He shakes his head. "But let me tell you, I did have a pity party. A huge one, where I jacked up my body with about every drug I could think of, and you know what? It made me feel better, and I guess that was the most fucked-up part of it all—that I was feeling good. Getting high, while people hurt because they lost a loved one, all because I couldn't put down the damn phone while I was driving." He pauses, lowering his head, and I think he might be crying.

A few people in the crowd nod, like they totally get what he's saying. Understand. I should. It's a story similar to mine, although my distraction wasn't a phone, it was Lexi sticking her head out the window. The distraction that led me to drive carelessly. Still, I should have just pulled over.

I'm not understanding, though. Not yet, but I feel something change inside me. Lighten. I'm not sure what it is.

He raises his head back up and I'm surprised there aren't tears in his eyes. "It took me years to figure out something. Years of drugs to finally realize one simple thing. That it's not about numbing the pain, but accepting it and doing something with it. Doing something good to make up for the bad." He starts walking back and forth across the front of the room again. "Doing something that helps people, instead of wasting away because I feel sorry for myself. Because I made a shit decision at the wrong moment and changed everything." He glances at the people in the room, like he's speaking to each one. "Make a difference. Make good in the world. You'll be surprised how much easier dealing with your guilt is."

He stops there and people start asking him questions. I stay quiet, though, getting stuck in my own head as a revelation hits me. Is that what I'm doing? Feeling sorry for myself? As I rewind through all my shit decisions over the last two years, I come to the painful conclusion that maybe I am. I mean, I haven't done anything good to make up for the lives I've taken. I've just slowly walked toward death myself, determined to die because it seemed so much easier than dealing with all the aching inside.

The more I analyze this, the more freaked out I get. I'm not sure what's worse, just letting myself drown in my guilt or seeing some sort of lighter side, like I'm starting to. I'm not even sure I'm ready to deal with it, and by the time the meeting ends, I'm ready to run the hell out of that church and go find someone to buy from so I can pump my body up with meth and focus on the adrenaline rush of that instead of the positive adrenaline I'm feeling.

But Wilson cuts me off at the doorway, stepping in front of me, appearing pretty much out of nowhere. "Hey, is the room on fire or something?"

I stop in front of him and give him a quizzical look. "What?"

He chuckles as he leans over and collects a Styrofoam cup

from the table beside the doorway. "You were leaving so fast, I thought maybe you saw a fire." He pauses like he's actually waiting for me to answer the question. "But by the confused look you're giving me, I'm guessing no to the fire, right?" Again, he waits for me to respond.

I slowly shake my head. "No . . . no fire."

"So then what's up with the rush exit?" he asks, reaching for the coffeepot. "Did my speech freak you out or something?"

I'm about to tell him no, but he seems like the kind of person who would call me out on my lie, so I warily nod. "Yeah, sort of, I guess."

He pours the coffee into the cup before returning it to the coffee maker. "Yeah, I tend to do that sometimes when I get really intense." He reaches for a packet of sugar. "It seems like the more speeches I give, the more passionate I get, but I think it's because I become more and more determined to try and help people like you and me see things in a different light."

I glance around at the few people in the room, feeling out of place. "Yeah, I can see that."

"You seem uneasy." He studies me as he rips the packet of sugar open with his teeth. "If I'm remembering right, Greg made you come to these meetings?"

"Yeah, he did."

He smiles to himself as he pours the sugar into his coffee, then tosses the packet into the garbage before grabbing a stirrer. "He's a pushy son of a bitch, isn't he?"

I nearly smile. "Yeah, sort of, but he's not that bad."

"Nah, he's not bad at all." He walks out the door and toward the steps that lead upstairs. The meeting room is actually located in the basement of a church, of all things. I'm not really a fan of going into the church. In fact, I feel like I'm being judged the moment I step over the threshold, whether by church members or God, I'm not sure, especially since I'm not really sure I believe in God.

"In fact, he actually helped me a lot by pushing me," Wilson continues as he jogs up the stairs.

"Really?" I ask with doubt, grasping the railing as I walk up.

He pauses in the middle of the stairway, glancing over his shoulder at me with a curious look on his face. "How long have you been seeing him?"

"A few weeks."

He nods, like he understands something. "You're a newbie, then." He starts up the stairs again. "Give it time. It'll get better."

I'm not sure if I'm completely buying his getting-better speech. "How long does it usually take?" I ask as we step out into the pew area and turn for the exit doors to our left, which have wreaths on them. Christmas cheer everywhere and yet I feel so bummed out.

"Take for what?" he asks, stirring his coffee, which I know is stale because I tried it the first time I came to one of these meetings and nearly threw up from the nasty taste.

"I don't know." I scratch the back of my neck, loitering in front of the doorway as the support group people leave the church. "To get rid of the weight on my shoulders...the guilt." I'm not even sure why I'm asking, because that would mean I believe it's possible. And I don't. Not really, anyway. But Wilson seems so easy to talk to, maybe because I know he once felt the same way I'm feeling.

He briefly stares at me before he takes a sip of the coffee, then stares up at the front of the church, where there's a lectern, rows of chairs, and a stained glass window that rays of sunlight shine through. "To be honest, it doesn't ever go away." He returns his attention to me. "Like I said today, it's always there, but you just got to learn how to deal with it and make your life good enough that good covers up the dark part of you."

"Dark part?" I pretend like I have no idea what he's talking about, when I do, way, way too fucking well.

He gives me a knowing smile, like he understands this. "You just got out of rehab, right?"

"Yeah."

"And how long has it been?"

"Since when? Since I did drugs?"

He shakes his head and pats the shoulder of the arm where the tattoos are hidden under the sleeve of my jacket. "Since the accident."

I swear the ink burns, scorching hot, my whole body igniting. "Two and a half years."

He grips my shoulder. "Give it time. I promise it'll get easier."

"How much time?" I ask, stepping aside as a woman with gray hair whisks between us and through the door.

He reflects on what I said and I think he's going to give me an estimated time frame, but then he says, "Have you ever volunteered for Habitat for Humanity before? Or any other organization like it?"

"Huh?" I'm thrown off by the abrupt subject change. "No, well, I mean I've been helping down at the homeless shelter and spending time with the elderly people in our community...why?"

He gives me another pat on the shoulder and it's starting to annoy me but I can't figure out why. I think it's because I'm not really used to people touching me and because his pats seem to be an attempt to convey compassion. "Can you meet me tomorrow at six?" he asks.

"Maybe...I mean, yeah, but why?"

"Because I want to show you something."

"If it's about building a house, then you should know that I'm working for a painting contractor right now so I'm already sort of doing that."

"Habitat for Humanity is a little different." He says it with passion, removing his hand from my arm and balling it into a fist in front of him. "Imagine, building a home for someone who really needs it." He reaches for the door and pushes it open, letting a cool breeze in. "There's a whole world out there, Quinton. Full of people who need help and full of people who don't want to take the time to offer help. But you and I—we see time differently. We get how important it is and how everything we do in this life matters. Good and bad. So it's important that we spend a hell of a lot of time doing good."

"Yeah, I guess." I still don't know if I'm completely on board with his speech and I think he can tell, but he refuses to give up.

"Meet me tomorrow at six at this house I'm working on," he says, stepping out the door. "And I'll show you."

"Six in the morning?" I ask, and he nods. "Okay, but I have to be at therapy by noon."

"That's plenty of time." His lips tip up into a smile and I follow him, letting the door bang shut behind me. It's a breezy, clear day, the grass covered with frost and browned leaves.

"For what?" I ask, drawing the hood of my coat over my head.

He walks toward the grass, which is shaded by trees. "For me to show you how wonderful life can be."

I honestly wonder if he's on crack or something with his positivity. He doesn't look like he's tweaking out, though, so I don't really think that's the case.

After I agree to meet him, he gives me an address and his phone number, then promises me a life-changing morning. I don't believe him, although part of me wants to. Wants to believe that one day I can walk around as happy as he is, living a drug-free life without feeling like I'm fighting not to sink into the ground.

&

Later that day, after I've gone and talked to Greg, who thinks it's a great idea to go with Wilson tomorrow, and spent a few hours at work, I go home to a half-packed house. My father's left me a voice mail, saying he has a meeting tonight so I should eat dinner without him. As I heat up last night's frozen lasagna leftovers, the quietness of the house and the boxes start to get to me. I can't believe this is happening. He's really going to move and I'm not ready for it. I don't want change. I want fucking stability. I want to be able to walk around and feel good like Wilson seems able to do. Jesus, I really do. Now whether I really believe that can happen, I'm not sure. But I'd like to find out.

When the microwave buzzes, I take the lasagna out and go upstairs to my room to eat it. As I sit on my bed, surrounded by the drawings and photos of Lexi, my thoughts drift to her. I can't help but think of all the times we spent in here. We'd kiss and touch each other, laugh, and sometimes Lexi would even cry if she was having a bad day. I'd listen to her vent and try to comfort her as much as I could. I'd sometimes talk to her, too, but not a lot.

I take out my notebook, feeling the need to write as my

emotions surface, connecting to my emotions, to Lexi, the accident, myself, because that's what Greg's been telling me I need to do.

I've never really been much of a talker, honestly. When I think back, I was always sort of the listener. When Lexi would talk, I'd give her my advice, but I never did seek advice, even when I felt confused, about school, life, my future. Sure, I was planning on going to college and getting married to Lexi, but deep down I always sort of wondered if she was on the same page as me—if she wanted to get married—because whenever I brought it up she would always just smile and avoid talking about it by kissing me or touching me. And I never did press, just held it all inside . . . kept it in until it was too late and there was no longer a way to get the answers. No way to find out.

I'm realizing I do that a lot. Avoid talking about stuff, like I did right after the accident, never dealing with the aftermath, never saying sorry for what happened, whether it was my fault or not. Even with Nova, I shut down when things get emotional or touching, although sometimes things veer in that direction without me even realizing it. Nova is easy to talk to. That's for sure and even though I hate to admit it, I've talked to her more openly over the last month than I have with anyone in my entire life. But I still struggle with the really

complex stuff. Like my feelings about Lexi. Or any time
I can feel my heart opening up to Nova. But Wilson, he
just fucking walks around in front of a room pouring his
heart out. I wonder how long it took him to get there. I
wonder if I can get to that place…I wonder if he has a
normal life? If he got forgiveness? Let go of the past? Has a
wife? Kids? A family? Could that be possible? No, it can't
be possible…can it?

As soon as I write it, I want to take it back. How can I be getting to that place? The one where I think of a future? No, I
take it back. But it's written in pen and can't be erased, just like
the brief second I had the thought can't be erased.

"Shit." I curse because my thoughts are suddenly racing
about a million miles a minute. I need to turn them off somehow. I know one way to…but no…I can't go there. In fact, I
don't want to. It's been so hard to come out of that dark place
and I don't think I have the energy to drag myself up from it
again.

I throw the pen across the room and ball my hands into
fists. Breathe in. Breathe out. That's what Charles had me do
when I was first in rehab and I was coming off the meds that
weaned me from my heroin and meth addictions. Breathe.
Breathe. Breathe. Let it pass. But it's not passing. I need something else. A hit. Yeah, that's the easy solution, but the harder
one has fewer long-term consequences.

I need someone to talk to. Greg. Wilson. It's after eight

and I don't want to bother them. I immediately reach for my phone and call the one person I know I can talk to and the only person I really want to talk to. The one person I know can distract me enough to calm me the fuck down.

I drum my fingers on my knee as I dial Nova's number and then listen to the line ring. As it gets to the fourth one, I think she's not going to answer, and I'm about ready to hang up and go over to Marcus's house and buy whatever I can off him. Get a hit. Feel the rush. Then the numbing. Thankfully Nova picks up before her voice mail clicks on and I exhale a breath of relief, realizing how weak I still am—how much help I still need.

"Hey," I say after she answers, instantly settling down, my pulse calming.

"Hey." She sounds breathless. "I was hoping it was you calling."

Her response makes me smile, but of course it also confounds me that she'd be that happy to hear from me. "Yeah, I just wanted to talk to you...but if you can't talk, then it's okay."

"Why couldn't I talk?"

"Because...I don't know. You sound sort of breathless."

She laughs and I close my eyes, relishing the tranquil sound of it. "That's because I was playing Twister with Lea and Tristan and I had to run to get the phone."

I lean back against the wall, my eyes opening. "Twister? Was that Tristan's idea?" I loathe that I sound jealous, but I can't help how I feel. That I wish I were the one living with her, playing games where I get to tangle our bodies together in awkward positions.

"No, it was actually Lea's," she says, and I distinctively hear a door close. "She said she was bored and that she needed to do something other than sit on the couch and watch reruns of *Vampire Diaries*."

"And Twister was that thing?"

"Yeah, it was the only game we had in the closet, and just in case you're wondering, it did belong to Tristan."

"I knew he had something to do with it." I remember all the times he wanted me to hook up with girls. Tristan always wanted to hook up with any girl he came across. God, it feels like years ago when it was only months. A whole different world, full of cracks, temptations, and unsteady footsteps. That's what life feels like when you've been on drugs for years and then suddenly you're sober.

"Yeah, I guess he's kind of a perv, isn't he?"

"Sometimes," I say, then decide I need a subject change because talking about Tristan's pervertedness isn't helping me calm down. "So I was thinking that you could put on the song first tonight and then we could talk."

"Yeah, I could do that." She sounds confused. "But can I ask you why?"

"I'm just having a rough day," I tell her, being more honest than I usually am. "And waiting to hear what song you're going to pick out for me always cheers me up."

"Okay, what kind of song do you want tonight?" There's cheeriness in her tone and I can feel my heart rate calming from it.

"How about a hopeful one?" I ask, unsure if she'll get what I mean.

But I quickly learn that I should never question Nova when it comes to music, because a few minutes later "Rise" by Eddie Vedder comes on. It's probably not what most people would have picked for a hopeful song, but leave it to Nova to pick something different that still gets the point across. She found me a song that's not talking about rainbows and sunshine, but that gives enough hope that it makes me feel better.

"So what do you think?" she wonders, getting back on the phone with the music playing in the background.

"I think it's good." I relax in my bed and shut my eyes. Breathing seems a little bit easier, just like thinking. In fact, everything seems easier at the moment.

"Does it give you hope?" she asks, and I can hear the expectation in her voice.

I keep my eyes shut, but a trace of a smile graces my lips. "You know what? It does. It really, really does." I pause, knowing that what I say next is going to be huge for me, but for some reason I want to do it, want to talk with her, because it always seems to make life just the tiniest bit easier. "Can I talk to you about why I was upset tonight?"

"Of course," she says, although she does seem nervous. "I told you that you can talk to me about anything."

I take a deep breath, then another, preparing myself to crack open a door. "It's about my future and how much it scares me."

"I get that," she says, and my eyelids flutter open. "But I promise that it'll get better—that moving forward will get better."

"I know." I stare at a photo of Lexi on the wall. She's laughing at something... I honestly can't even remember what it was. Something I said, I think. She looks so happy. So alive. Eyes bright. Heart beating. Happy. "But it's hard to think about a future when it feels like every time I do, I'm leaving someone behind."

I hear her breath hitch in her throat, but Nova being Nova, she sounds calm when she speaks. "I actually get that really well. That's the way I felt about Landon."

I swallow hard. "Did you love him?"

"Yes," she utters softly. "He was actually my friend for a few years before we got together, but that helped me get to know him more." She sucks in a breath and releases it gradually, like she's on the brink of tears. "I thought I was going to marry him."

I can feel tears prickling at my eyes as I realize what I'm about to say. "I thought I was going to marry Lexi, too... although I'm not sure she was on the same page as me. She was cryptic like that. And restless. And she didn't like the idea of settling down." And when she died, I saw our future together slipping away, but I was okay with it because I was dying, too, but then I came back without her and that future was gone forever.

"Landon didn't like talking about the future at all," Nova says sorrowfully. "Sometimes I think it's because he knew he was...well, you know...and he either didn't let himself talk about it, didn't want to make any empty promises to me, or just didn't ever think about it."

I've been close to that place where taking my life seemed like the way I was going to go. Being there, I didn't really think about my future, but I don't want to tell her that because she deserves a better answer. "I'm sure he thought about it," I say. "Even though he might have never said anything, he had to think about it a little. Being with you forever."

"You think so?" she asks hopefully.

"I know so." It's a lie, but for a good cause. She deserves it—deserves the world and more.

"Quinton?"

"Yeah." I'm getting choked up and even one word conveys all the grief, agony, regret, and sorrow surfacing inside me.

"I know it's really hard to think about the future and everything," she says. "But I have this really good feeling that yours is going to turn out a lot better than you think it is."

"I hope you're right," I reply, massaging my hand over my aching chest, the scar across it a permanent reminder of what happened that tragic night. "But I don't even know what I'm going to do in the future. I keep thinking about where I could possibly be a few years from now..."

"And what do you see?"

"I don't know...nothing, really, at the moment."

"Well, what do you hope to see one day?"

I roll on my back and glance at another picture of Lexi, one where I have my arms around her in a tight embrace. She's in a red prom dress and I'm wearing a black tux. It was taken only a few weeks before the accident. "I hate seeing anything, because it makes me feel guilty that I'm...not having a future...with her..." I get really unnerved as the topic drifts toward Lexi. In a way it makes me feel like I'm almost cheating on Lexi by talking to Nova about her, yet I feel guilty talking to Nova about my old girlfriend because I'm sure she doesn't really want to hear about her. It's very confusing.

"Do you think she'd want you to have a future still?" she asks in a tentative voice.

That wasn't what I was expecting. "I'm not sure..." My thoughts wander to that night she died and begged me not to forget her. "There's actually something that happened...that night of the accident that makes me think she might not have wanted me to."

"What was that?" she asks, then quickly adds, "You don't have to tell me if you don't want to."

I've been asked by my therapists several times to talk about that night. What happened. How I felt. I always refused to give details, but with Nova, I feel like I can finally talk about it. Maybe because I know she's seen things like I have. Death.

135

Or maybe it's that over the last couple of months I've come to trust her.

"She asked me to promise her that I wouldn't ever forget her...when she was dying...and I did..." My voice is so strained and so quiet I'm not certain Nova even hears me. I wish I couldn't hear me, because as soon as I say it, I want to take it back. But I can't. It's as permanent as the scar on my chest.

Nova is silent, probably trying to figure out how to respond to such an alarming statement. I feel bad for putting her in such a position, letting horrible secrets like that slip out that no one wants to hear about. I'm about to tell her that I should probably go, when she finally speaks.

"You don't have to forget her to move forward in your life," she says. "You can still remember her. And I'm sure you will, without even trying. In fact, I think it's impossible to forget about someone that you loved once. They always stay with you."

"But you know what happened with me...you know that I was the one driving during the accident." I've never wanted a hit more badly than I do right now. The idea of sniffing, injecting, hell I'd go for inhaling, anything that could distance me from my emotions, sounds amazing right now.

"I know what I read from the newspaper." Her voice is so soothing that it's making my heart stay steady despite how much it wants to speed up. "But it doesn't mean I understand what happened. I know from experience that hearing about stuff is way different from the actual experience."

136

I think she's trying to press me to tell her, but I can't. There's no way I can tell her the details of that night. What went on. How responsible I am for the lives lost that night. What exactly happened. Knowing Nova, she'll definitely tell me that it wasn't my fault when she hears everything, but that's not what I need from her right now. I just need her. The sound of her voice. The image of her in my head.

"I can't," I whisper, feeling strangled. "It's too hard to talk about."

Her soft breathing flows from the other end and I match my own to the rhythm because it helps me to breathe through the weight bearing down on every inch of my body, helps keep me afloat even though I feel like I'm on the verge of drowning.

"Do you know what Landon and I were doing the night he took his life?" she asks. "We were lying in his backyard stargazing. And it seemed like such a perfect night, except for one thing... something Landon said to me that just didn't sit right with me, yet I wouldn't press him to talk about it."

"You can't force people to talk about things they don't want to." I'm not really sure if I'm referring to Landon or myself.

"Yeah, but I should have tried harder," she insists. "He'd always say these things to me... these dark, disturbing things that still haunt me to this day because most of the time I'd just shrug them off, too worried that he'd, like, break up with me or something if I pushed him too far."

"Nova, what happened wasn't your fault." I attempt to

comfort her, but I'm not sure how good a job I'm doing. "You can't blame yourself for that."

"He said, 'Do you ever get the feeling that we are all just lost? Just roaming around the earth, waiting around to die?'" Her voice trembles at the end and she takes a moment to pull herself together. "It was one of the last things I heard him say before we fell asleep on the hill together. When I woke up, he was gone. I couldn't figure out where he was, because it wasn't like him to just leave me like that." She laughs, but it sounds so warped and wrong, laced with pain and sadness. "Go figure, it ended up that he left me forever…something I found out a few minutes later when I found him in his room."

Each one of her words stabs at my skin, sharp and painful, as an aching need to make her feel better arises within me. "Nova…I don't even know what to say." I drape my arm over my head and try to shut out the aching inside me.

"I don't want you to say anything." Her voice balances out and she almost sounds like her normal self again. "I was just telling you my story, because I'm the only one who can really tell what happened—at least with me. And I hope one day you'll tell me yours, but it doesn't need to be today. Just one day." She pauses. "In the future."

She mentioned the word *future* on purpose, probably to make the point that I'm going to have a future, at least in her eyes I am.

"I wish I could make you feel better," I tell her, rotating back onto my side so I can stare at the wall instead of the

138

pictures around me, so for a moment it can be just her and me. "I wish I could take all your pain away."

"Yeah, but you and I both know that's not possible," she reminds me. "And I've learned to deal with it. And you know what? It's not as bad as it used to be."

"I hope so," I say, fighting to keep my voice even. "I hope one day I can be okay with everything and so can you."

Is it possible, though? After the last few years, to heal and live a life where I'm not drowning? I used to think no and part of me still thinks there's no way. But there's a small part of me that has to wonder.

Does hope still exist for me?

139

Chapter Six

December 10, day forty-two in the real world

Quinton

I'm feeling pretty good when I wake up early to meet Wilson, especially after my talk with Nova last night. It's amazing how good she makes me feel. I just wish I could hold on to the good feeling because the more time goes by since our conversation, the more the heaviness returns to me.

Still, I get up, trying to grasp Nova's positivity. There are clouds in the sky and a little bit of frost on the grass, so I put on my coat, gloves, and boots, even though I have no idea if I'm actually going to be working outside.

After I get all bundled up, I go downstairs to have breakfast and pack a lunch. My dad's sitting at the table with a slice of toast and coffee in front of him, and he's reading the newspaper, surrounded by boxes. The sight of them makes it hard to stay optimistic, reminding me that I still have that problem to deal with.

When I enter the kitchen, my dad glances up and then offers me a small smile, but then he takes in my outdoor wear and it falls from his face. "Where are you going?" he wonders, reaching for his coffee mug. "I thought you had your therapy session today."

"I do," I tell him, getting a Pop-Tart out of the cupboard. The kitchen walls have been sunshine yellow forever and the countertops a deep green. It's a ghastly sight, but my dad always refused to change it because it was the color palette my mom picked out. "But I have to go somewhere else first."

He folds up his newspaper, seeming skeptical. "Where?"

I rip open the wrapper on the Pop-Tart. "Remember that Wilson guy I was telling you about?"

He raises his mug to his mouth and takes a sip of his coffee. "Yeah, the one that runs those meetings for people who . . ." He trails off, uncomfortable with the subject. Always is.

"The meeting for ex–drug addicts who are dealing with guilt and loss," I say bluntly. If I can say it, he should be able to say it.

He nods, setting the mug back down on the table. "Yeah, that one."

"Yeah, that's the guy." I bite the corner of the Pop-Tart off as I pull out a chair and take a seat at the table. "And he wants to show me some house he's building for Habitat for Humanity. I think he wants me to get involved or something."

"But you're involved in a lot of stuff already." He doesn't seem that thrilled.

I shrug as I get up to pour myself a cup of coffee. "What else am I going to do with my life?" I ask, getting a mug out of the dishwasher.

"I don't know." He bites his toast and chews it slowly as he thinks. "I just don't want you to get too involved when we're going to be moving soon."

"I never said I was moving," I say bitterly as I grab the pot of coffee. "You said you were moving."

"But I thought we agreed you'd come with me," he says with a hint of sadness.

"When did I ever agree to that?" I ask, confused, as I pour some coffee into the mug.

He glances around the room at the packed boxes on the countertops and on the floor. "Well, you never argued when I started packing and put the house up for sale, so I just assumed you were okay with everything."

"Well, I'm not," I say, shaking my head. "I'm almost twenty-one years old and I shouldn't even be living with my father to begin with. Let alone moving across the country with him." I take a swallow of my coffee, hoping that I'll be able to calm myself down. There's no reason to get angry. After all, he wants me to come with him. But for some reason I do feel a little resentful and I can't even figure out why. "For the first time since the accident, I have some sort of structure in my life and I already told you I don't want to just give that up—I don't want to start over again. It's too fucking hard."

He stares at me with wide eyes and I realize how loud I'm talking and how much I'm trembling. I don't say anything else and neither does he as I finish my coffee and he cleans up his plate and cup. After I make my lunch, I leave the house and take the bus to where I'm supposed to meet Wilson, because I don't want to ask my dad to lend me the car or give me a ride. I just want a break to clear my head.

It's a fairly long bus ride and I end up getting there about half an hour late. The address Wilson gave me ends up being that of a small, single-story house that's almost completely finished, except for the yard work and a few spots that need siding. There are a few guys working on it right now, out in the cold, with their hammers and power tools, dressed in heavy coats and boots. Wilson is one of them.

I stand at the curb for almost an eternity, because I can't seem to bring my feet to move. I'm puzzled by Wilson and his freeness. He can't be real. He has to be fake. There's no way anyone can live with that kind of guilt and laugh like that. It can't be possible.

But the longer I stare, the more I realize he just might be real and that he really does seem to be at some sort of inner peace with himself. I'd call it a miracle, but I don't believe in miracles, not since Lexi and Ryder died and I lived. That would mean my life was the miracle, but it's not. It should have been the other way. They should have lived and I should have died. That would have been the miracle.

"So are you just going to stand there and stare all day?"

Wilson's voice interrupts my thoughts, crossing the front yard toward me.

"Sorry, I was just admiring the house," I say, then start across the yard and meet him in the middle.

"It's nice, right?" He nods at the almost-finished house.

"Sure." I honestly wouldn't call it nice. It's small, with plain tan siding, no grass in the narrow front yard, and no front porch or shutters.

"For someone who hasn't ever had a home, it's nice," he tells me, and then motions for me to follow him as he walks back to the guys working on putting up the siding.

When I get over there, he hands me a nail gun. "Get busy," he says.

I gape at the nail gun and then at him. "You want me to help you put up siding?"

"What else are you going to do?" he asks. "Stand around and watch us put it up?"

I admire him for being so blunt and follow him over to the small pile of siding that needs to be put up. He quickly introduces me to everyone and then we pick up pieces of siding and he shows me where to put the nails. We don't really talk about anything except lining up the siding and putting the nails in right.

There's country music playing from an old stereo near the tools and the air smells like cigarette smoke because everyone keeps taking smoke breaks. About halfway through, I realize how comfortable I feel, but the revelation freaks me out more than it calms me.

"So what do you think?" Wilson asks as he holds a piece of siding on one side and I hold the other side.

I put the tip of the nail gun up to the siding and shoot a nail into it. "About what? Building the house?"

He nods as I put another nail in. "Yeah, does it make you feel invigorated?"

"I don't know. Maybe." I move the nail gun to put another nail into the siding, but he stops me, grabbing my arm.

"You want to hear the story of the family the house is for?" he asks, taking the nail gun from me.

I dither, almost afraid it's going to be too much for me to handle. "I guess so."

He gives my unenthusiastic attitude a disapproving look, but tells me the story anyway. "It's for a widow and her three daughters."

Normally I don't ask about stuff that I know is going to be dark, but for some reason I find myself asking, "How'd her husband die?"

I can tell the moment I ask the question that it's going to be something bad. Something that he worries I'm going to react to.

"A drunk driver."

"Oh." It's all I can say. While I wasn't drunk when I crashed the car into another car that night, I was driving too

145

fast. It triggers something inside me and for a brief moment I think about running the hell away from this place and shoving as much crystal up my nose as I possibly can. Maybe even shoot my veins up, although it's only part of me that wants it. The other never wants to go back to that wandering, pointless place again.

But before I can even take a step, Wilson picks up another chunk of siding and pretty much throws it at me. "Here, let's switch jobs," he says as I catch it with a grunt. "You put the nails in and I'll hold up the siding." He rolls his shoulder. "My arm's getting fucking tired."

I end up staying there until a couple of hours later when all the siding is put up, listening to country music and breathing in the cigarette smoke. With each piece that goes up, I feel a little bit lighter. It's kind of amazing when I think about it. How at the moment I'm not beating myself down, but holding myself up without feeling guilty. But maybe that's because I'm doing something good for someone who needs it. Maybe it's because I'm making up for what I did. Who the hell knows? But I'll take it for the moment.

After we're done, the guys start to pack up their tools with pleased looks on their faces, like they feel the same way. Wilson explains to me that three out of the four of them are exchanging their time in order to get help on their own houses.

"Did you get a ride here?" he asks, after we've packed all the tools and scraps of siding into the back of an old pickup truck.

"No...I don't have a car and my dad couldn't drive me

this morning." I lie about the last part but only because I don't want to think about the little argument I had with my dad. And I'm hoping that when I get back to the house, he'll be there to take me to therapy. "So I took the bus."

He nods at the old pickup parked in the driveway. "Come on. I'll give you a ride."

"You don't have to do that," I tell him, not wanting to be a burden.

"Quinton, quit trying to be nice and get in the fucking truck," he says in a joking tone. "I have nothing better to do anyway."

Again, I want to ask him if he has a family, but I don't dare. "Thanks," I say, then hop into the passenger side of the truck and slip off my gloves.

He climbs into the driver's side and shuts the door, then starts up the engine. The truck backfires and he laughs as he pats the top of the steering wheel. "Got to love old cars, don't ya?" He grabs the shifter and puts it into reverse. "I personally love the classics, though."

"What year is it?" I ask, buckling my seat belt.

"A 1962 Chevy," he tells me as he backs up into the street. "It was actually my dad's." He aligns the truck and drives toward the corner of the road. "He left it to me when he died."

"My girl...a friend of mine," I correct myself, "got a Chevy Nova when her dad died."

He seems really interested as he heads out of the neighborhood and toward the city. "What year?"

"I think it's a 1969," I reply, unzipping my coat. "It's completely restored and everything."

"I bet it's a nice ride," he remarks as he turns out onto the main road, where the lampposts are decorated with Christmas lights along with the houses.

"I guess so."

"Has she ever let you drive it?"

I shake my head and then shrug. "I never asked her if I could."

He gapes at me like I'm crazy. "Why the hell not? Do you know how badass those cars are?"

I shrug again. "Things are complicated with Nova." That would be the understatement of the year.

He arches his brows as he pulls the beanie off his head and tosses it onto the seat between us. "Things are complicated with the car or is the girl's name Nova?"

"Yeah, her dad named her after the car," I explain as I put my frozen hands up to the heater vent, wishing we could get off the subject.

He appears impressed by this. "A girl named Nova," he muses. "I'd really like to meet her."

"You can't," I say hastily. "She lives in Idaho."

"Okay, then I'll visit her when she comes here next time."

"She never comes here." I'm being vague because the last thing I want to do is talk about my issues with seeing Nova. How I desperately want to, but at the same time I'm afraid to.

"Are you going to tell me the story behind why she doesn't?" he asks. He shifts the truck and the engine groans in protest.

"There's no story," I tell him. Not one I want to share, anyway.

He looks me over with doubt as he presses the brake and stops at a red light. "Yeah, I'm not buying it."

I drum my fingers on my knee, getting agitated. "Fine, there is a story behind it, but it's a really long, fucked-up story and I don't want to talk about it."

"We have about a twenty-minute drive to your house," he says. "You could at least start explaining why just the mention of her has gotten you all worked up."

"Why are you being so pushy?" I ask. "You barely even know me."

"But I do know you," he insists, looking back at the road as the light turns green and he starts driving again. "You blame yourself for the accident and think self-punishment is a way to make up for the lives lost. You don't have any friends or a girlfriend because you don't think you deserve them. You did drugs because it helped you forget and because it was easier to deal with life when you were high. And maybe even because it was a way to slowly kill yourself."

"Those aren't the only reasons I did drugs." I feel this compulsion to prove him wrong—to prove that he doesn't know as much about me as he seems to. "And how do you even know all that? Did Greg tell you?"

He shakes his head. "Greg can't tell me. Doctor-patient confidentiality, remember?"

What the hell? "Then how do you know?"

He presses his lips together as he watches the road, his jaw taut, his eyes hued with pain and penitence, and I swear for a moment I'm looking into a mirror. "Because I wasn't describing you. I was describing myself about seven years ago."

"Oh." I'm not sure what else to say and I end up saying the first thing that pops into my head, which seems stupid after I say it. "Sorry." Jesus, that was probably the stupidest thing I could have said. I know, because I hate when people say that to me. Sorry for what? That I made a huge, irreversible mistake and now I have to live with it forever?

"For what?"

"For flipping out."

"You're allowed to get pissed off sometimes. In fact, it's good for you." He pauses, pondering something as he slows down for the speed limit change as we get closer to a section of the city where stores line the streets instead of homes. "However, you could always tell me what's up with the girl and that might make up for the bad attitude." He grins at me.

I shake my head, but calm down inside. "Nova's just..." God, how do I begin to explain what Nova is to me? "I'm not even sure what Nova is."

"How did you meet her?" he asks interestedly.

I shrug uneasily. "She was going through a rough time in her life and sort of wandered into the house I was staying at...

in the beginning we spent a lot of time getting high, but then she got better."

"So that's why you don't see each other anymore?" he inquires. "Because she got better and you're still working on stuff?"

"No, that's not it." I rake my hand through my hair, struggling to put my thoughts into words. "It has to do with the fact that she saved me and I…" I trail off as I almost start talking about my feelings for Nova, ones I'm still trying to figure out how to deal with now that I'm sober. "It's really fucking complicated." And it is. Because I'm in love with her, something I realized in Vegas. But I can't admit it aloud because then it'd mean I was accepting it—accepting that my feelings for Lexi have changed. That I've broken my promise to her. Let go. Replaced her.

He considers what I said as he flips the blinker on to change lanes. "What do you mean when you say saved you?"

My pulse is hammering as I recollect everything that Nova did for me to bring me fully alive again when I was walking the line between life and death. "When I was doing drugs and stuff she came down to Vegas and tried to get me to stop," I tell him. "She never gave up on me and she was there when I decided to leave the streets and get myself cleaned up—she never gave up on me."

He takes in what I said with great interest. "She sounds like a good person."

"She is," I say, nodding in agreement. "Too good, probably, at least to be with me."

"Ah, and there it is." He points his finger at me with accusation in his eyes.

"There what is?" I ask, puzzled.

He glances at me and I see something in his eyes I don't like. Understanding. "The reason why she doesn't visit."

"Yeah, so. It's a good reason."

"I completely agree with you."

I'm stunned by his response and the frankness in his tone. "You don't think I should see her, then?"

"Not until you're one hundred percent ready for it." He steers off the main road and drives down the side road toward my neighborhood. "Relationships are complicated and can be messy and, for people like you and me, dangerous. You need to make sure you're ready to handle whatever comes from it, good or bad."

I nod, not necessarily liking his advice, but understanding it. "So distance is good for now?"

"If you think so," he says, slowing the truck down to make a turn.

I'm not sure if I do or don't. Part of me wants to see her all the time. Be with her. But part of me is terrified of how it would make me feel and what it would mean, not just for me and her, but for the memory of Lexi. Would I be able to just do it? Let her go? I'm not sure if I'm ready to do that, not when I haven't even begun to make up for what I did. I need to do more—I need to apologize to the people who lost loved ones during the accident, before I can even think of letting myself be in a relationship. And I need to keep doing good things to make up for the bad I've done.

"And what about you?" I ask.

He looks lost as he glances at me. "What about me?"

"Do you . . . are you in a relationship?" I wonder if it's even possible.

He shakes his head. "No. No girlfriend."

"So you're not ready?" I can't hide my disappointment because I was hoping he'd say yes and give me some sort of hope that eventually Nova and I could possibly be together.

"No, I'm ready," he assures me. "I hate living alone, but I haven't found the right person yet."

That makes me feel a little better until we're pulling up in front of my house. It seems like all my problems come crashing down on me all at once. My dad. Moving. The fact that I still haven't been able to take the sketches or photos of Lexi down, even though everyone keeps telling me to. The fact that I've been sitting in this truck, wishing I could be with Nova. *I want her. I want her. So badly.*

"So what did you think of today?" Wilson asks as he parks behind my dad's car in the driveway, glancing at the neighbor's Christmas decorations flashing brightly. In fact, almost all our neighbors have lights up, except for us, but my dad never did like to celebrate the holiday. Said it reminded him too much of my mom because I guess she loved this time of year.

"It was okay," I tell Wilson, unbuckling my seat belt.

"Okay enough that you want to do it again?"

I think about it briefly. "Yeah, I think so."

"Good, because we're going to be starting on a new one next week." He puts the truck into park and the engine backfires. "Call me this weekend and I'll give you the info."

"Thanks." I grab the handle and open the door. "And thanks for the ride." I want to say, "and for the talk," but I can't quite get the words to come out, mainly because the talk made me feel uncomfortable, but in a good way I think.

"Any time," he says as I hop out of the truck. "And Quinton?"

I pause as I'm shutting the door. "Yeah?"

"Things will get better," he assures me with an encouraging smile. "I promise."

I want to believe him. I really, really do, but I can't see how it's possible. For things to get better. Still, as I head up to the house, I can't help but think that maybe, just maybe he could be right somehow.

Chapter Seven

December 11, day forty-three in the real world

Nova

"God, the last couple of days have been kind of downers," I say to my camera phone as I leave campus building and hike across the campus yard, the leafless trees creating shadows over the screen as I walk beneath the branches. "I just finished up my film class for the semester, and turned in my film project. My professor asked me if I was interested in being part of his project. I told him I wasn't sure. When he asked why, it took me a second to answer because what I really wanted to say was, 'I do want to go. So, so, badly. Please let me be part of this.' But instead I told him it was complicated. Which was my way of saying without having to say that I have people here who need me and who I worry about. He gave me the information and told me to think about it."

I stop talking for a moment as a guy jogs by to catch a Frisbee and I have to dodge to the side to avoid being run over.

"But anyway," I say, smoothing my wind-kissed hair into place, "I can barely focus on if I should go because I have so many things on my mind. The biggest one is Delilah. I can't get her out of my head. I'm not even sure why. It's not like she's dead." I pull the collar of my coat over my mouth because it's colder than a Popsicle today. "But I keep thinking about the fire and the gunshot and how Dylan had a gun. I think about the few conversations we had in Vegas. How different she was from the girl I first met, how bitchy she was. How broken. Then there's Dylan. I'd disliked him from the first time I met him, but I never did much but occasionally express that I didn't like him. That's it." I stop talking as I reach the busy sidewalk where students walk to and from class. There are usually more people, but most of the classes have ended. "I wish I had someone to talk to about this, but Lea's been busy with her secret stuff and Tristan and Quinton both get uncomfortable whenever I talk about it, so I always drop it because I hate pushing them... still, it'd be nice if just once I could call up Quinton and pour my heart and soul out to him." I sigh and then decide to end the recording there, because it's only bumming me out more.

I'm putting my camera phone into my bag, figuring I'll wait until I get home before I start chattering away to it, when someone comes running up to my side. My body goes rigid as their body lines up with mine and an arm goes around my shoulder. Out of reflex I'm about to smack them away, but they catch my arm in midair.

Tristan starts laughing and I shake my head, breathing

profusely. "Holy crap. You scared the living daylights out of me," I gasp.

"Sorry," he says, pressing his frozen lips together. They're outlined with a bit of blue. He has a hat pulled low on his head, and his coat is zipped up to his chin. "I yelled your name, but you were talking to yourself and didn't hear me, I guess."

"I wasn't talking to myself." I tuck my hands into my pockets, trying to ignore that he's still got his arm around me. "I was recording."

"You really get into that stuff, don't you?" He blows on his free hand, trying to warm it up.

"Yeah, I guess." I round the corner and then step off the curb to cross the street.

"So what were you recording about?" he asks, glancing over his shoulder as someone hollers out, "Yo, Tristan!"

"I…" I stop in the middle of the road and turn around with him, because he doesn't let go of me, and he stares at a lanky guy with brown hair who's wearing a bright-yellow coat. The guy is walking toward us and he's got this look on his face that I can't quite place. Like he's about to start some trouble and is glad about it, maybe.

"Hey man," the guy says to Tristan with a chin nod. "You bailed so quickly after class I didn't get a chance to discuss that thing we were talking about."

I feel Tristan tense beside me and his arm suddenly falls to his side as he puts some space between us. "Yeah, I actually have a doctor's appointment so I have to hurry my ass up."

"You do?" I say, relieved he's finally going to go get himself checked out. His cough's gone away, but he's been extra tired lately and it has me worried.

Tristan nods, glancing at me and then back at yellow coat guy. "Can I catch up with you later, man?" he asks edgily.

"Sure, but we're still doing that thing, right?" the guy asks, discreetly glancing at me, then pressing a look at Tristan.

"Yeah, sure, of course," Tristan replies nonchalantly.

The guy looks at me again with a wary expression on his face and it feels like he's trying to read my vibe or something. "You cool?" he asks me.

I know he's asking if I'm cool with drugs, which makes me want to shove Tristan down and beat some sense into him.

"Hey, let's talk later, okay?" Tristan says through gritted teeth.

The guy nods, shuffling back onto the sidewalk, his eyes fastened on me until he turns around near the trees in the campus yard. Tristan hurries and grabs my sleeve to pull me out of the way as a car rounds the corner a little too fast.

After I get safely onto the sidewalk and start heading toward the apartment again, I ask, "So who was that?"

He shrugs, putting his hands in his coat pockets. "His name's Jazz. He's in my philosophy class."

"Jazz? That's an interesting name."

"About as interesting as Nova." He playfully prods my side with his elbow.

The ice on the ground crunches under my shoes as I walk

quietly with my head down, deliberating if I want to ask him, if I want to take a risk that I might be wrong and piss him off. But I need to know, so...

"What did he mean by if I was cool?" I ask, even though I know. I'm hoping I'm wrong.

Tristan doesn't answer right away. "Nothing. Jazz is just weird like that."

I'm not buying it at all. "Tristan, you're not..." I blow out a stressed breath and then tip my chin up to meet his eyes. "You're not thinking about doing drugs, are you?" I search his eyes for a sign that he might be doing them already, but they look clear, haze-free, although they do carry a little annoyance.

"Wow, I'm glad you have so much faith in me," he says, his tone as sharp as the icicles dangling from the rain gutters on the houses around us.

"I do have faith in you," I try to assure him. "It's just that that Jazz guy and you seemed to be...I don't know...talking in code."

"That's just how he is." Tristan steps to the side, moving away from me. "Jesus, Nova, I can't believe you're accusing me of anything. I've been good, you know, despite how fucking boring as shit this normal stuff is."

That right there is what makes me nervous. The fact that he thinks normal life is boring—that he's bored.

"I'm sorry," I say, feeling bad, but also really concerned. "I just worry about you—about everyone, really. And I've been really stressed out over this Delilah thing."

He glances at me from the corner of his eyes. "Why are you worried about Delilah?"

"I told you already, because she's missing." I hop over a patch of snow blocking the entry to the apartment complex. "And because of how things were the last time I saw her."

"But you weren't friends with her anymore, really. I mean, not since she moved to Vegas and you barely talked to her."

"We were once, though, and I still care about her." I try to explain how I feel, but I can tell he doesn't get it.

"I'm sure she'll be okay," he says unconvincingly. "Disappearing is just part of the life of a crackhead, mainly because we'll do anything and go anywhere to get our next bump." He gazes off into the distance as if he's remembering his time spent in that world. "It's all that matters to us."

"Don't say *us*." I loop my arm through his to bring his attention back to reality. "You're not part of that group anymore."

He nods, but there's something in his eyes I don't like. "Yeah, I know."

"And you're going to stay away from that group, right?" I ask as we hike across the parking lot and to the sidewalk.

"Of course, Mother." He flashes me a grin, breaking the tension between us. "So, *Mom*, can you give me a ride to the doctor's later today?"

"Why yes, *Son*," I joke back, and then stick out my tongue. "You know, I should take it offensively that you call me Mom all the time when you don't like your mom very much."

"It's not that I don't like her," he says, stopping as we reach the doorway to the stair entrance of our apartment. "It's that my parents don't like me."

"How do you figure?" I ask as he opens the door and I step inside, slipping my arm out of his.

He shrugs, the door slamming shut behind us. "Basic observation." We start up the stairs side by side. "Like for instance how they completely and utterly ignored me after Ryder died."

"I'm sure they didn't ignore you," I tell him. "They were probably just distracted by their own pain, like my mom was right after my dad died."

"Well, distracted or ignored, it was still hard, you know. I mean, it was like I was a ghost, and trust me, I tried to do everything to get their attention. Rebelled. Let my grades drop." He pauses as we approach the second floor. "Did drugs."

"Is that why you started?" I open the door and enter the hallway lined with numbered doors.

He shakes his head, following me down the hall. "Nah. I started getting high when I was fourteen. I just started doing more drugs after Ryder died and was a little more obvious about using." He fidgets uncomfortably, tucking his hands up into his sleeves. "I guess you could say I pretty much stopped caring about stuff, just like they did."

"Tristan, that's so sad, but I guess I sort of get it—how easy it is to stop caring."

"Yeah, it really, really is."

We pause in the middle of the hallway. I don't know about him, but my thoughts drift off to my past and how I stopped caring about everything at one point. Finally, after we stand there long enough that it starts to get weird, I blink myself out of my daze.

"Well, don't stop caring ever again," I say, waving my finger at him sternly. "Or else you'll be grounded."

"Got it," he says with a smile and then shocks the bejesus out of me when he leans forward and presses a kiss to my forehead. "I have no idea what I'd do without you," he says, heading for the door to our apartment, leaving me standing there with my jaw hanging to my knees. "You can always get me to smile when I feel shitty."

I let out a nervous laugh as he unlocks the door and then pushes it open, stepping aside to let me enter first. I don't really say much to him after that, telling him I'm going to go call my mom before I have to take him to the doctor. He easily lets me go, sitting down on the sofa to watch some television.

After I get into my room and shut the door, I let out a breath of relief. "I'm getting in over my head," I mutter to myself, pressing my hand to my forehead. "I really am and I have no idea how to fix it."

I slide to the ground and stare at the wall, wishing I could just walk out there and tell Tristan we should just be friends and to stop the flirting. And that he'd understand. Then I'd get a phone call from Delilah's mother and she'd tell me she found her and that Delilah was okay.

"I just want everything to be okay," I whisper, taking a deep breath and then another, wishing I had someone to talk to about my problems. I briefly consider calling Quinton and just letting it all out, like I've been wanting to, but I know I can't overwhelm him like that, so all I can do is tell myself that everything's going to be okay.

It has to be.

Chapter Eight

December 22, day fifty-four in the real world

Nova

Things have been getting really unbalanced in my life. My mom informed me that Delilah's mother needs help looking for her daughter and that she's going to help her. I'm not even sure why my mother is helping, but she said it was because Delilah's mom asked, after the two of them ran into each other at the store. They aren't really friends or anything but I guess Miss Pierce hasn't been doing that well lately and kind of broke down about Delilah and also revealed that she's been having health problems. Maybe that's why she suddenly decided to start searching for her daughter after all this time.

I told my mom what Quinton told me about the fire, the gun, and the gunshot. She said for me not to worry about it. That she had a feeling everything was going to turn out okay, but she always says that, mostly because she worries I'm going to break apart anytime life gets hard. But I've never really given her much of a reason to think otherwise.

Then there's Tristan. Heavy sigh. Tristan is a huge complication at the moment. He's been acting really weird, although his health has been improving. He actually had some sort of infection and had to be put on antibiotics. The doctor said he has a really weak immune system and I got the impression that he suspected something more serious, but I'm not sure what exactly. I have some guesses that involve him doing drugs again, but he doesn't show signs of it, at least when it comes to track marks and red rings around his nostrils. He's been really nice lately, too, and if I've learned anything it's that Tristan is an ass when he's high.

Still, overly nice Tristan is making things slightly complicated. I'm actually starting to loathe being at my apartment, worried he's going to finally actually try to kiss me, and I have no idea what the hell I'm going to do. I've been spending extra time at work and at the hotline center because of this, but I can't stay away from my home forever.

It's late when I get home and as I head up the stairway to my apartment, I find myself dreading going inside. I have a few sacks of Christmas presents in my hands. I've always been a last-minute shopper, which probably seems a little strange to some people since I have OCD and like order. It's mostly because I hate the busyness of the stores. I shopped online for most stuff, but Lea dropped a hint the other day that she wanted a vintage Pink Floyd record, so I had to run to the music store downtown and try to find one. Lucky one of my band members works there and was able to track one down.

When I get to my apartment, I stick my head in, instantly catching a scent of cigarettes. "Lea?" I call out. "Tristan?"

"Lea's not here," Tristan replies, and I hear something banging around.

I push the door open and walk in, slipping off my coat as I enter the living room. Then I stop dead in my tracks at the sight of Tristan hurrying to turn the television on while Jazz quickly stuffs something into the pocket of his yellow coat, a faint trail of smoke lingering in the air. I know what pot smells like and that's definitely not the scent of pot. Still, the situation seems a little bit sketchy to me with how nervous they're acting.

"Hey, Nova," Tristan says casually as he sits back in the couch and puts his feet up on the coffee table with the remote in his hand.

"Hey," I reply, glancing back and forth between the two of them. "What's up?"

Tristan shrugs as he aims the remote at the television. "Nothing much. Jazz and I were just hanging out. Being bored and shit."

Jazz looks at Tristan, then smiles at me as he puts on a beanie. "Yeah, just fighting the boredom of the potato state." He gets to his feet, running his hands across the front of his coat like he's smoothing the wrinkles out of it. "I'll check you later, man," he says to Tristan, and brushes past me and out the door without so much as an introduction.

As soon as the door shuts, I target my attention on Tristan. "So what was that about?"

He shrugs, pretending to be fixated by the news on the television screen. "Nothing much. We were just hanging."

I don't believe him. "You guys were acting a little weird," I point out as I set the presents down on the coffee table.

"Weird how?"

I shrug, setting my coat on the coffee table, eyeing his arms for signs he's been shooting up, but he looks clean and honestly I don't think that's what was going on here. Still, something's off. I can feel it in the air.

"Tristan, you're not...I mean, you're not doing..." I scratch my tattoo as I inch up to his side, wondering if accusing him is the right thing to do. I know if my mom had accused me back when I was getting high I would have either lied or gotten pissed. But I also feel like just letting it go means I'm not caring. "You're not doing drugs again, are you?"

His expression hardens as he glares up at me. "Is that what you think? That I'm sitting here getting high?" He spreads his arms to his sides and glances around the clean living room. "Does it look like that's what I've been doing?"

I shake my head, but something still doesn't feel right. "No, but I saw that Jazz guy put something into his pocket."

Tristan gets a confused look, like he has no clue what I'm

referring to, but the realization crosses his face. "Oh, that was his lighter. He was going to smoke in here, but I told him to put it away," he explains.

I fan my hand in front of my face. "It smells like he did."

He presses his lips together, brushing his hair out of his eyes. "Fine. If you want to know what's up, then yes, he smoked in here. Sorry for breaking the rules." He's mad at me and I open my mouth to say…well, I don't know, but he reaches forward and threads one of his fingers through the belt loop of my jeans, pulling me toward him. His anger turns to dead seriousness as he looks me straight in the eye. "Nova, I swear to you that I'm not doing drugs."

I study him, something still off, but ultimately I nod. "All right, I'm sorry for accusing."

"I forgive you, but only if you'll watch a movie with me." He yanks on my belt loop and pulls me forward until I stumble onto the couch beside him, pretty much landing on his lap.

I start to move off him, but he yanks me back so I am sitting on his lap. My lips part and my eyes widen as he snakes his arms around me, the scent of cigarette smoke and his cologne surrounding me. "Tristan, I—"

It's at this moment that Lea decides to stroll into the house. As she shuts the door behind her and turns to face us, her expression changes from elated to shocked.

"Holy hell." She takes in the sight of us and her jaw nearly drops to her knees.

I press her with a look, begging her not to say anything to make the situation worse. *Help me*, I mouth.

She takes the hint and then, being the awesome friend that she is, says, "Nova, can I talk to you in my room for a minute?"

I gratefully nod and then get up from Tristan's lap like it's on fire. Then Lea and I leave the living room with Tristan giving us a weird look as we duck down the hallway. Once we're in Lea's room and the door is closed, she spins toward me with her hands on her hips. "Holy shit."

"Yeah, holy shit," I say, shaking my head in disbelief as I pace her room.

"What the hell was that?" she asks, unbuttoning her black plaid coat.

I shrug, counting the number of nail polishes she has on her vanity, not really caring at the moment that I'm reverting back to my bad habits. I'm stressed out and I need relief. Just a minute or two and then I'll stop. "I have no idea what happened. One minute I was making sure everything was okay with him and the next he's pulling me down onto his lap."

She tosses her coat onto her bed, frowning. "I knew this was going to happen."

I stop pacing and look at her. "How?"

"Because I can see it in his eyes every time he looks at you," she says, unlacing her boot as she sits down on her bed. "He likes you. And I mean like-likes you."

I want to argue with her, but only because I don't want to

accept the truth. "I know…he had a thing for me once a year or so ago."

"I think he's never gotten over it," she says, kicking off her boot. "But the question is: do you think of him that way?"

I immediately shake my head. "No, Tristan's just a friend."

"Are you sure?" There's accusation in her tone. "Because you don't really crush on guys and I'm starting to wonder if maybe you just don't realize when you have feelings for someone."

"I know when I have feelings." I sigh and sit down on the bed beside her. "I've had them before once…twice."

She wiggles her foot out of her other boot. "With Landon. And….?" She waits for me to say it, even though she knows.

"You know it's Quinton," I say, pulling the elastic out of my hair and combing my fingers through it.

"How would I when you never say it?"

She's right. Way too right. I never say much aloud unless it's to my camera.

"It's hard to say it sometimes," I disclose, side-braiding my hair and securing it with an elastic. "When I don't know how he feels or if I'll ever see him again."

She takes a shimmering, knee-length black dress off a hanger. "I'm sure you will."

I shake my head as she steps deeper into the closet to change. "I'm not so sure. Every time I talk to him…it seems like he thinks that it might be too hard to see me again…he keeps saying one day down the road but I don't know…" I rest back on my elbows and sigh.

She steps out of the closet, wearing a tight sheer black dress with sparkling heels. "You could always just ask him." She reaches for the silver jewelry box on her vanity.

"I don't want to push him," I say, sitting up. "He always gets uncomfortable whenever I say something about visiting him."

"You don't need to be pushy when you ask." She takes out a black diamond earring and clips it on her ear. "Just make it a question and be okay with whatever answer he gives you." She puts the other earring in and then does a little twirl with her hands out to her sides. "How do I look?"

"Super fancy." I stand up. "Where are you going?"

"Out." She winks at me as she collects her purse.

I hurry and cut her off as she strides toward the door. "No way." I span my hands out to the sides, trying to block her path. "Enough with the secrecy. Fess up."

She rolls her eyes at me as she reaches for her coat on the bedpost. "I'm just going out with some friends." She drapes the coat over her arm. "Jesus, Nova. You need to chill out." She pushes past me, but halts before the door. "Look, I'm your best friend so I can say this. Do yourself a favor and let Tristan know where you stand, wherever that may be." She grabs the doorknob and pulls the door open. "And let Quinton know where you stand. It'll be good for you, I think."

I want to be angry with her for telling me to do things I don't want to, but I can't. "Thank you, Lea," I say, following her out the door. "But I still think you're lying to me about where you're going tonight."

"Think what you want." She grins in response. "Totally off the subject, but can I borrow your car, in just a bit, for a couple of hours?"

I think about telling her no unless she'll fess up to where she's really going, but I'm not that big a bitch. "Sure, but you'll have to drop me off at practice and then pick me up afterward."

She frowns, because she hates taking me to practice. She actually probably would have been in my band if she hadn't broken the heart of Jaxon, the lead singer. "Fine, but I'm staying in the car."

"That sounds good to me," I tell her. "But then again, it's totally okay for you to come in and say hi. In fact, I know Jaxon would love it."

"Nova, I love you to death, but you need to get over the idea of Jaxon and me ever getting together again."

"I am over the idea, but at the same time, if you guys get back together I wouldn't mind."

"We won't get back together. *Ever*," she says, frustrated. "Seriously, Nova. You need to let go of the past... this is why I don't tell you stuff." Then she hurries down the hallway and leaves me standing there with her words replaying in my mind.

Getting stuck in the past is an issue I've struggled with for quite a while. I have a hard time letting go. I thought I was getting better, though, but she pretty much just threw in my face that I'm not.

I try to decide whether I should go out and tell Tristan there will be no more forehead kisses or lap-sitting. But after lurking in the hallway for a moment, I decide to go back into my room and get ready for band practice, even though it's not for a few hours, because I'm a big chicken who's not ready for confrontation at the moment.

❧

Thankfully, band practice gives me time away from my thoughts. After an hour of playing, I feel good. And the amazing feeling only increases after we're done playing. I'm bouncing up and down like a little kid strung out on candy as I'm informed that my band got a gig. And not just any gig, but one where we get to open for Peaceful Injustice, one of my favorite indie rock bands of all time, next weekend on New Year's eve. Jaxon announces this to us in the garage of his house, the place where we practice because we're all broke students and can't afford to rent a studio space.

Jaxon is a pretty good-looking guy, if you like that whole mysterious rock-star look. He's tall and kind of lanky with dark brown hair that hangs in his eyes, but in an intentional kind of way. He's dressed head to toe in black today, with a studded belt, boots, and leather bands on his arms.

"So what do you think?" Jaxon asks me after he's made the epic announcement.

I tuck my drumsticks into the back pocket of my jeans as I search the garage for where I left my jacket. "I think it rocks. But what I'm wondering is how the hell you managed to get them to let us open for them."

"He's got connections," Spalding calls out as he unplugs his guitar from the amp. He's got longer hair, too, like Jaxon, only his is jet black. He has a pierced eyebrow, and colorful artwork is tattooed all over his arms to create full sleeves. He's got gauges in his ears and he's also wearing all black, but that's normal for him.

Nikko snorts a laugh as he puts his guitar away. He's got short hair that sort of spikes up at the top and his eyes are crazy intense because if you stare at them long enough they almost look gold. His taste in clothes is a little more eccentric. Right now he's wearing this bright-red fitted shirt and these baggy black pants with zippers and buckles all over the front. His black boots have gray skeletons on them and his fingernails are black. He's the baby of the group, only eighteen; he's also Jaxon's cousin.

"The only reason we got the gig is because Jaxon hung out with Stella." Nikko laughs under his breath and then sticks out his tongue, making an obscene gesture with his fingers, and Spalding rolls his eyes.

"Children." Spalding shakes his head and I laugh. Spalding's twenty-two, but he acts like he's thirty, which from the tidbits of information I picked up from Jaxon is because he became the legal guardian of his sister when he was eighteen. I'm not sure why, though, and I don't have the lady balls to ask because, more than likely, there's a tragic story behind it.

"Shut the fuck up," Nikko says hotly as he picks up a bottle of water from the top of one of the speakers. "You're only four years older than me, dumbass." He takes a swig of the water and then sets it back down.

They start arguing and I turn to Jaxon as I pick up my jacket off the floor in the corner of the garage. "So did you get the gig because of Stella?" I dare ask. Stella is the owner of Black & Red Ink, the place where we'll be playing, and a very popular club in the potato state.

He shakes his head, getting a little bit uneasy as he pretends to search for something behind the freezer. "No...well, yeah, I mean she's how I got the gig, but I didn't like sleep with her or anything." He turns in a circle as he looks around at the floor. "Have you seen my cell phone?"

"Yeah...it's in your hand." I hate the awkwardness between us, but until Lea and he can come to terms with their breakup, I think it'll always be there, especially since I have a hunch she was out on a date earlier today.

He glances down at the phone in his hand and then shakes his head. "Sorry, I guess I'm tired or something."

I offer him a smile. "Yeah, it happens sometimes." I slip my arms through the sleeves of my jacket and then take the drumsticks from my pocket. "So what time are we practicing tomorrow?"

"About six," he says, checking his cell phone screen. "I know we usually do it earlier, but I have to go out with the family for an early Christmas dinner."

"Early Christmas dinner?" I ask as I zip up my jacket. "But

175

Christmas is in three days, so why don't they just wait two extra days?"

"Yeah. I'm going to be gone for Christmas and my parents think they need to have an early one for me," he says. "I'm flying out to New York with Spalding to hang with his family for the holidays."

"Oh. Well, I'm glad my parents don't want to have a makeup dinner for me," I say, ignoring the bang as Nikko bumps into one of the cymbals. "I mean, I love going home and everything, but I can't go anywhere right now. Not when I just picked up some extra hours at work. Plus the band and our stellarly awesome gig we just got on New Year's eve." There's also the fact that Tristan won't go home and I don't want to leave him here for so long. My mom's planning on coming out after New Year's so everything should work out.

The corners of his lips quirk. "I'm glad to see where we are on your list of importance."

"Hey, you guys are totally important," I say, heading for the door. "However, my job pays the bills and my education will hopefully be able to pay the bills in the future."

"What? You're not planning on becoming a rock star?" he jokes as he follows me, weaving around my pink drum set, the one Landon gave to me on my birthday years ago. It's sad he never got to see me perform, just practice. He didn't get to see a lot of things, which makes me even sadder. But it's an obstacle that I've overcome and I can find solace in playing now.

I pause, contemplating what he said. "I'm honestly not sure what I'll do...what about you?"

"I'm not sure, either," he says. "I mean, I'm majoring in general education so I have no idea what the hell I'm going to do with that or if I want to do anything with it at all." He hurries to my side and opens the door to the wash-room for me. "Honestly, if I could make a living singing, I would, but there's a slim chance that'll ever happen."

"Maybe you'll be one of the lucky ones." I step into the room and breathe in the warm air and faint scent of cookies flowing from the kitchen.

"Maybe," he says, but doesn't seem too optimistic. And I don't blame him. There is very little chance that he'll be able to actually become a famous rock star. Life doesn't work that way. You can try and try but it doesn't mean you'll get what you want. You just have to make do with what you have.

He continues to walk me to the front door and I'm hoping he'll say good-bye to me there, since Lea's outside. But he doesn't and ends up walking out with me to the driveway, where Lea is waiting in my car.

She gets out to let me drive and tenses as her eyes meet Jaxon's and Jaxon freezes in the middle of the frosted lawn. No one speaks and I can hear Christmas carolers down the street singing a very cheerful "Joy to the World."

"Hey," she says, cracking the tension like the ice on the ground. She glances around at the yard, the front door, the garage, pretty much everywhere but at him.

"You cut your hair," he says, his brows knitting as he takes in the sight of her as she steps around to the front of the car. "It looks good."

Lea touches a strand of her hair, finally looking at him. I remember that when I first met them, over a year ago, there was a sparkle in her eye every time she looked at him, but it's not there anymore and that makes me sad. What makes me even sadder is that I wonder if that's how Landon and I would have gotten if he were still alive. Would we have gotten to this point? I believed at the time that we'd always be together, but it's hard to say now, especially when my feelings for Quinton are so strong.

"Thank you," she says formally, her hand falling to her sides as she reclines back against the front of my car and crosses her arms. "I thought it was time for a change."

That comment makes Jaxon sad. I can see it in his fallen expression and the way his shoulders sort of slump in. "Yeah, change is good, I guess," he mutters.

Poor guy. I feel so bad for him. He's actually been writing really depressing songs lately and I sometimes wonder if they're about Lea.

"So we should get going," I say, attempting to break the awkward tension as I head toward the driver's side. "We have to go pick up some stuff for Christmas dinner."

"You're not going home?" Jaxon asks Lea as she heads for the passenger side of the car.

She shakes her head, opening the door. "Nah, I thought

I'd stay here and catch up on some schoolwork. I've kind of fallen behind the last few weeks."

Probably because she's been spending a lot of time at football games and restaurants, and swimming, or whatever the hell she was doing that day.

"Are you going home?" she asks Jaxon, holding the door open and looking at him.

He shakes his head, fidgeting with a leather band on his wrist as twinkle lights sparkle in the background, highlighting the sadness in his eyes. "Nah, I'm actually going to New York to hang with Spalding and his family."

"New York. Holy shit. How fun." She rests her arms on top of the car door while I debate whether I should just climb into the car and let them chat or stop them from chatting to avoid Jaxon getting more attached. "I've always wanted to go there."

"I know you have." He steps toward her with this look in his eyes like he's about to ask her something really important.

That's my cue to stop the conversation. "Hey, Lea, we gotta go, otherwise Tristan's going to head out on his own to go shopping and, well, I can only imagine what he'll buy for us to eat for Christmas dinner."

"Probably TV dinners." Lea chuckles under her breath. "Yeah, we should get going." She waves at Jaxon, who looks crushed. "It was nice catching up with you. Hope you have a blast in New York." She lowers her head into the car and climbs in.

I wave at Jaxon and he gives me the dirtiest look, like I've just hit him in the face or something. I'm guessing it's because I broke up the conversation, but it's for his own good. I know for a fact that right now Lea's not looking to get back together with him. Maybe in the future, but I won't say for sure because the future is always changing.

After I get into the car, buckle my seat belt, and drive down the road, Lea turns to me with excitement in her eyes. "I have a huge favor to ask you."

"It wouldn't by chance be helping you get back together with Jaxon, would it?" I ask with false hope.

"No." She frowns. "Nova, I already told you that isn't happening."

"I know what you said, but I'm always hoping you'll change your mind," I say. When she scowls at me, I opt to change the subject. "Okay, tell me what your favor is."

She lightens up a little. "I need you to play with my band tomorrow at Red and Black Ink."

I gape at her as I slow the car down for a stop sign. It's fairly late, the sun descending behind the hills, but there's still enough light that I can see Lea's face clearly. "Band? Since when are you in a band?"

She pulls a whoops face. "Oh yeah. I should probably explain that part, huh?"

I nod as I press on the gas. "Yeah, that would be awesome, since I have no idea what the hell you're talking about."

"Hey, there's no need to get snippy," she says. "I kept it a secret for a good reason."

"And what's that?"

She bites her thumbnail as she gazes out the window at the sliver of sunlight left, painting the sky bright orange and pink. "Because..." She sighs, lowering her hand onto her lap. "Look, I get that you like Jaxon, but he just wasn't the right guy for me, so I need you to remember that when I tell you what I'm about to tell you."

"I don't think you need to tell me," I say to her. "You're dating one of your band members, aren't you? And that's why you've been acting so vague about what you've been doing the last couple of months."

She hesitates and then nods. "Well, that and I've been sneaking off to band practice."

"But what about the football game? And the face painting thing?"

"Oh, Brody also plays football."

"Brody's the guy you're dating, I'm guessing," I say, unable to hide the disdain in my voice. Brody? What kind of name is Brody anyway? It sounds like a meathead's name. *Jesus, what the hell is wrong with me?*

She tucks a fallen strand of her hair behind her ear, then she slouches in the seat so that she can put her feet up on the dashboard. "Yeah, he's also the guitarist of Moon Glory."

"Moon Glory?"

"Yeah, it's the name of our band," she says cheerfully. "A band in desperate need of a drummer, since our old one decided to bail out on us last week. Just up and quit." She throws her hands in the air exasperatedly. "Can you believe that?"

"Kind of." I turn the car onto the main road in town. "Bands break up a lot."

"Yeah, you're right." She sighs and then looks at me with a silent plea in her eyes. "So what do you think? Can you be our drummer?"

"I'm already in a band," I remind her. "And I like them."

"Yeah, but I'm your best friend," she says, lowering her feet onto the floor and sitting up in the seat. "And I've been there for you a lot in the last few months."

"I know you have," I reply heavyheartedly. "But I can't just up and quit when things are going so great right now...I don't get great a lot."

"But it's our first gig and if we bail out on it, then Stella might not give us another chance." She pouts, giving me her saddest puppy-dog face, trying to guilt-trip me into it.

"I'll tell you what," I say, turning onto the side road that leads to our apartment complex. "I'll fill in until you can find your own drummer, but I'm not quitting my band."

She claps her hands and bounces up and down excitedly. "Thank you. Thank you. Thank you."

I force a smile, hoping this doesn't come back to bite me in the ass. For one thing, I can picture Spalding getting pissed off because he thinks I'm cheating on the band or something. And Jaxon…well, God knows how that's going to go over if he knows I'm in a band with Lea and her new boyfriend.

❧

"So what's the hell's bugging you?" Tristan asks me later that night as Lea, he, and I wander around the grocery store, attempting to plan some sort of Christmas eve meal for the three of us to have in just a couple of days. I can still feel the awkwardness from earlier and it only builds every time he gives me a more-than-friendly look, which has happened four times so far.

"What do you mean?" I ask as I assess the frozen vegetable selection, tapping my finger on my lips as I decide which one to get.

"I mean, why have you had a permanent frown on your face since Lea and you showed up at the apartment earlier?" he asks, rolling up the sleeves of his blue hooded jacket, which matches his eyes.

"I'm just tired." I yawn, pretending to be exhausted, and I am, kind of. Mentally exhausted, anyway.

He flirtingly bumps his shoulder into mine. "I know you're lying, so fess up. What the hell is making you so down?" He pauses. "It's not something with Quinton, is it?"

I quickly shake my head. "No, nothing like that." I reach for the handle of the freezer door. "In fact, now that you've said that, it seems really stupid."

"Tell me anyway," he says, reclining against the cart as he studies me. "Maybe I can help you with a problem and pay you back for all the times you've helped me out."

I shouldn't do it. I know that.

I glance around the aisle. Lea wandered off to get rolls, but that was a few minutes ago and I worry she might come back and hear me talking to him. "It's nothing. Just band stuff."

"Like what?"

I open the door and the freezer air hits me. "Lea wants me to help out in her band. Step in for the drummer until they can find a new one." I grab a bag of frozen corn and drop it into the cart. Then I let go of the door and it slams shut.

"She's in a band?" he asks. "Since when?"

"For a while, I guess."

"So that's why she's been acting so weird, then?" he asks, and I nod. He muses over something, then adds, "And you don't want to help her band out because she lied to you?" He turns around and pushes the cart forward.

"It's not that," I say, stopping in front of the frozen pie selection. "I don't want to help out because I worry that my band's going to get pissed off at me and kick me out."

"Because the singer is Lea's old boyfriend?"

"That, and Spalding takes everything so seriously."

"That he does," Tristan agrees, opening the freezer door to pick up an apple pie. "And I think that after only meeting him, like, twice."

"So you get why I'm worried." I squeeze up to his side and select a chocolate pie.

"Aha!" he practically screams, pointing a finger at the pie in my hand. "I picked the healthier choice."

I roll my eyes as he grins. "Just because it has apples in it, doesn't mean that it's healthier."

"It so totally does." He snatches the pie out of my hand, flips it over, and starts reading the back. Then he puts it into the cart and skims over the back of the apple pie, his goofy attitude dissipating. "Shit, the apple sounds almost worse than the chocolate."

"Told ya." I give him a cocky grin as he puts the other pie into the cart.

"And I'm telling you that everything's going to be okay with your band," he says, draping his arm over my shoulder. I tense. Stop breathing. My mind searching for a way to shrug him off without being too obvious. "You don't give yourself enough credit for how much people love you. If they get pissed, just show them that sweet smile and I'm sure they'll forgive you."

"You're giving me and my smile way too much credit." I pretend to step forward and assess the selection of pies again.

"No way." He moves forward with me and touches my bottom lip with his fingertip. "I'm not giving it enough credit." His tongue slips out and wets his lips as his eyes zone in on mine.

I swallow hard. *Shit. This can't be happening. This can't be happening.*

As he looks at me with this sort of lustful gaze, I realize I just might have more problems than my band getting mad at me. I can see it in his eyes—he's thinking about kissing me. Right here in the grocery store. I should take off running, right down the aisle, but I freeze in place, worried that if I reject him like that, it could mess up how good everything's going.

My thoughts are racing in a distorted stream that doesn't make sense and the closer Tristan's lips get to mine, the blurrier everything around me becomes. I feel a shift, one I want to run the hell away from. Not just out of the store, but back in time to when life didn't seem so complicated. Back when I was sure about everything. Yet I keep standing in place. Motionless. About to ruin everything.

Thankfully, Lea turns the corner with two bags of rolls in her hand. "Okay, so I couldn't decide what kind to get," she says, dropping the bags into the cart. "So I got both." She gives us a funny look as Tristan steps back, stuffing his hands into his pockets, and I start picking at my nails.

"Two bags is fine," Tristan says indifferently. "You never can have too many rolls."

Lea looks at him like he's crazy, but Tristan ignores her and roams up the aisle, glancing at the crackers-and-cookies section like it's the most fascinating thing in the world.

"Did you guys almost just kiss?" Lea hisses as I wrap my fingers around the handle of the cart.

I swiftly shake my head. "No."

She raises her eyebrows at me. "Don't lie to me, Nova Reed."

"I'm not," I say in a low voice, pushing the cart forward.

But I am lying. Because I know I wouldn't have moved away if he'd kissed me. But for what reason, I'm not sure.

By the time I get back to the apartment, I feel like a terrible person. I end up going into my room, locking my door, cranking up my music, and pretending I don't hear Tristan when he knocks or Lea when she hollers for me to come watch a movie with her. Instead I sit on my bed and take out my photo album dedicated to Landon. I relax, leaning against the headboard, and start turning the pages. I can't help but smile at the good pictures, the ones where Landon looks really happy. The ones of our good moments. There weren't many, which makes it hard to remember them sometimes and easier to remember the sad times because there were so many. But when things were good, they were amazing.

Finally, after I'm on the verge of tearing up, I decide to get out my camera and record myself. I set the camera on my nightstand and aim it at myself as I flip the pages of the album.

"Once upon a time, there was a girl who liked to look at things on a positive side a lot," I say as I stare at a picture of myself grinning at the camera, a picture Landon took; his finger ended up covering part of the lens. "She had such hope inside her that everything was going to turn out okay. That despite the tragedy with her dad, she would grow up and be happy." I turn the page and then run my fingers across a picture of Landon with his head tipped down as he stares at something on the ground, his backyard in the background. "What she didn't realize is that tragedy was going to hit her again and her happily-ever-after wouldn't exist anymore. And she'd be left feeling lost for the longest time." I flip the page over to a picture of Landon and me together, one where he's kissing my cheek and I'm laughing because his hair tickles me. I think it might be one of my favorites. "She'd eventually find her way back to a good life again, for the most part, anyway. But when it came to relationships, she'd be confused and she'd analyze it all the time, who she was supposed to end up with in life. But an answer would never come to her and she'd eventually start wondering if maybe she was just supposed to be alone in the world." I sit up and pull my knees up to my chest, resting my chin on top of them, and stare down at a picture that captured a moment that was gone as soon as the flash died. "That maybe her heart would always belong to a ghost." As soon as I say it, though, I know it's not true. Yes, Landon did take a piece of my heart with him the day he died, but not the entire thing. I know because I can feel a pull to someone else at the moment.

I lean over to my nightstand, open the drawer, and take out Quinton's sketches, which I picked up from his apartment floor in Vegas when he disappeared from my life. I unfold them and then run my fingers across the lines and shadings. One of them is of Lexi, his girlfriend who died in the car accident. The way he captures her, the dark lines drawn with such passion, lets me know how much he cared about her. The second is a picture of himself, only half of his face is skeletal, and then the final one is of me. The lines aren't dark and full of passion like Lexi's. They're actually really light, like he was afraid to draw me or something. I wonder if he was—if he still is afraid of me.

I get up and turn my music down, then go get my phone out of my jacket pocket before returning to my bed. Once I get situated on the bed, I take a deep breath and dial Quinton's number. I haven't told him I have his drawings, because I'm not sure how he'll react.

But he doesn't answer and I end up lying in my bed, feeling so alone.

Chapter Nine

Quinton

I'm feeling decent today after I get back from work. Tired, but tired can be a good thing. It helps me block out all the boxes in the house when I walk inside, and the fact that in about ten minutes I'll be heading right back out the door isn't too bad, either.

"Hey, you're home early," my dad says, cutting me off in the foyer. He's dressed in old jeans and a faded shirt and he's wiping his hands on a towel.

"I could say the same thing to you," I tell him, reaching for the phone in my pocket as it vibrates, but I get distracted by something. "Why are you home?"

He tosses the towel down on the back of the chair in the living room. "I actually have some news," he says. "My boss wants me to go over to Virginia a little bit early. Next week, actually."

"Are you kidding me?" I frown, pulling my hand out of my pocket without checking my phone. "Please tell me you're kidding me."

He shakes his head with an apologetic expression. "But don't worry. It's going to take me a few weeks to get a place set up there, so I figure you can stay here while I do."

"Stay here for a few weeks and then what? I move to Virginia?" I shake my head, hurrying for the stairs. "I already told you I don't want to do that."

"I know what you said, but that's just how things are," he says, catching hold of my arm before I get too far. It's weird that he's touching me because he never does. In fact, when I really think about it he never has. I can even remember thinking how weird it was when he gave me a handshake at my middle school graduation.

"Well, I'm not moving." I turn to face him and he swiftly lets go of me.

"Quinton, I understand how you feel." He gives me a look of pity as he rolls up his sleeves. "But sometimes we just have to do things we don't want to do."

"I know that, but I just can't move across the country," I say, folding my arms. "I'm going to find somewhere else to live."

"Do you have enough money saved up for that?" he wonders as he reaches for a folded-up box on the floor near the front door.

I unzip my coat. "No, but I'll figure something out." I think about what Nova said about getting a roommate. "I'll get a roommate or something."

"Are you sure that's what you want to do?" He places the

box on the floor beside his feet. "Because…" He massages the back of his neck tensely. "Because I was really looking forward to you coming to Virginia with me."

I'm wondering if he really means it or not. It's hard to tell with him, but I want to believe that he does, so that's how I'm choosing to see things. "I want—need to stay here."

"But I worry about you living alone and what might happen," he says. "I worry that you might relapse."

"If it's going to happen, then it's going to happen," I say, rubbing some paint off the back of my hand. "But I don't want it to happen and staying here and doing what I'm doing is going to make it more possible for me to stay out of trouble." I hope. I've been doing good. Haven't wandered in places I don't belong. Haven't lost control. I just hope nothing triggers me to do otherwise.

He unfolds the box. "Well, if you absolutely need to stay at the house, then you can until the new buyers move in, which I think is next month." He backs into the living room and picks up the packing tape from the sofa. "But Quinton, I just want to make sure that you stay in touch with me this time."

I nod and then go up into my room to change out of my painting clothes and get my work clothes on. I put on holey jeans, an insulated coat, then some gloves, pulling a gray beanie onto my head. I'm glad my dad and I finally talked and everything, but I still have the huge problem of finding a place and saying good-bye to this home and all the memories it carries.

As I'm getting ready to head down the stairs, I glance around at the sketches and photos on the wall. I still haven't taken them down. Still holding on. I stare at a picture of Lexi on the wall, the one where she's smiling so brightly it makes me want to smile with her. I lift my hand and touch my finger to the photo, noting how badly my hand shakes.

"Will you forgive me?" I ask, my hands still shaking as I pull the photo off the wall, feeling something break in half inside me. "If I keep going forward this way...keep healing instead of dying?" I wish I could hear her say yes. I wish that for just one moment I could hear her voice and she would let me go.

But of course the only response I get is silence and I know that I'll never hear her voice again. As I go to put the picture back on the wall, I draw back and decide that maybe this is the first step to moving forward. That this is it.

"I can do this," I tell myself, then walk over to my nightstand and put the photo in the drawer. The moment I do, it feels like I've done something wrong. But I still walk away from the room. Step by step. Trying to move forward, even though I can feel an invisible pull drawing me back. To her. Begging me to put that picture on the wall and never let go. Never change anything. Just keep holding on until it kills me.

❧

"Do you want to tell me what's got you so upset?" Wilson asks me as I hammer a nail into a piece of wood. We're inside the house, although it's not really inside. Two-by-fours make up the walls, the floor is plywood, and the roof isn't even close to being finished. The air smells like sawdust and my hands feel like sandpaper. The sound of power tools encircles me and it just quit raining so everything's wet and the temperature is low. But I like everything about it. It helps me somewhat forget that I took down one of Lexi's photos today. And that I'm going to be homeless soon. And that through all of this I have to feel everything because I decided to become sober.

"I'm not upset." I toss the hammer aside and then reach for another board. "I'm just working through some stuff."

"Well, maybe if you tell me what, then I can help you work through it?" He rolls up the sleeves of his worn plaid jacket, even though it's cold, because we've been working hard so it feels hotter than it is. I align the board into place and he steps up with the nail gun. "Come on, Quinton," he says, putting the tip of the nail gun up against the wood. "Just give it up and share what the hell's got you looking so cranky."

I hold the board in place while he shoots some nails into it, then he sets the nail gun down and picks up his water bottle. "Fine," I say, stepping away from the now-sturdy board. There are rows around us and soon the Sheetrock and insulation will go up to make walls. It's an amazing thing to be a part of—it really is. "My dad's moving to Virginia in like a week and I have no place to stay because he's selling our house."

He takes a swig of his water while I sit down on the floor and retrieve my pack of cigarettes from my pocket. "Why don't you just go with him?" he asks.

"Because of all this." I remove a cigarette from the pack as I gesture around the partially built house. "I don't just want to give it all up."

He sits down on the floor beside me and stretches out his legs in front of him. "You know you can do this stuff anywhere, right? You can even do other stuff and still get the same experience."

"Yeah, but." I put the cigarette into my mouth and reach for my lighter in my pocket. "I'm comfortable here." I cup my hand around the end of the cigarette. "And I like how things are going here." I light the cigarette and inhale before blowing out smoke. Part of me wants to run and call Nova, because she'd try to cheer me up and figure out solutions, instead of telling me that I should probably go with my dad. And she probably could even help me deal with taking down the photos. Talk me down. Get me to see things in a different light—a brighter light. Because she always makes things seem ten times better.

Wilson takes another swig of his water before screwing the cap back on. "All right, I'm going to throw an idea out there and see where it goes." He rises to his feet and sets the water down before picking up the nail gun again. "Why don't you live with me for a little while? At least until you can get on your feet."

195

I give him an unfathomable look. "Are you seriously offering me your place?"

He shrugs as he lifts the cord of the nail gun over a pile of wood it's snagged on. "Sure, why not?"

"Because it would be weird," I point out. "Having a twenty-year-old ex-junkie living with you."

"Well, since I'm a thirty-five-year-old ex-junkie, I don't think that's too big of a deal," he says. "Besides, I'm barely there anyway."

I get to my feet, grazing my thumb across the bottom of the cigarette and scattering ash all over the floor. "Why?"

"Because I travel around a lot to do this." He gestures around the construction site, where the sounds of hammers and power tools are going off all around us. "In fact, you could always do that, too. You'd have a place to live while we're on the road and when you're here you can stay at my place, until you're ready to get a place of your own." He points his finger at me. "Now there's an idea."

For a second I actually consider it. Just going. Leaving. Taking off and working the crap out of myself to help others. I'd have to say good-bye to a lot of things, though, and I'm not sure I'm ready for that yet, since an hour ago I nearly cracked saying good-bye to a photo.

I put the cigarette into my mouth and take a slow drag before exhaling. "It seems too easy just to move in with you."

"What? Things can't be easy?" he asks as he puts the nail gun up to a board. "Life's not right if it isn't hard?"

"It's not supposed to be easy for me," I say. "It's supposed to be difficult and a struggle to pay back for what I..." I stop talking, not wanting to go down that road right now. It's weird, but the only person I've really talked to about this is Nova, which I think says a lot about her...a lot about how she makes me feel.

After putting a few nails into the board, he places the gun down on the floor. "You know, I get the whole self-punishment thing and wanting to pay back for what you did by slowly torturing yourself," he says. "However, do you really want to be homeless again? Living outside in the fucking cold? Behind a Dumpster or in a crack house with a bunch of other crack addicts? Holes in the wall. Probably no plumbing. Doing God knows what? Snorting lines? Shooting up? Whatever your drug of choice was."

I hate how direct he is sometimes and the images he's vividly painting are crawling under my skin. "No, but if I did end up that way I'd probably deserve it...maybe that's why this isn't working out for me." I drop my cigarette to the ground and put it out with the tip of my boot. "I'll never be able to deserve much of anything, but I'm going to make sure I keep trying to pay everyone back until the day I die again." I bend down to pick up my hammer, realizing I let something slip out that I'm not sure he knew yet.

"Wait. What do you mean *again*?" He waits for me to explain, but I don't, instead going up and hammering a nail that doesn't necessarily need to be hammered. "Did you die at the scene of the accident?" he asks, and I pound the hammer harder against the wood. "Quinton, talk to me."

My heart misses a beat as I ram the hammer into the nail repeatedly. "Yeah, so what if I did?" I shrug, like it's no big deal, even though the urge to go find a bump is hitting me harder than it ever has. "Shit happens sometimes."

"Shit happens sometimes?" He's astounded, standing there with the nail gun loosely in his hand, about ready to drop it. "Quinton, you're a walking miracle."

Miracle? *Miracle*? Is he fucking kidding me? One pound. Two pound. Three pound. The nail is so far in that the wood is starting to split around it. But I can't stop until he stops talking. "Yeah, try telling that to Lexi's parents," I say, wiping the sweat from my brow with my arm, and then move to another nail. "Or Ryder's. They'll tell you how delusional you are."

He shakes his head and then snags hold of my arm as I swing back to hit the nail again. "Quinton, you can't expect them to think any differently," he says, looking me directly in the eye. "They lost their children and are probably never going to forgive you." His words are sharp and jagged like the shrapnel that cut open my chest and nearly killed me.

I jerk my arm away from him. I'm not really mad at him; it's more that there's so much panic and anguish in me that I can't figure out any other outlet than to yell at him. "I need to tell them I'm sorry at least...I never did that."

"I don't think you should, at least until you can deal with what's probably going to come after you say it," he explains as

198

I drop the hammer on the ground. "I think what you need to do is work on forgiving yourself, because it's all you can do and life will get easier when you do. It might even end up being good."

I cross my arms, wishing I could curl up in a ball and erase the last few minutes, go back home and put that picture up on the wall. "I'm not sure I can do that. Forgive myself when they haven't yet."

"Sure you can," he assures me, picking up my hammer and extending it in my direction for me to take. "It'll just take some time."

I don't take the hammer from him and instead storm away, the knife in my chest digging deeper as I think about how I wanted to say sorry to Lexi's mom one day, hoping that something might come out of it, but now he's saying I shouldn't because what I want—need—to happen probably isn't going to. Then I think about how I just took down her photo and put it away and I start to regret it.

"Quinton, come back," he shouts out after me.

I shake my head as I keep walking. "I need to take a walk and think," I say to him, trotting down the stairs of the house and onto the bottom floor. There are a few guys at the site, but I barely pay attention to them even when they wave.

When I get outside, I dash across the parking area and to the sidewalk. Then I start walking toward the corner. I don't look back, looking straight ahead as I wander toward the unknown, one foot in front of the other, focusing on that instead of how I feel. I'm not even exactly sure what I'm upset about. I think it might be a combination of everything that's happened today and the difficulty that just comes with living life.

Life.

It's so fucking hard.

One minute things are fine. The next they change into something painful. Every day just moving. Changing. And I'm left coping. Is that what I want? To go through day after day like this? So up and down? I'm not sure I can do that.

Not sober, anyway.

The last thought guides my feet to a place where I can start making everything easier. I don't stop walking, going for at least an hour, passing blocks and blocks, until I'm standing in front of Marcus's house, staring like a fucking psychopath at the door with a flowery wreath on it. I can't seem to bring myself to walk away, yet at the same time, I can't get my hand to knock on the door. I'm getting so furious with myself for even coming here. Why did I do it? I don't want to be here.

What do I want?

What do I need?

Why do I feel this way?

Why can't I bring myself to walk away?

Questions are racing through my head so quickly I'm hardly aware of anything around me. It's like me and what's on the other side of that door are the only things that exist. That's it. *I need to walk away. I need to knock. Go. Stay. Go. Stay.*

My phone starts to vibrate in my pocket and the sound brings me out of my daze. I don't want this—I remember that. I've been to this place and even though it's easy, I chose to leave it for a reason—I chose life.

I turn to walk away even though my body's so stiff it feels like it's going to crack apart. But when I'm in mid-turn the front door of the house suddenly swings open. Marcus looks a little startled as he stumbles back in the doorway. He's wearing a white T-shirt, jeans, and no shoes. His black hair is thinner than the last time I saw him. Not from old age— he's only twenty-two. But because he's gotten into harder stuff since then. The scabs on his face and arms and his major decrease in weight are evidence of that. And also evidence that he has what my mind is craving at the moment.

"Wow, where the fuck did you come from?" Marcus says, scratching his arm as he glances around at the front yard behind me, which is decorated with a giant inflatable Santa. "Quinton, my man, how the hell have you been?"

To him it's probably such a casual question, but to me the answer is more complicated than living. "I've been good," I lie, and then exchange a handshake with him. "How's things going with you?"

He shrugs, glancing over his shoulder into the house. "Not too bad. Just been living life."

201

I nod with uneasiness. "That's good." I'm about to say good-bye and walk away because things feel really awkward.

But then he looks back at me and says, "You want to come inside for a bit? Dan's here chillin'."

Fuck. Shit. Fuck. What am I doing? "Maybe…I mean, yeah. Sure." *Walk away.*

Marcus steps back to let me in and I stare down at the threshold, watching in slow motion as I lift my foot over it and step inside. Just like that I enter the world that nearly killed me.

I'm trying to decide how I feel about that as I follow Marcus down the hallway and toward the basement where I used to spend a lot of time getting high. Marcus is chatting about something, but I barely hear him because I'm too distracted by the way my mind and body are reacting to the pungent scent flowing up the stairway. I'm sure a lot of people probably wouldn't notice the increase in moisture in the air, but having craved the sensation before, my senses heighten.

I know what I'm walking into before I walk into it, which means I should turn away. But I don't. I walk right into it. Part of me wanting it. Needing it. Seeking the quiet.

Dan's sitting on the leather sofa when I enter the room at the bottom of the stairs. He looks about the same as the last time I saw him, maybe a little scragglier and his hair a little shorter. He has a light bulb up to his mouth and he's heating the glass with a lighter. He glances up when I walk in and then lowers the light bulb.

"Quinton, what the fuck," he says with a surprised laugh. Smoke leaves his lips and enters the air around me and I helplessly feel myself crave it. He gets to his feet and sets the light bulb and lighter down on the table. "Where the hell have you been for the last year or two?"

"Around," I tell him, being purposely vague. That was always the thing with hanging out with people who were high. Nothing mattered. The future. The past. If you wanted to dodge questions, they'd let you, because they were too fixated on getting the next hit. So different from spending time with Nova. Or even Wilson.

He nods, like I've said something that actually means something. "Cool. Cool."

"I heard you were in Vegas," Marcus says as he winds around me and plops down into the sofa, reaching for the light bulb.

"Who'd you hear that from?"

He shrugs as he collects the lighter. "I heard my mom talking. I guess she heard it from your dad or something."

My dad's been talking to people about me? That pisses me off a little.

I go over and sit on the couch beside Dan, knowing I'm probably about to ruin the last few months of getting clean, and desperately searching for the will to get up and walk the hell out of here. "Yeah, I was there for a few months," I say, blinking as Marcus blows some smoke out.

"I heard that city was pretty crazy." Dan is fixed on tracing the cracks in the leather with his finger, spun out of his mind I'm sure.

"Yeah, it was pretty fucking crazy, I guess," I tell him vaguely as I watch Marcus take another hit, my mouth starting to salivate for a taste myself. But there's also conflict within me. I want it, but I don't want it. Do. Don't. What do I do? *Why am I here?*

Marcus must notice me staring, because he holds up the light bulb and says, "You want a hit?"

Four words. One question. But my answer is going to be huge. Life-changing. God dammit. Why did I come here? I don't even want to be here at the moment. Yet now that I am, it feels nearly impossible to walk away.

What the hell is wrong with me?

I'm about to nod. I'm not even going to lie. I have every intention of taking that fucking light bulb out of his hand, putting it up to my mouth, and messing up everything for myself. But then the damn phone rings inside my pocket. Over and over again. I hit silence without checking who it is and then reach over to take the light bulb from Marcus. But then the stupid phone rings again.

"Dude, someone wants to get ahold of you bad," Dan remarks as he starts drumming his fingers on his knee.

I take the light bulb from Marcus, set it on my lap, then reach for my phone. I'm pissed off and totally ready to give whoever it is a mouthful. But then a text message flashes across the screen.

Nova: I know I'm probably bugging the crap out of you right now, but I really, really need to talk, so if you can call me, please do. And sorry for bothering u.

"Jesus fucking Christ," I mutter because the moment I see her name on the screen, I know I have to get up and walk out. I can't be here. If not for myself or anyone else, for her. Nova. The girl who brought me back the first time, despite how hard it was on her own life. The girl I look forward to talking to every day. Jesus, she's become more important to me than drugs. More important than maybe anything else.

Marcus looks confused, but I get up, terrified by my thoughts. "I have to go," I say, and then I hand him back the light bulb, despite how much I don't want to.

Marcus's brows furrow as he takes the light bulb from me. "You sure?"

I nod, putting my phone into my pocket. "Yeah, I have to call someone."

He gives me a baffled look, which is completely understandable—walking away is hard. Everyone in this world knows that and yet here I am doing it, even though it's almost physically painful to leave.

He gets to his feet, sticking his hand into his pocket as he walks around the coffee table. "I'll walk you out."

I can't believe I'm doing this. I'm baffled. Stunned. Shocked beyond reason, as my feet guide me toward the door, away from the need, the craving, the want, all because Nova texted me and reminded me that unlike the first time I did drugs, I'd be messing something of a life up this time by making the choice.

When we get to the front door, Marcus finally takes his hand out of his pocket and I notice he's got a plastic bag in it. "So here's the down low. Since you were such a good friend of mine before you took off, I'm going to give you a freebie." He sticks his hand toward me. "I don't usually do that for clients, but I'm gonna for you because I know once you get a taste, you're gonna be back." He grins like he's got everything all figured out.

I stare down at the bag filled with tiny white crystals. "I don't…" *Give it back to him.*

"You don't what?" His forehead creases. "Shit. Did I read you wrong?" His fingers close around the bag with panic in his eyes. "I heard you were into this shit, but I guess I heard wrong."

I shake my head. "No, I was…am…it's just…" I don't even know what I'm saying, so instead I stick out my hand, my fingers trembling, and I wonder if he notices or if he's too high.

He drops the bag into my hand. "It's the best in town," he says, like it matters. It doesn't. Not to most crackheads, anyway. "And it can be an early Christmas present." He says it like he's doing me a favor giving it to me. But he's not. I know it. He knows it. Because we both know that if I do the line, I'll more than likely be back for more.

"Thanks," I mumble, putting it into my pocket and then

reaching for the doorknob, both relieved that I have it and at the same time angry with myself. "I'll catch you later."

"Definitely." He backs away toward the hallway. "In fact, I'm betting you're going to be back really soon for more."

I force a smile and then open the door and step out of the house. The cold air hits my lungs like bricks and my legs feel like lead as I trudge down the stairs and head for my house a few blocks down. I feel like I'm dragging weights behind me and the bag of crystal in my pocket starts to take over my thoughts. Finally I take the phone out of my damn pocket and dial Nova's phone number, just so I can stop thinking about what I almost did. What I still may do.

"Hey," she answers after two rings, and it's clear she's been waiting for my call, which makes me feel bad, especially because of what I was just doing.

"Hey," I reply, rounding the corner. "What's up? Your text message sounded sort of panicky."

"Yeah, sorry about that," she says with a sigh. "I'm just having a rough day and needed to talk so I don't have to think."

Sometimes she sounds so much like me it freaks me out. Although my reasons are different, we still both like to avoid thinking sometimes.

"Why was your day rough?" I shove my hand into my coat pocket and grab my cigarettes, hoping a little nicotine will calm me the fuck down and maybe give me the strength to throw away the crystal in my pocket.

"I don't know..." She wavers. "A lot of things, but one is that Lea wants me to cheat on my band."

"Cheat on your band?" I take a cigarette out of the pack and put it between my lips. "How exactly does that work?"

She sighs. "By playing for her band, which is going to upset my band members."

I cup my hand around the end of my cigarette and flick the lighter. "So why didn't you just tell her no?" I blow out smoke as I take the lit cigarette out of my mouth.

"Because I owe her," she explains to me. "For being there for me."

"Oh, I get it." I head up the sidewalk toward my house; the porch light's on because it's nearly sunset. "So why don't you just explain that to your band? Maybe they'll understand."

"Because it'd be weird," she says. "One of them is really serious and then the singer...well, he used to date Lea and any sort of mention of her makes things awkward." She blows out a deafening breath as I enter my house. "But anyway, can we talk about something else?"

I glance around at my empty house, pulling a face at the boxes. In most houses there's probably Christmas presents and I get packing boxes, reminding me that I'm going to have to make a huge decision soon. "Yeah, like what?" I trot up the stairs, slipping off my coat.

"I don't know." She hesitates. "Actually, I do have something to tell you, but I'm not sure how you're going to take it."

I kick my bedroom door open with my foot and toss my

coat onto my bed. "Should I be worried?" I stuff my hand into the pocket of my jeans, take out the bag, and stare at it with a familiar needy burn inside my chest. *What do I do with this? Throw it away? Keep it? Devour it?*

"Well, I'd say no," she says as I clasp my hand around the bag, my palms coated with sweat. "But I might be wrong."

"Okay, well, tell me. I think I can handle it." Such a lie, especially since I have a bag of crystal in my hand, waiting to soothe me if I need it. But I don't want to need it. I just want to be free, yet I can't let it go.

"I have some of your sketches," she blurts out.

"What? How?" My hand tightens around the bag as I try to focus on Nova and not it.

"Because when I went back to look for you after you'd disappeared in Vegas... I picked some up off of your bedroom floor."

"Why would you do that?" I wonder, not upset, but a little puzzled.

"Because I was worried they'd be lost if I didn't," she explains. "And I know they're important to you."

I sink down on my bed, staring at the empty spot on the wall where the photo I took down used to be. "What were they of?"

"Um... you... me..." She catches her breath. "Lexi."

Elongated silence follows. I'm not sure how to react to hearing her say Lexi's name. It feels warped and wrong, but at the same time I can't get mad at her. In fact, the idea of yelling at her is impossible.

As I sift through my emotions, trying to figure out what I feel, I distractedly put the bag of meth underneath my mattress beside Nova's unopened letter. "I don't know what to say," I tell her as I get up from the bed. "I mean, I'm sort of glad you have them, because they're my sketches and everything, but still…I drew them when I was high." High on the same thing I just hid under my mattress. Jesus, I just need to find a way to throw it away. I never should have taken it to begin with.

"That's okay. I just wanted you to know that I have them in case you want them back," she says. "I could mail them to you if you want me to."

"No, hold on to them." I grab a pair of pajama bottoms and a T-shirt and head for the shower, needing to get space from the crystal. Plus, the walk home was freezing and I need to thaw out, wash the crappy day off me.

"Are you sure?"

"Yeah, I'm sure." I push open the bathroom door and shut it behind me, releasing a breath of relief at the distance. I didn't even realize what it was doing to my body and mind just having it on me. So heavy and weighted. Such a burden.

I turn on the faucet water, letting it warm up, then unbutton my pants. I decide to get rid of the crystal when I get out of the shower. Then I won't choose the empty path.

"What's that noise?" Nova asks.

"I turned the shower on," I tell her, even though I don't really want to get off the phone with her. Just talking to her…

well, I've calmed down a lot. "I was outside working and I'm frozen to the bone and filthy."

"Oh." She pauses, then asks, "Are you going to talk to me while you take a shower?"

I'm unzipping my pants but pause, trying to decipher if there's a hidden meaning to her words. If she's just asking a simple question or trying to be dirty with me. She never usually is, so I don't have a clue how to read her. "Do you want me to keep talking to you?"

She wavers with uncertainty. "Well, I don't want to stop talking to you, so..."

I still can't read her at all. "But the phone will get wet."

"Put it on speakerphone and set it close to the shower," she suggests, and I can detect the slightest bit of nervousness in her voice, which makes me wonder what she's thinking. "And turn the volume all the way up."

"But won't it be weird?"

"Why would it be weird?"

"Because I'd be...taking a shower while we were talking."

"Yeah, so?" The nervousness in her voice is more attractive to me than it should be.

I'm definitely starting to get the impression that she's not just being naïve about the situation. That she knows exactly what she's doing and is enjoying herself. I hesitate. I know I'm being a fucking pussy about it, which is weird because I've slept with a lot of women over the last couple of years. But I barely knew any of them and there was no emotional connection.

Plus, I was always either drunk or high. Being sober is different because I *can* feel. Everything. And the whole point to having sex, at least in the past, was to numb myself. Plus, I just brought drugs home with me, which makes me feel like a dick because she doesn't know that.

"But I can let you go if you want me to," she says, almost saddened.

It's her sadness that makes me say what I say next. "No, it's fine…we can keep talking." I start to get undressed. "Tell me more about your band," I say, hoping to sidetrack myself from how unsteady I feel at the moment, wobbling on the tightrope, about to fall.

"There's not much to tell, really," she replies. "It's just three guys and myself hanging out in a garage most of the time."

"It sounds like I should be jealous." I shuck off my shirt while holding the phone, which is difficult, but I manage to get it done.

"Of the band? Nah, they're harmless. Besides, I think they think of me as one of the guys."

"I doubt that." I set the phone down on the countertop beside the shower, then turn up the volume.

"If you say so," she says with uncertainty. "But anyway. There is something pretty cool happening."

"And what's that?" I raise my voice as I pull the shower curtain back.

"We got our very first gig," she tells me as I step into the shower. Her voice fades a little but I can still hear her, even

212

when I step under the stream of water. "And I'm not talking about playing at some club because it's open band night. I'm talking about opening for another band because we were chosen to. How cool is that?" She sounds so happy.

I smile as I let the water run over my body. "Pretty fucking cool." I rub the water away from my eyes. "Who's the band?"

"Peaceful Injustice."

"Never heard of them."

"Yeah, they're not that well known, but I love them. In fact, I have a huge band crush on them."

I reach for the soap, her comment deflating my mood. "Sounds like I should be worried."

"Nah. I promise you have nothing to worry about." Silence takes over the line, but I can hear her softly breathing when I strain my ears and listen. "What are you doing right now?"

I pause, so many dirty responses racing through my mind I can't even think straight. "Taking a shower."

"Yeah, I know, but..." She trails off, breathing profusely. "But what exactly are you doing at this very moment?" She sounds really fascinated, which makes me wonder what she's thinking.

I think about telling her that I'm touching myself and thinking about her. Starting something up because it's been a while since I've gotten any. God, just thinking about it turns me on, but at the same time, do I want to go there yet? "I'm not sure..."

"You're not sure what you're doing?" She sounds lost.

After some more internal conflict, I decide to just spit out what's floating around in my head. "Nova, I'm picking up this vibe from you and I'm not sure but…it sounds like…" I swipe my hand across my face, wiping the water away. "It sounds like you're trying to have phone sex." And just like that I've changed everything and I have no idea how it even happened. One minute I'm freaking out, and the next I'm calmed down and all I can think about is her.

She doesn't respond right away and I worry I've read her wrong.

"Jesus, I didn't mean that," I say, feeling like a moron. "Please, just forget about it. Please."

"I don't want to forget about it." Her voice is uneven. Scared. Nervous. All of her insecurities are coming through. "I just don't know what to say…I'm not an expert at this."

"At phone sex?" There's a hint of amusement in my voice that accidentally slips out.

"Hey, don't laugh at me." She tries to sound offended, but I can tell she's on the verge of laughing. "I'm in no way an expert at this…any of this, actually. The last time I came close to even doing anything with a guy was…well, with you, at the lake."

She's being so honest it shocks me. But what really shocks me is that she hasn't been with anyone else since then, which would also mean she's still a virgin. That no guy has touched her the way I did since we made out in the lake. It makes me feel twistedly happy, but at the same time sad, because that isn't the best memory in the world. For her or for me.

"I'm not sure what to say," I tell her as I rinse my face off in the water.

"Do you think I'm a freak?" she asks. "Because I haven't done anything."

"Not at all. I don't even think I could ever think of you as a freak, no matter how goofy you got."

"Then what do you think of me?" The nervousness in her voice reemerges and I think it's a signal that she wants to head down that road, which makes me both wary and eager. Makes me want to hang up, but at the same time push the conversation further. This is Nova. If there's anyone in the world I'd want to be doing stuff with sober, it's her. Yeah, I probably don't deserve her, but I want her. So fucking badly.

I shut my eyes and picture the many things she could be doing right now. "You want to know what I think of you?"

"Yes, please."

I take a deep breath. "That you're the most amazing person that I've ever met." My voice cracks and I cough to cover it up. "That you're nice, caring, way too perfect to be with me." I put my hands up on the wall and lower my head, letting the water run over my body. "That you're sexy as hell, from your freckles to your long legs... I can still remember how fucking amazing it was to have those legs wrapped around me."

"Yeah?" she asks, and I can tell she likes what I'm saying, so I keep going, despite how unfamiliar it is.

"Absolutely," I assure her, with a hint of nervousness in my voice. "Even though I haven't really touched you in a year—not

215

the way that I want to, anyway—I can still remember how perfect it felt to run my hands all over your body…kiss you…" I shut my eyes tightly as my heart pounds deafeningly inside my chest. "Slip my fingers inside you." I grip the tile wall for support, because it feels like I'm falling into a unknown place, one where I've never been, but one I want to keep falling into despite where I might end up.

"Would you do it to me if you were here?" she asks timidly. "Touch me like that, I mean."

"Yes," I say in a low, husky tone that surprises me. "God, I would do more than that if you were here."

"Oh yeah? Like what?" Her voice is a little off pitch, but in the most adorable way ever.

Jesus, she's killing me. "Like kiss you while…I slip inside of you," I say, and she starts to breathe heavily. I want to keep going, but at the same time, there's a voice in the back of my head telling me it's wrong. Not like this. Not over the phone. Not when I just hid a bag of crystal underneath my mattress.

Right and wrong. Which one is right? Which one is wrong? How much do I care for her? A lot. More than a lot. I care for her so much that I want everything to be perfect when we finally do get together, so even though I've got the hugest hard-on, I force myself to step away and wait for the perfect moment to continue this.

"Nova, I…I think we should slow things down a little." I'm one step away from touching myself and it's almost physically impossible to pull my hand away, but I still manage to.

"Oh, okay." Her voice falters and I feel like the biggest ass that's ever existed.

I push back from the wall and turn the shower off, gradually turning the knob so that for a brief moment I get sprayed by icy-cold water to help cool me off and settle me down. "Hey, I'm getting out and I wanted to talk to you about something." I pull the shower curtain back and step out, reaching for a towel. "Something pretty important."

"Sure. What's up?" She's working hard to hide her disappointment, which makes it harder to dry off and start getting dressed.

"It's actually about something I did," I say, tugging a T-shirt over my head. "But give me a second because I want to tell you when I'm in my room." As I slip into my jeans, I think about which thing I'm going to tell her. That I managed to take one photo of Lexi down or about what I have underneath my mattress. If I can confess that to her, I know I'll be able to get rid of it. I just have to decide if I want to.

I go into my room, barefoot, my hair damp, and shut the door behind me. I turn and look at the spot on the wall where the photo of Lexi was, so lonely, surrounded by sketches and photos. Then I look down at my unmade bed, deciding. Which path do I want to go down here?

"I took down something from my wall today." I sink down onto my bed and lower my head, pressing my fingertips to the bridge of my nose as I squeeze my eyes shut. "A picture of Lexi." It's excruciating to say it, blinding pain within my skull and heart, but at the same time I feel lighter.

"Oh my God, Quinton," she says with empathy in her voice. "Are you okay? Jesus, if I would have known I wouldn't have…" She trails off, feeling guilty.

"It's okay, Nova. I'm okay." I look back up and skim the four walls of my bedroom. "I've still got a ways to go, too… there are still a lot of photos and pictures up."

"But that's a step in the right direction and each time it'll get easier. I promise."

"I hope so," I tell her, then slide to the floor and kneel down at the side of my bed. "I have to tell you something else, but it's not good—it's bad." Before I can chicken out, I hurry and sputter, "Someone gave me a bag of meth today and I have it underneath my mattress." As soon as I say it, I wonder why the hell I thought this was a good idea, throwing this on her. I need to stop relying on her so much—need to stand on my own two feet.

I'm about to hang up, because really it's the only choice, but then she says, "Did you do any of it?"

"No." My voice shakes as I grip the side of the mattress and battle to breathe evenly.

"Do you want to?" she asks calmly.

"Yes." My voice is full of desperation.

"Are you… are you going to?" There's a hint of worry in her tone.

"I'm not sure," I admit. "I want to, but I also want to throw it away."

"Then throw it away," she says, as if it's the easiest thing in the world to do.

"I don't think I can." My hands quiver just at the thought of it and I rest my forehead on the mattress, still on my knees "It feels fucking impossible."

"Yes, you can." She sounds so certain and I have no idea how she's doing it—managing to sound so calm when I know she can't be. "Just take it and dump it down the toilet. You can do this. I know you can."

"You have too much faith in me," I say, slipping my fingers between the bed and the mattress, fighting the urge to hang up on her and turn to what's only inches away from my fingertips.

"No, I have the right amount," she replies. "Now let me know when you have it and you're headed to the bathroom. And don't hang up on me." It's like she can read my mind.

I sit there forever, going back and forth with what I want and need to do. At one point I grab the bag of crystal and put it back. Then pull it out again and open it, staring at the white crystals so close I can almost taste them. But I can also hear Nova breathing on the other end. Soft and full of concern. Acting calm, when I'm sure she's freaking out. I want to throw them away just for her, but I have to wonder if it's possible to care for someone so much that I'd give this up. Do I care for her that much?

After a lot of deliberating, I come to one simple answer.

Yes. I care about her that much.

I get to my feet and make my way to the bathroom, not speaking. Then I lift up the toilet seat and, shutting my eyes, I tip the bag over, pour the contents into the water, and flush them down.

"Did you do it?" Nova asks at the sound of the flushing.

I press my lips together, resting back against the bathroom wall, realizing how sweaty I am and how much I'm gasping for air. "I did."

"See, I knew you could do it," she says with relief in her voice. "I knew you'd do the right thing."

The right thing? Is that what I just did? Sometimes it feels like it is, but there are other times when it feels like what I'm doing is so wrong and disrespectful to Lexi. But through the right and wrong, there's always one thing that gives me hope and that's Nova. She's what keeps me going.

Chapter Ten

December 23, day fifty-five in the real world

Nova

Quinton freaked me out yesterday, but I think I did well hiding it and calming him down. At least I hope so. But part of me can't help but wonder if he'll end up doing drugs again. I can't stop obsessing over it and all I want to do is go to Seattle and see him—make sure everything is going okay.

On top of everything else, Tristan's freaking me out, too. He keeps giving me these come-hither looks from across the room, and while I was taking a shower this afternoon, he walked into the bathroom to brush his teeth. This is not good at all. I can see it leading to a very bad place where everything is going to crumble. I need to find a way to talk about it with him, tell him how I feel, but I'm worried about how he's going to react.

"Oh, Nova Dova," Lea singsongs as she comes skipping into my room with a grin on her face. "Are you ready to rock and roll?"

She's dressed up in a torn shirt, cutoffs, fishnet tights, and boots. Her hair's been teased and her eyes lined with liquid liner. My outfit's a little mellower: black plaid skirt, a tank top with a vest over it, and minimal eye shadow, but I did stain my lips red.

"As ready as I'll ever be, I guess," I say with zero enthusiasm as I get up from my bed. Not only am I unenthused to play tonight, I'm also not thrilled to be meeting Lea's boyfriend, either. I've been a downer lately and I can tell Lea is picking up on this, although she thinks it has something to do with the band.

She puts her hands on her hips and narrows her eyes at me. "Hey, cheer up. Everything's going to be fine. You're going to rock tonight."

"Rocking is the least of my problems," I tell her, grabbing my leather jacket from my bedpost. "I'm worried the wrong person's going to see me and then I'm going to get kicked out of my band."

"How would anyone see you?" she asks, lowering her hands to her sides. "Aren't Spalding and Jaxon in New York right now?"

"Yeah, but Nikko's not." I put my jacket on and flip my hair out of the collar. "Plus, we have to go pick up my drums from Jaxon's house, which is going to come off a little bit suspicious."

"No it won't," she says, backing toward the doorway of my room and spinning around on her heels. "Just tell them you're bringing your drums home to practice over the week-end. You've done that before."

I follow her into the living room. There's a candle burn-ing, a soothing lavender scent, but it does nothing to settle the restlessness inside me. "Yeah, before the Millersons from the apartment below complained about the noise."

"So what?" she says, leaning over and blowing out the candle. "Jaxon, Spalding, and Nikko don't need to know that."

"We'll see." I button up my coat and head for the front door, ready to get the night over with. It's probably the first time I haven't been excited to play and I'm not sure if it's because I feel like I'm cheating on my band or because my head's in another place. "I just hope this all doesn't blow up in my face."

She picks up the car keys and tosses them to me. "It won't. I promise."

Sighing, I open the front door to head outside. But Tristan walks out of his bedroom and I pause as he picks up his jacket like he's about to go somewhere.

He's dressed in a plaid shirt and nice jeans, and his hair's a little damp like he's just gotten out of the shower. "So what time do you guys go on?" he asks as he walks past the kitchen and heads toward us.

"In a couple of hours." My brows knit as he slides his jacket on. "Are you coming with us?"

"Yeah," Lea answers for him as she slips a pair of finger-less gloves on. "He said he wanted to come and I said he could because I thought we could use a man's help getting the drums out of the garage and into the trunk of your car." She gives me an apologetic look and mouths, *I'm sorry*.

"We're not helpless women," I say, trying to make it sound like I'm joking, but I'm not. I don't like that Tristan's going. Not after what happened in the grocery store yesterday. In fact, I was hoping to get a little space tonight and clear my head. I want to be mad at Lea for asking him to help us, but I can't, because I understand where she's coming from. Lea's a lot like me when it comes to being rude to people and I'm sure the last thing she wanted to do was tell Tristan no when he said he wanted to tag along.

"I know you're not helpless," Tristan says, stopping in front of me as he zips up his jacket. "But I figured I could come watch you rock out for the night instead of hanging out here by myself."

I liked it better when Tristan and Lea didn't like each other. In the beginning Tristan would never have gone any-where Lea was, because they clashed so badly. But now they've warmed up to each other.

"Unless for some reason you don't want me to." There's a challenge in his blue eyes like he's daring me to say it—that I'm afraid of being near him because we almost kissed.

I shake my head, pretending to be indifferent. "No, you can go." I fake a smile, feeling like a jerk because of my feel-ing toward him. Or lack of feeling, anyway. Part of me wishes I could reciprocate but I can't make myself feel that way, especially when my head's stuck on someone else with honey-brown eyes and a sensitive heart, who had me so turned on yesterday when he was in the shower.

Tristan grins at me. "Good, because I really want to see you play."

I keep smiling as I exit the apartment and the two of them follow me. They start chatting about what songs we're going to play and Lea starts listing them. They're all covers, something she told me the other day when I tried to use the excuse that I wouldn't know the songs they were playing, to get out of going. Turns out I knew all of them, so that didn't work.

It's okay, though. Things could be a hell of a lot worse, something I tell myself in order to keep moving as I walk out of the apartment.

It's dark and breezy outside and I immediately wrap my arms around myself, shivering as the breeze hits me. "Jesus, wearing a skirt wasn't a good idea," I remark as I rush for my car.

I feel someone move up to my side, but I don't turn my head because I know it's Tristan as soon as I hear the lighter flick. "I think you look good," he says with a wink.

"Thanks," I say, rubbing my hands up and down my arms. "But I'm not sure it's worth freezing to death."

"I'll keep you warm," he jokes, smoke encircling his face.

I don't know how to respond, so I just offer him a smile and head for the driver's side of my car. After we get inside, Lea in front, thankfully, I back out of the parking spot and head for Jaxon's garage. His parents said they'd be home when I called earlier and told them I needed to pick the drums up, but part of me is hoping that they won't be. But the lights are on inside the house when we pull up and I can't help but sigh, heavyheartedly.

"Don't look so down," Tristan leans forward and says in my ear as Lea gets out of the car. "Everything's going to be fine."

"I hope so," I mutter, reaching for the phone inside my pocket as it starts to ring. I think it's going to be Quinton, wishing me luck or something, but it's my mom.

I answer as Tristan moves the seat forward and gets out of the car. "Hey, can I call you back?" I ask her, preparing to get out. "I'm getting ready to play in about an hour."

"Oh, was that tonight?" She sounds distracted and a little out of it, not like her usual self. "I'm sorry. I'll call you back later."

"What's wrong?" I think I know, though, without hearing the answer.

"It's nothing. I just…call me when you're done."

"Mom, I can't wait now," I say, growing more worried by the second. "Not when you sound like something tragic just happened…does…does it have to do with Delilah?" I hold my breath, remembering when I was twelve and I had to meet her in the waiting room at the hospital right after my dad died.

She was crying when she walked through the door,

frantically looking around like she was expecting my dad to walk out from one of the rooms. Then she spotted me sitting in the chair by myself and she panicked.

"Oh my God." She rushed to me, clutching her purse. "Are you okay?" She threw her arms around me and I can remember thinking how strange that was, since after all she'd just lost her husband.

"I'm fine," I said in an eerily calm voice. "But Mom... Dad's gone."

She only pulled me closer, hugging me so tightly I had to stand up out of the chair. "I know, honey. And I'm so sorry."

I wrapped my arms around her, even more confused over her worry for me. "I'm okay, Mom, but are you?"

That set her off and she started to sob onto my shoulder. I held on to her as she nearly collapsed to the floor, telling myself that I had to be the strong one. And I was, helping out with the funeral arrangements, calling up my grandparents and telling them what had happened. I was always better at that stuff, dealing with other people's issues instead of my own.

"Nova, I'm going to tell you something, and yes, it's about Delilah," my mom says, bringing me back to reality. "But I need to know you're not alone... is Lea around?"

I glance out the window at Lea, who's saying something to Tristan in front of the car as she bounces up and down from the cold. "Yeah."

"Good." She lets out a breath of relief. "Because I need to know that you'll have someone there for you."

"I do." My heart tightens, death in the air. "Delilah's mom found her, didn't she?" I say, gripping the steering wheel, trying not to hyperventilate. "And she's dead."

"She's headed down to Vegas to . . . God, I don't even know how to say this." She pauses, looking for the right words, but what she doesn't get is that they don't exist. I'm familiar with the routine by now and nothing she says is going to change the outcome of the situation. "She's going down to identify a body . . . see if it's Delilah's."

I smash my lips together, feeling the numbness flow through me as I fight to shut myself down. I've been through this before. I know what to do. Just like I know that in a few minutes I'm going to start assessing every single thing I did wrong, like the time I walked away from that apartment and left Delilah there sobbing, strung out, and with an asshole of a boyfriend. God, this never ends. Death. Regret. Remorse. Guilt. It's a stupid cycle and I want it to stop.

"Do they know how she died?" I ask in an uneven voice.

"Well, they don't even know if it's her yet," my mom says, keeping her voice gentle in an attempt to soothe me, but there's an underlying ache to it, one that leads me to believe that she's pretty sure it's Delilah. "Nova, are you going to be okay? You've got that tone—the one you get before you shut down."

"I'm fine." I sit up and extend my hand for the door handle. "Thanks for letting me know, but I have to go get ready to play tonight."

"Nova, I—"

I hang up on her, not wanting to talk about it anymore. I'm done talking about death. I can't do it anymore. I just can't. Yet it keeps pushing its way into my life. And not just my life. Everyone's, really. It haunts everyone and everything and I wish I had the power to make it go away so that no one would have to feel the ache, the cracking apart, the inability to process it because it doesn't make any goddamned sense.

After taking so many breaths I become light-headed, I put my phone away and get out of the car. Lea immediately gives me a worried look, which makes me wonder what I look like at the moment. But before she can say anything, I head for the front door, calling over my shoulder to Lea and Tristan, "Are you guys coming?"

They quietly follow me, Lea boring a hole in my head, while Tristan seems a little oblivious. But it's not his fault. He doesn't know me like Lea, and I know that as soon as the night's over, she's going to corner me and start yammering questions. I wouldn't even be surprised if my mom calls her and tells her what's up, which makes me want to bail out somehow.

In fact, it's all I can think about as Jaxon's parents let us inside. There's this awkward sort of exchange between Lea and Jaxon's mom as she walks us to the garage, and Lea ends up talking to her while Tristan and I load up the trunk of the car and the backseat with my drums, my thoughts refusing to be quiet. I keep picturing scenarios of what happened and they mix with all the good memories I had of Delilah. Like

229

the first time we actually hung out. I was sad and she made me laugh by making a joke about our English teacher having a mustache. It was the first time I'd laughed since Landon died. Then we went to college together, and while we weren't always on the same page, things were still good. She still made me laugh. Forced me to go out into civilization once in a while. Forced me to try to live when all I wanted to do was let myself die inside.

"You're awfully quiet," Tristan comments as he puts my drumsticks into the backseat.

"I'm fine." I shut the trunk and climb into the car as Lea walks out the front door, carrying a plate of cookies.

Tristan gets into the backseat and buckles his seat belt, watching me in the rearview mirror. "Are you sure? You look like you're going to be sick."

"I'm fine," I repeat, and then remain silent as Lea gets into the car. I should probably tell him about Delilah, but I can't bring myself to talk about it at the moment. I also worry about how he's going to react when I do. I'm not sure how close they were, but they did live together and that has to mean he cared about her in one way or another.

"What's with the cookies?" I ask as Lea balances the plate on her lap.

"Jaxon's mom gave them to me...she also said how much her family misses me." She sighs and then starts rambling about how uncomfortable that was as I drive to Red & Black Ink. I'm relieved by the distraction of her chatting, nodding and agreeing in all the right places. But as soon as we pull up to the back parking lot, I feel nauseous. Why didn't I do something to help Delilah? Why is death always happening? Why? Why? Why?

I need to calm down somehow, because I don't even know if the body is Delilah's yet. But I can't and things only get worse the longer the night goes on. *I'm stronger than this. Tough. I've been through this before.* Nothing works. Breathing. Counting. God, I'm counting everything, my mind racing a million miles a minute. But I can still feel myself about ready to fall apart the moment we step into the club and the madness surrounds me. My mind seeks structure but there's nothing around me and I can feel myself falling.

"Nova, get your head in the game," Lea shouts over the chatter of voices around us. We're seated in a booth, waiting to go on. The whole place is decorated with red Christmas lights and the cheeriness of them clashes with the black walls and makes the place seem eerie. Tristan wandered off to the bathroom, but he's been gone for over ten minutes and I'm wondering if he took a detour. I hope it's to find a girl and not get a drink or something even worse. This place is making me uneasy because it's crawling with temptation. I know because I've seen a few drug exchanges happen. Jesus, why did I let him come? Especially with all the sketchiness with that Jazz guy. I was so distracted by his overly friendly attitude that I forgot how this place was.

Lea waves her hand in front of my face and I flinch. "Earth to Nova."

"Sorry." I blink my attention from my glass of water and look at her. "I'm dazing pretty badly, aren't I?"

"Yeah." As soon as she says it, I glance at the crowd again, thinking I see Tristan, but it's just another blond-haired, boy-band-member-looking guy.

Lea crosses her arms and assesses me from across the table. "Okay, what the hell is your problem?"

"Nothing," I say, not ready to talk about it—say it aloud—deal with it. I wonder if Delilah's mom will find out exactly how she passed away. I wonder if it matters, because in the end it doesn't change anything. She'll still be gone.

"I know when you're lying," Lea says sternly, and then she puts her hand on the table. "So just fess up."

"It's nothing," I tell her, slumping back in the booth. "My mom and I just had a fight. That's all."

"Over what?"

"Over me coming home for Christmas."

She takes a drink of her water. "I thought she was okay with you staying here for the holidays just as long as she gets to see you for a few days around New Year's?"

I scratch my tattoo, hating that I'm lying, but talking about Delilah isn't an option yet. "Yeah, I thought so, too, but she changed her mind."

She gives me a sympathetic look. "You could always go home."

I shake my head. "No, I have too much to do with work and stuff."

"Well, then cheer up, missy." Lea points a finger at me. "Your mom will get over it, just like she does with everything you do. Besides, tonight's going to be so awesome, you won't even have time to think about being bummed out."

"I'm sorry. I'll try not to be a complete downer tonight."

"Good." She smiles and then turns in the booth to look at the dance floor. "I wonder where Brody and Braxton are?"

"Maybe they got cold feet," I say. "And it'll just be you and me."

She turns around and scowls at me. "Stella would never allow that. You know she hates when people try to do solo acts."

"It wouldn't be a solo act." I stir my ice with my straw. "But I'm sure everything is going to be okay . . . I'm sure they'll show up."

She considers what I said and then takes her phone from her jacket pocket. "I'm going to call them and see what's up."

I zone out as she yammers on the phone with Brody. I can tell by the way she keeps laughing and twirling her hair that she's really happy right now. I need to make myself cheer up and be a better friend, like I wasn't with Delilah. So I sit up straighter and put on my best happy face as she hangs up the phone.

"They're running late," she announces as she picks up a few fries from a basket between us. "But they'll be here in just a few minutes."

I grab a handful of fries. "You seem happy, when you're talking to Brody, I mean."

233

She pops some fries in her mouth. "I am." She grins from ear to ear. "He makes me really happy, Nova."

"How long have you been seeing him?"

"It's about damn time you asked," she says, wiping her fingers on a napkin.

"Hey." I frown. "You're the one who kept the secret from me. How was I supposed to ask questions about him when I didn't even know about him?"

"Yeah, you're right... still, you barely seemed interested in him, even after I told you." She scoops up another fry and dips it in the cup of ranch. "But that's okay. You've been sad lately." She pauses, the fry in her hand, dripping ranch on the table as she waits for me to say something, probably for me to give an explanation as to why I've been so sad.

"I've just been bummed out over silly things," I lie, afraid that if I start talking about everything, I won't be able to stop. The floodgates will open and I'll lose it, right here in the bar. "Work and school stuff." I sit up straighter in the booth. "But I'll try to cheer up, and I want to hear about Brody."

She seems unconvinced, but says, "Well, I've been seeing him since the middle of September."

"That long?" I ask, and she nods. "Jesus, how did I not know this?"

She rotates in her seat and points at Tristan, who's standing at the bar chatting with the bartender. "Because that one's had you distracted, along with the sad, brown-eyed one you spend all your time on the phone with."

"Dammit," I curse, getting out of the booth and shoving through the crowd toward Tristan. Why does he have to choose to drink tonight of all nights, when I'm already cracking apart?

When I arrive at the bar, Tristan's laughing at something the bartender is saying.

"Hey, I was just talking about you," he says, smiling at me.

I smell the Jack Daniel's on his breath as soon as he speaks, and then notice the glass on the counter. "You drank." I sound horrified.

He rolls his eyes, like it's the most absurd thing he's ever heard. "I had one drink." He holds up his finger. "And I'm a recovering drug addict. Not an alcoholic."

Jesus, can this night get any worse? "Yeah, but you told me once that one can easily lead to the other. Remember?"

"I say shit all the time." He dismisses my worry, turning to face me. Then he leans against the bar and puts his elbow on it, all casual and relaxed, but definitely not sober. "Besides, I only did it because of you."

"Because of me?" I ask, confused. "Why? What did I do?"

"It's not what you did," he says, his gaze flicking to my lips. "But what you didn't do."

God, please don't let this conversation go where I think it's going. "I'm sorry if I forgot to do something," I say, noting that he's sort of acting like an ass, which is his telltale sign that he's been doing drugs.

He lets out a soft laugh, his forehead furrowing. "You're so naïve sometimes."

"Hey, I am not," I say, turning my back on him, offended because I'm not naïve. I know exactly what he's talking about. I just don't want to deal with it tonight.

He catches my arm and stops me from leaving. "Nova, I'm sorry. I didn't mean it like that." He draws me back to him and just like that my crappy night gets even worse. Because without warning, he kisses me, tasting like Jack Daniel's and vulnerability and reminding me of our first kiss, only I was trashed then and there was a lot more tongue involved. This time it's just on the lips, no tongue, thankfully.

When he pulls away, he mutters something that sounds an awful lot like "Wow." Then he lets go of my arm and slants back to look me in the eyes. "I've been wanting to do that for a few months now."

"I..." I open my mouth to say something—anything—to salvage this situation, but I just struggle to find my voice.

As it starts to click that I'm not on the same page as him, his expression sinks. But before he can say anything, Lea shows up and interrupts us. "We're on in like twenty, so we need to get your drums out of the car and into the back area." She's bouncy and buzzing with adrenaline and excitement.

"Okay." I glance at Tristan. "Can we talk about this later?"

He shrugs, his expression cold. "Is there anything to talk about?"

"Maybe." I scratch my tattoo, wishing there were an answer there in the words, a solution that would fix this. "Just please don't go anywhere."

He doesn't answer and I end up walking away, feeling guiltier than I already did tonight. I worry about what he's going to do, especially if he finds out about Delilah, and I'm going to have to tell him eventually.

Lea grabs my arm and guides me toward the back door, hissing under her breath, "What the hell was that about?" She pushes the door open and we step out into the cold, where she lets go of me. "The tension was so thick, I could seriously cut it with a knife."

"I'll tell you after we play," I mutter as I hurry across the icy parking lot toward my car.

She shuffles after me, her heels clicking against the ice. "Why can't you just tell me now?"

"Because you're going to freak out," I say, sticking my hand into my pocket to get my car keys out. "And your head needs to be in the game right now."

After that, Lea and I start unloading the drums from my car. It's late, the stars are shining, and I can't help but think of the many times I spent staring up at the stars with my dad, Landon, and Quinton. At some point, I've lost them all. Quinton did come back, though, but at the same time he's still distant. And now there's another person gone and I swear my heart can't take it anymore.

Knock it off, Nova. You don't even know if she's gone yet.

As we carry the last of the drums inside, Lea lets the door shut and then smiles at something over my shoulder. She raises her arm and waves at someone behind me. "Hey, we're over here." Then she whispers to me, "Nova, smile. You look like your dog just died."

I prepare myself the best I can, trying to get my head into the game, and fake a smile as two guys walk up to us. One of them is taller, with spiky blond hair and colorful tattoos covering both his arms. The other guy is a little bit on the short side, but good-looking, with brown hair that hangs over his ears and forehead and these really blue eyes that match his shirt. He's really stocky, too, and I'm guessing he's Brody, the football player/guitarist.

Lea introduces us and I find out that I was right. Brody is the stockier one and seems nice enough, at least I'm guessing he is. I barely get two words out before Lea and he start making out behind the stage.

Braxton, the taller one and the bassist, seems a little uncomfortable, with his hands stuffed in his pockets as he glances around the bar, trying to avoid looking at the heavy amount of PDA going on beside us.

"Hey," he finally says, looking at me. His eyes scroll up and down my body and he seems a little confused. "So you're the drummer Lea's been talking about?"

I smile, despite the massive amount of surprise in his tone. "Yep, that would be me."

He gives me a look of annoyance mixed with disbelief. "Yeah, I think I'll have to see it for myself because I'm not buying it, especially since you're in a band with that Jaxon dude, who sucks."

I glance over at Lea, who's still in a lip lock, pressed up against the wall, then give a haughty look to Braxton. "Yeah, you will see. Trust me." I'm not normally a mean person, but he's being an ass and tonight I'm about to lose it. I can feel it.

"A little cocky, aren't we?" he asks in a snide tone as he arches a brow at me.

"Only because you're being a douche bag." I feel like a terrible person as soon as I say it. "I'm sorry."

"Braxton, knock it off," Brody interrupts, still holding on to Lea. There's lipstick all over his mouth and jaw and Lea's is smeared. "Nova's helping us out here and you don't need to be an asshole."

"Sorry," Braxton mutters, and then Lea and Brody go back to making out. Braxton scratches at the back of his neck, looking over at the bar. "So do you want a drink? I could go get us a couple of shots and maybe we could try to chill out." He sounds doubtful.

"No thanks. I'm not a big drinker and I don't do shots at all."

"Okay, I guess that's cool." He pauses and I can tell he's struggling for something else to say. He stuffs his hands into his pockets and rocks back on his heels. "So how long have you been playing the drums?"

"A few years," I say, and he nods with vague interest, staring over at the tables, where a waitress is bent over, her dress so short she's flashing the entire room.

Things get quiet after that. I think about leaving, but I'm

239

worried that the moment I step away, we'll be called to go on. Finally, after a very painful twenty minutes, Stella comes back and tells us to "Get your asses up there."

"Wait, we need to decide what song we're going to open up with," Lea says as Brody picks his guitar up off the floor and starts heading for the stage area.

"You guys haven't picked out your lineup?" I ask, ready to get this show on the road, ready for a break that only my drums can give me. I just need to clear my head for a moment. Think about music. Forget about all the crap that just hit the fan. Braxton shakes his head and then the three of them start arguing about what cover would be the best one to start with. I try to stay calm as I lean back against the wall and watch Stella get impatient with their lack of organization. I know she might very likely kick them out of the lineup and so I finally step forward and offer what I think would be a good song to start out with.

"How about 'Tears Don't Fall,' by Bullet for My Valentine?" I suggest, because I want to really beat my drums up at the moment.

"That's a dude's song and Lea's a girl." Braxton gives me the hardest look I've ever seen.

"I'm sure she can handle it." I look to Lea for help. "Can't you?"

She gives me a smile. "I think that's the perfect song. Great choice, Nova."

Braxton utters something under his breath that sounds an

awful lot like "Stupid bitch." I take a deep breath and brush it off because it doesn't really matter. Not when so much other stuff is going down. Then Lea and I go up onto the stage and set the pieces of the drums down at the back, so they're organized perfectly just behind the microphone, while Braxton and Brody plug their guitars into the amp.

The lights shine down on us and the people sitting at the tables below, and over at the bar, are barely paying attention to us, but there are still enough people that it gives me butterflies. But I like the feeling. In fact, I welcome it. That's what drums are to me. A distraction. From everything going on around me. All my problems. The aching inside. The confusion. My thoughts.

"Braxton hates me," I say to Lea, setting the last piece of my kit down on the floor.

She shakes her head, tucking strands of hair behind her ear. "He's just upset because Spike isn't here to play with us."

"Spike?" I ask, rearranging the drum pieces to get them exactly where I want them.

"Yeah, our old drummer." She adjusts the height of the microphone stand.

"Your old drummer was named after a character from *Buffy the Vampire Slayer*?"

She snorts a laugh. "Well, it wasn't his real name. Just a nickname he gave himself because he hated his real name."

"What was his real name?" I ask, picking up my drumsticks and twirling them through my fingers.

The corners of her lips tug upward. "Larry."

I stop twirling the drumsticks. "Okay, I get the name change now."

She starts to laugh again, but her laughter quickly turns to nervousness as Stella yells that we're up. Seconds later we're all ready to go, moments away from playing. Lea looks nervous as she stands under the lights, drumming her fingers on the side of her leg, and I feel the same way, but at the same time I crave the different feeling inside me, because it wipes out all the other stuff stirring within me.

"You'll do fine, babe," Brody says to Lea, giving her an encouraging kiss that seems to settle her down.

I think it's then that I realize two things: one, Brody's not so bad, and two, I really, really want to see Quinton. More than I ever have. I want to get lost in him. Hold on to him. Be held by him and just know that he's there. Maybe if he kissed me, it could relax me. Or maybe it's not necessarily him that I crave, so much as the need to just get out of here. Run away. Take a break.

I try to shake the thought out of my head the best I can and focus on playing. As soon as I raise my drumsticks, I sort of zone out as the bright lights wash over me. This is solitude. My peace. Nothing exists here but the music, and part of me wishes I could exist in this moment forever.

Seconds later the guitar and bass start playing, and the first notes of the intro blast through the amps. I get ready, waiting for the right moment to connect, waiting until I get swept away in the music. It gets closer and closer and I bring my sticks over my head. When I slam them down, Lea's voice and the banging of my drums collide and flow out over the room.

I slam my foot against the pedal, pouring my heart and soul out with the rhythm, putting enough energy into it that I can barely breathe. I drown in the music as the sticks and drums collide. Beats. Notes. Vibrations. It overtakes me. Nothing exists in this moment but the music. Not Tristan. Not Delilah. Not even Quinton. This is just about me.

As the song picks up, so does my energy. I'm sweating, panting, fueling the song with every part of me. My foot slams on the pedal, in sync with my hands. Over and over again. The song ends, but another one picks right back up, "I Miss the Misery" by Halestorm. I keep going, draining all my energy, hoping it's enough that when I stop, I'll be too tired to think. Too tired to focus on my problems.

But as soon as we're done playing the last song, a wave filled with all the pain I've ever felt in my entire life rushes over me. The pain grows with every song we play, and after our set is done I can't find Tristan anywhere. I finally take out my phone to call him, telling Lea I'll be right back before walking out the back door to get some quiet.

"Hey," I say after he answers. "Where are you?"

I can hear commotion in the background. "At a party."

"Tristan." Disappointment laces my voice. "Are you serious?"

"Does it sound like I'm serious?" he asks as someone shouts something profane in the background.

"Maybe, but I'm hoping you're not." I turn to the side and plug my finger in my ear as someone walks out the door, talking loudly. "Look, I get that things are a little weird between us, but just come home and I'll try to fix it. You've been doing so well and I'm sure you don't want to ruin that, right?"

"You can't fix everything, Nova." His tone lightens a little. "And besides, this isn't even about you."

I inch toward the side of the building, trying to get farther away from the door because people keep walking out and being noisy. "Then what is it about?"

"Life and how shitty it is and how it just loves dealing me the shitty-ass cards."

"Why is it shitty? Because you're sober?"

"No, it has nothing to do with that or with you," he says, and then he sighs. "Look, I get that you want to help me. I get that I've been doing good. I get that what I'm planning on doing in the next ten minutes is probably going to fuck up my life, but you know what, I don't really have a life anymore. Not a good one, anyway."

"What are you talking about?" I ask, and when he doesn't answer I say, "Tristan, talk to me—" He hangs up on me.

"Shit." I try to dial his number again, but it goes straight to voice mail. I try to text him, but he still hasn't responded by the time I get into the car and am heading home.

"What party do you think he's at?" I ask Lea as we make

the short drive home. She was planning on hanging out with Brody, but she said their plans got canceled. I think she's worried about me, though, and that's why she decided to come home with me.

It's after nine, the sky starry and the moon a crescent in the sky, and I can't help but count the stars repeatedly, every time I have to stop at a red light. "Maybe we can track him down," I say.

Lea seemed mildly upset when I told her what happened on the phone with Tristan, but she's not freaking out as much as I am. "Nova, there's no way you're going to be able to track him down. It's Friday night, for God's sakes."

"Lea, you didn't hear him on the phone," I say, making a right onto the main road, which is glossy with ice so I have to drive slowly. "He's going to do something to ruin his sobriety. I can feel it."

She lets out a slow breath, her head turned toward the window as she watches the Christmas lights strung across the trees to the side of the road. "Nova, we've been through this before. You can't just save everyone, especially when they don't want to be saved." She looks at me with what seems like pity in her eyes, but I don't know why she's feeling that way toward me. "So just let it go. When he comes home you can see where he stands and go from there."

I shake my head, tears about to pour out. "I can't take this anymore."

"What? Tristan? Or are we talking about something else?"

I have to work to keep my eyes open, the tears bubbling their way up as I turn into our apartment complex. "Tristan. Delilah. Quinton. Myself. I'm so sick of just sitting by and watching people fall apart."

She reaches across the seat and gives my arm a gentle squeeze. "Well, you have me."

I know she's right, but at the moment her touch only feels cold. I park the car and we head inside. She follows me, not saying much until we're inside the apartment and I'm heading to my room.

"Nova, please, just stop fighting to save everyone," she says. "You need to learn to just let some things go."

I step into my room, turning to face her as I make to shut the door. "Do you know what happens when you let things go?" I ask, and she just stares at me. "People fall apart and die. And even though it might be a lost cause and you might think I'm crazy, I'm still going to do it, because no one else seems to be." And with that I shut the door.

I think about calling Quinton and talking to him about everything, but I'm tired of talking to him on the phone. I just want to see him—want to hold him and know that through this entire mess at least he's doing okay. I know it's crazy. Selfish. Impulsive. I know that I have work and other things— life—and I can only go for a day. But I need that day more than I need anything at the moment. So before I can chicken out, I quickly start packing my bags, hoping that when I get there, he won't send me away.

Chapter Eleven

December 24, day fifty-six in the real world

Quinton

I wake up in the middle of the night with the strangest feeling. I was dreaming about Nova and seeing her again. How she'd feel...the scent of her...how she'd taste. I flip on the lamp and lie in bed for a while, staring at the ceiling, thinking about how not too long ago I was staring at a different ceiling, one that was cracked and warped, but the one above me now is flawless. All because of Nova. She got me here because she never gave up on me and she talked me out of going back to a life of getting high all the time.

Nova...my thoughts are flooded with her...what she thinks...I'm struggling with my emotions all centered around her...how much I want her. I'm afraid, though. So afraid that I haven't even opened the letter that she wrote me while I was in rehab.

Before I can chicken out, I roll over to my side and reach

247

underneath my mattress and take out the envelope. My fingers are tremulous as I carefully tear it open and pull out the letter inside. Then, taking a preparing breath, I unfold it and start to read.

Dear Quinton,

I'm writing to you mainly because you don't seem to want to talk to me. And I can understand that. You're working on healing right now and probably have to focus on yourself a lot. But we never did really get to say good-bye the last time I saw you and I hate not having the chance to do that. If there's one thing I've learned, it's that saying good-bye is important.

But as I'm writing this letter, I realize that that's not what I want this to be about. I don't want to say good-bye to you yet. Actually, I don't want to say good-bye to you ever. I know that's probably freaking you out right now, but it's the truth. The idea of losing you is too much to handle. I want you in my life always, either as a friend or more. And I know you probably think I'm crazy. That we barely know each other and in a way you're right. We do barely know each other, but at the same time I think we've been through more than the average person, which makes us able to understand each other more than a lot of people could. And I honestly can picture us one day down the road, super old and just hanging out, again as friends or more—your choice.

And if you've learned anything about me over the last year or so, it's that I'm stubborn. When I want something, I sort of latch on to it. In fact, that habit can be a huge issue for me—the inability to let go. But that's the thing. Everyone keeps telling me that I need to work on that and I know I do, but I don't necessarily believe that I need to let go of everything. I can hold on to the things that are important to me. And one of those things is you. So even though you might not want to hear this, I'm not letting you go. I'm always going to be here for you no matter what.

Your friend forever,
Nova (like the car)

I stop reading it. She's right. No matter what happens, I want Nova in my life. I never want to stop talking to her. Listening to her. I want her with me. I just need to make sure I create the sort of life that's worthy of her being a part of. Can I do that for her? Let go and move forward toward a future with her? I glance around the room. Can I let all of this go for her?

Swallowing my nerves, I get up and circle around my room, taking in each sketch and drawing and feeling the powerful memories connected to them. How much time I spent drawing them or the moments captured within the photos. Then there's my mom. I don't want to say good-bye to any of this and maybe I don't have to completely, but I can let go a little.

One step at a time.

Sucking up the full amount of strength I have in me, I start to take the photos and drawings down. One by one, holding them in my hands as if they were the most delicate things in the world. With each one that comes down, I feel different, as if I've stepped into someone else's body, the body of someone I don't know. Someone stronger, new. Reborn.

When I'm finished, I haven't taken all of them down, but enough that they don't overtake my room. There's one photo of my mom in a rocking chair, her belly big because she is pregnant with me, and a photo of Lexi and me sitting on her back porch, posing for the camera. There's also a sketch of her... one I drew a few days before she died. That one I hold on to to remind me of her, because I may be trying to let go, but forgetting her completely isn't right. She deserves to be remembered, never forgotten. Despite the fact that I'm choosing life, I don't have to break my promise to her.

"I'll remember you forever," I whisper to the air, wondering if she can hear me. "No matter what. I promise... but I think I have to let go just a little..."

By the time I'm done saying it, I'm crying. Tears pour down my face as I take in the bareness of my room, the past no longer overtaking my future, just a ghost, distant memories, and it hurts, yet there's this strange freedom in the pain because I'm feeling it, not running away from it.

I'm starting to sob, tears choking me, refusing to stop flowing, when my phone starts ringing. It's five o'clock in the morning and I wonder who the hell would be calling this early.

Quickly pulling myself together, I wipe my tears away, then lean over to pick up my phone and check the glowing screen. When I see Nova's name on it, panic slams against me as I worry that something might be wrong. "Hey, is everything okay?" I ask as I quickly answer it, worried she'll be able to tell I've been crying.

"No." She sounds strange. Not necessarily sad, but like she's repressing something...numbing her emotions. I hate hearing it in her voice and immediately want to fix it, my problems at the moment shrinking inside me.

"What happened?" I ask. God, please don't let anything be wrong.

"A lot of stuff really, but I..." Her voice catches, her emotions on the verge of spilling out. "I have to tell you something and I need you not to get mad at me."

"Okay...what is it?" I ask cautiously. She doesn't say anything right away and I can hear a lot of commotion in the background. "Where are you?"

"At the airport." She sounds guilty. "The Seattle airport."

A bundle of emotions rush through me all at once and I almost hang up on her. Nova's here. In Seattle. This is bad. Really bad. I'm not prepared for this. And I wanted to prepare myself for the first time I saw her again. Wanted to be completely stable instead of sobbing my heart out because I just took a bunch of photos of my old girlfriend down.

"You're here. In Seattle. Seriously?" I can't conceal my shock or the fact that I'm on the edge of crying again, just from reliving the memory of taking down the sketches and photos.

"I know you said you didn't want me to come here," she says, sounding upset. "But some stuff happened and I just...I just needed to get away from it all, so I packed up my bags and headed to the first place I could think of."

"You made the decision to come here tonight?" I ask worriedly, not just because she's sitting in the airport by herself, upset, but because something made her upset enough that she just took off. "Just up and left. Just like that."

"Yeah. I just really needed to get away before my head exploded. And it was either go to you or have a meltdown."

"How did you even get a flight?"

"It was a pain in the ass," she promises me. "I was on a plane for six hours and normally it's like a two-hour flight."

"I bet." I'm not sure what to say to her because I'm still attempting to process that she's here. Only miles away. "Are you just sitting at the airport now?"

"Yeah...I'm trying to figure out what to do next," she says miserably. "I know what I want to do and that's flag a taxi down and come see you, but I totally get it if you don't want me to do that."

I wonder what she'd do if I said I couldn't see her. Would she just hang around in the city or get on a plane and fly back home? That's probably the best option, since I'm still not as stable as I wanted to be when I saw her again.

But the idea of her being so near and my not seeing her makes my heart throb. "Don't take a taxi," I say, getting to my feet. "I'll come get you."

"Are you sure?" she asks. "Because I don't want to force you to do anything you don't want to do."

God, she's killing me. Too nice for her own good.

"Yeah, of course I'm sure." But I'm not. At all. Then again, I'm not sure I'll ever be, but I guess I'm going to have to rip off the Band-Aid.

"Thanks," she says, getting choked up. "And Quinton, I'm really, really sorry for springing myself on you like this."

"You don't need to be sorry," I say, opening my dresser drawer and grabbing a shirt. "Now stay put. I'll be there in about twenty to thirty minutes." I hang up, get dressed, then go into my father's room to ask him if I can borrow the car. He's hesitant at first, until I tell him why. He reluctantly gives me the keys and tells me he'll take the bus to work. As small as the gesture is, it means a lot to me, and I wholeheartedly thank him.

I have to let the car thaw out for about five minutes and let the frost melt away from the windshield, so I climb in and dial Wilson's number, cranking up the heat. After about four rings, he picks up, sounding extremely exhausted.

"This better be really important," he says, and then he yawns. "Because I am not a morning person."

"Nova's here," is all I say, staring up at the gray sky as the sun begins to rise and kiss it with a hint of orange.

It takes him a moment to say anything. "Right now. In Seattle. At your house."

"She's at the airport." I flip on the wipers and watch as they scrape off the rest of the frost. "I'm headed to pick her up right now."

"Why didn't you tell me she was coming?" he asks, yawning again.

"Because I didn't know she was coming." I turn the wipers off and buckle my seat belt. "She called me a few minutes ago and said she was at the airport…she sounded upset. And I need for you to tell me that I can handle this."

"Do you think you can handle this?" He uses psychology on me like Greg does all the time.

"I don't know…maybe…" I put the car into reverse and back out of the driveway. "I had all these pictures up on my wall….ones of Lexi and my mom. I kept them there because they reminded me of everything I lost…to hold on…I just took them down."

"When did you do this?" His voice is cautious.

"Like five minutes ago." I turn the wheel and drive down the road, heading toward the freeway.

"And how do you feel?"

"Weird." It's the first word that comes to mind, but it seems fitting. "Wilson, I'm not sure I can do this…see her… I'm not ready…" I stop the car at the stop sign, wishing I could be happier about her being here, but I can't. "Tell me what to do. Should I just tell her to go home?"

He contemplates what I said. "Why would you do that?"

"Because I just said I wasn't ready...and the idea of seeing her is freaking me out." I lower my head onto the steering wheel and stare at the floor. "And you told me not to get into a relationship until I was ready."

"Just because she's here, doesn't mean you're in a relationship," he tells me. "And besides, it might be good for you to help her out with whatever she's going through, since, from what I understand, she's really helped you in the past."

As soon as he says it, I know he's right. I'm being really selfish at the moment, thinking about how her being here is going to affect me when really I should be thinking about what happened that she needed to get on a plane and come see me. "Yeah, you're probably right."

"Of course I'm right," he says arrogantly. "I'm always right."

Right or not, it doesn't make it any easier to drive to the airport. But I make it there. And even though it probably takes me a little longer than most people to actually get to baggage claim, mainly because my feet seem to weigh a fuckload, I do get there.

It takes me a minute to spot her because it's the holidays and the place is pretty packed. But when I do, I swear to fucking God something changes inside me at that moment. Something good, I think, although I'm not 100 percent sure yet.

She's got her hair pulled up and a backpack by her feet as she leans against the wall with her eyes shut, the crowd moving around her. But the longer I stare at her, the more the crowd doesn't exist. I don't even care how fucking cheesy that sounds. It's just her and me and the past sort of washes over me. I start remembering everything. How she made me feel. How she refused to give up on me. How powerful it was just to be near her. This girl saved me and I love her for it. I know that now. My heart knows it. My head knows it. Even my legs do, because they're about to give out on me and I have to reach out and grasp the wall before I collapse. I can barely breathe as I work to stand up, the feelings inside me potent and over-whelming. I don't know if I can handle it—feeling this way for her while I'm sober.

The fear only intensifies when she opens her eyes and her gaze sweeps the room. A heartbeat later she spots me. She doesn't move. React. Neither do I. I want to, but I can't. Luck-ily she manages to unglue herself from where she's standing. She scoops up her backpack from the floor, swings it onto her shoulder, and heads for me. With each step she takes, her mouth turns up more, and by the time she reaches me, she's almost smiling.

"Hey," she says, and then without any warning she throws her arms around me, embracing me in a hug that's so tight, it feels like she's trying to survive through it. The heat of her body courses and rushes through me. Regardless of how terri-fied I am to touch her, I find myself wrapping my arms around her and hugging her so tightly my arms start to tremble. I fight the immensely intense urge to fall to the ground, but it's hard to stay up as adrenaline and emotions pulsate through me. I feel like I'm tipping sideways, falling off the tightrope. But she's holding on to me so I don't fall completely and I end up suspended in the air. I didn't even know feeling this way was possible and it's scary as shit.

I shut my eyes and breathe in her scent. "Wow," I whisper, breathless, as she presses her face into the crook of my neck, my hands shaking so badly I'm sure she can feel it.

"Yes, wow," she agrees, placing a kiss against my neck. She does it over and over again and with each one, I calm down inside. Still.

Suddenly, coming here to get her doesn't seem as terrifying as before. In fact, I'm glad I did. A feeling that grows when she moves away from me and, before I have any time to react, leans forward and kisses me right on the lips.

Chapter Twelve

Nova

I probably shouldn't have kissed him. It's not what I came here for. I just needed to get away from all the sadness and pain over Delilah and Tristan, and when I thought of the one place that I might be able to do that, being by Quinton's side was the first thing that came to mind.

Just friends, I kept telling myself during the airplane ride. *We're just friends.*

But seeing him in the flesh, healthy, honey-brown eyes more full of life than I've ever seen, it ignited something inside, and without thinking, I found myself placing my lips to his. I start to pull back when I realize I probably shouldn't have done that, but to my surprise, he presses his hand against my back and crushes our bodies together, deepening the kiss. My body conforms to his as I grasp on to him, my lips willingly part as his tongue slips deeper inside my mouth. The longer the kiss goes on, the more intense it gets, and before I know it my legs end up latched around his waist as his hands explore my body while he backs us up against the wall. I can barely breathe, only coming up for air when my lungs feel like they're going to explode. I can't take it anymore. I seriously want to tear off his clothes and run my hands across every part of him while he does the same to me.

But then suddenly he's pulling away and the noise around us washes over me and I remember that I'm in a very public place.

"God, I've missed you," Quinton whispers, resting his head against mine, his breathing ragged, my legs still fastened tightly around him.

"Yeah, me, too," I whisper back, basking in the feel of him, from the warmth of his skin to the feathery touch of his breath.

We stay that way for a moment before, finally, he lowers me back to the ground and lets go of me. Then he tucks a strand of my hair behind my ear, observing me intently. "Do you need to pick up anything from baggage claim?" he asks.

I shake my head and then reach around and pat the bag on my back. "This is all I brought," I say. "I was in sort of a rush and I'm not even sure if I remembered to bring deodorant."

He stares at me with a quizzical look, his eyes skimming over me. "Do you…do you want to talk about what's going on?"

I press my lips together and shake my head, refusing to think about what made me run. Not right now, when the moment is so good. "No, not yet, but later."

He cups my cheek in his hand. "Tell me what you need me to do . . . anything you need and I'll get it for you."

"Even if I said I needed a unicorn?" I shake my head at myself. I don't know why I crack a joke but I do.

He smiles, his eyes crinkling, and it's the most beautiful sight I've ever seen. "That might be possible to be arranged, if I have some time," he says. "But until then, what else do you need from me?"

My stomach grumbles in response. "How about breakfast?"

With a small smile, he nods and then takes my hand. "Breakfast it is, then."

We walk out the door and head to the parking garage, holding hands, the clear sky above us. It feels weird but at the same time right. It feels like this is where I belong and I love the feeling, yet at the same time I hate it, because I know that I won't be able to keep it this way. I have to start talking about what made me run.

"So you cook?" I say as he stirs some eggs in a pan. I honestly expected him to take me to a restaurant or McDonald's to get breakfast, but instead he took me to his house, which is about as bare as a home can be, completely filled with boxes.

He shrugs, turning down the stove temperature as the eggs sizzle. "Yeah, I mean, nothing fancy." He smiles at me over his shoulder. "But I can hold my own."

I grin back at him from the kitchen table. "Can you make bacon, too?"

"So you're picky," he jokes with a chuckle. "But if anyone deserves to be, it's you."

My expression falters. "I'm not as great as you think."

He grabs a plate from the cupboard. "Please talk to me." He sets the plate down on the countertop and scoops up some eggs. "I don't like seeing you sad."

I trace the lines on the table with my head tipped down. "I'm worried if I tell you what's going on . . . that it'll upset you. And I don't ever want to upset you."

He doesn't answer right away and when I hear him moving around, I force myself to look up. Our eyes meet as he sets a plate of eggs down in front of me. "Try me."

I give him a wary look and then swallow hard. "Are you sure? Because it's heavy stuff and I know you've been struggling with heavy stuff."

Now he swallows hard as he sits down in the chair across from me. "Yeah, I'm sure." He reaches across the table, his hand shaking as he gives my hand a soft squeeze. "I want to be here for you, and like I've said on the phone a hundred times, I'm not as fragile as you think."

His touch makes it the slightest bit bearable to speak. "I'm not even sure where to start," I say quietly. "It was like one minute I was completely okay and then all this stuff happened at once and I just needed to get the hell away from everything."

"Life can be that way," he says, letting go of my hand. "But I'm sure whatever's happening with you, you'll be able to handle it." He offers me a smile as he picks up a fork. "You're amazing with the heavy stuff."

I poke at my eggs, deciding that the only thing I can do is rip off the Band-Aid. "I think Tristan might be doing drugs again."

His arm muscles tense, his eyes widening for a split second, but then he quickly tries to compose himself. "For how long?"

"I'm not sure," I mutter, playing with my eggs, feeling too nauseous to eat. "I've had my suspicions for a couple of weeks now, but last night some stuff happened and when I called him, he told me he was at a party and that he didn't really care what happened to him, because life was shitty." I leave out the kiss part. It's irrelevant in my opinion because it didn't mean anything to me.

Quinton doesn't say a word, his fork still in his hand, his face masked with confusion. "Did he flat-out say he was doing drugs again?"

"No, but he said he was about to," I say, nibbling on my eggs. "He's been acting so weird lately. Hanging out with this sketchy guy, and I was worried that if I called him out on it, he'd get mad at me." I blow out a breath, drop my fork on my plate, and massage my temples with my fingertips. "There's more, but you can tell me to stop if you need me to. I don't want to overwhelm you."

He sets the fork down and rubs his hand down his face so roughly he leaves red marks on his skin. "No, I need to do this. I need to be here for you like you were for me."

"Are you sure?"

He vacillates, then nods. "Yes. I'm positive."

My stomach winds in knots and I hope that he can handle it like he says. "Remember how I told you about Delilah? And how she was missing and her mom was looking for her?"

He nods again and then his eyes enlarge. "Wait, did they find her?"

"I'm not sure." I shut my eyes to keep tears from falling. "I got a call from my mom last night and she said that Delilah's mom was heading down to Vegas to...identify a body...see if it's hers."

Silence surrounds us. I want to open my eyes and look at him, but at the same time I'm afraid. Afraid that I'll see that darkness return to his eyes. Afraid that I'll see the need to feed the darkness. But then I feel his hand on top of mine and the connection causes my eyelids to lift.

"It's going to be okay," he says, his hand trembling on mine. Or maybe mine's the one shaking—it's hard to tell.

"I know it will be eventually," I say. "Because I've been through this before...but I'm...afraid..."

A pucker forms at his brow. "Of what?"

"Of shutting down." I slip my hand out from underneath his and place it on top of my erratic heart. "Of counting. Of going back to my OCD so I don't have to deal with this." I'm

263

about to cry but I'm trying my hardest to suck back the tears, hold it all in, be strong. "Life was going so good and I just want it to stay that way." But the tears start to slip out and stream down my cheeks.

"Hey," he says, getting up from the chair and rushing to me. "Everything is going to be good still, even if it gets a little bumpy for a while." He kneels down in front of me and touches his hand to my cheek, smearing some of the tears away with his thumb. "And you want to know how I know that?" he asks, and I nod my head as more hot tears spill down my cheek. "Because I'm here. With you. And we're both sober." He gives me a lopsided smile and then wraps his arms around me, pulling me toward him. "And we both can get through this together."

My arms instinctively circle him and pull him closer as I rest my chin on top of his shoulders. "But what if it is her?"

His muscles spasm, but when he speaks his voice is calm. "Then we'll deal with it together."

"Can you . . . can you deal with it?" I wonder, looking him in the eyes. I honestly don't know, if it comes down to it, if he can be there for me without it hurting his recovery. If it is Delilah's body, will he be able to handle it? I don't think they were that close, but death is death. It's hard. Painful. And the weight of it grows with each person who passes, and never fully lightens again. Quinton's lost a lot and I worry the weight of another death will push him down.

"I think so." His voice falters, but he quickly recovers.

"I will for you…but Nova, let's not go to that place until we know for sure, okay?"

I nod, reaching up and wiping some more tears away with my fingertips. After I pull myself together, I lean back and look him in the eye. "You're pretty good at this. You know that?"

He raises his eyebrows with a look of disbelief. "Well, if that's true, then you can thank Wilson and his constant nagging words of wisdom."

"Do I get to meet him?" I ask, changing the subject to a lighter tone. "While I'm here?"

"Do you want to meet him?" he asks in surprise, his hands resting on top of my legs.

"Of course. You've been talking about him nonstop for a couple of weeks now," I say, but when he frowns, I add, "But you don't have to introduce me if you don't want to."

"No, I want to," he replies with reservation. "It's just that…" He scratches the back of his head. "It's just that it makes things so real." He gestures between us. "You and I."

"It doesn't have to mean that," I say, hiding my disappointment. "We can still just be friends."

His lips smash together as he holds my gaze. "I'm not sure if I can do that. Not when you're here now." He shuts his eyes and his chest rises and falls as he breathes in deeply and exhales. "Not after that kiss."

"I'm sorry about that," I apologize, even though I'm not that sorry. "I feel like I just put a ton of pressure on you by showing up here. I should have thought this all through a little better."

He opens his eyes, honey brown and reflecting the light of the room. I remember when I first met him how much pain they carried and in Vegas how empty they looked. But now they're different...he's different—more alive. "No, I want to be here for you...you've been there so much for me." He deliberates something with a lost look on his face. "Just tell me what you want to do and I'll make it happen."

I consider what I want, but a lot of impossible scenarios come to mind, like making it so Delilah will be okay, so I decide to settle on something simple. "I want to see the city," I say. "I've never been here before."

"How long are you planning on staying?" He gets to his feet and sits back down to eat breakfast.

"I have to go back home tomorrow...I have to work the day after Christmas and I promised Lea I'd spend Christmas day with her."

I can't tell if he's happy about this or not, but then he smiles. "Only one day in Seattle. I know just the place to go."

"Oh yeah? Where?" I dig into my eggs.

"It's a surprise." Then he winks at me and just seeing him happy makes me think that, despite all the darkness and wrong going on right now, everything's going to turn out okay.

Chapter Thirteen

Quinton

It's strange having Nova here, but not as strange as I thought it would be. In fact, despite my nervousness, it feels oddly right having her by my side. I wonder what this means. That it doesn't feel as wrong as it used to.

But the settled feeling leaves me a little as we get onto a bus and head toward town to see the Space Needle. I keep thinking how Lexi and I used to do this and how I shouldn't be doing it with Nova, yet as I sit by her, holding her hand, I can't seem to bring myself to put any sort of space between us.

"Seattle's a lot bigger than I thought," she says as she observes the city through the window. She has her phone out and every once in a while she records the stuff around us, always wanting to see everything through a lens.

The city is extra busy right now, being that it's the day before Christmas. More people walk the streets, carrying bags. Lights sparkle around windows and everything seems to shine cheerfully.

"It's definitely no Maple Grove," I tell her, leaning over her shoulder to stare up at the buildings with her. Her vanilla scent floods my body and I can't help it, I brush my lips across the side of her head. Just a soft kiss, to still the craving to smother her with passionate kisses.

"It's so tall and busy," she says, leaning into me and sighing contentedly. "And shiny. Like a big mirror...and all the Christmas stuff...I swear I can actually feel Christmas in the air."

"I used to draw it all the time," I divulge, turning my legs inward in the seat when a lady on crutches comes hobbling by. "I even won an art contest with one of my drawings when I was a senior in high school."

She turns her head and we're so close our lips brush against each other. "I want to see some of your sketches while I'm here. Ones that you used to draw."

My brows furrow as I realize that I think I might be able to handle that. "You know what? I think I'd like you to see them, too...I'd like you to see that I wasn't always so tripped out and could draw stuff with meaning behind it."

"I think everything you draw has meaning behind it," she says, the sunlight illuminating her greenish-blue eyes. "Some of the meaning is just sadder."

Her words hit me in the heart. She's so understanding and all I want to do is kiss her. Without any warning I press my lips to hers, startling her. But she doesn't pull back, falling into the kiss, opening her mouth as I slide my tongue deep inside. I'm sure we have an audience, but I don't care as I lean into her, forcing her to lean against the bus wall.

And that's how we stay until we reach our stop, almost missing it because we're so consumed in each other. We get off holding hands, the icy air just a bit more bearable as we walk side by side.

"Did you come here a lot?" she asks, angling her head back to look up at the top of the Space Needle stretching toward the sky as she raises her camera phone to get a shot of it.

I nod, not looking at the building, but at her. The awe in her expression is more fascinating than anything else going on around me. The way her eyes look crystal blue in the shadows, but greener when she leans into the light. The way strands of her hair move with the wind and the way she's biting her bottom lip nervously. Watching her makes me still inside and I wonder if this is how it could have always been with her if my mind had been undiluted enough to be aware of it. Although I feel high on her right now. Nova high. I wonder if that's okay.

"What?" she asks, suddenly looking at me, and our gazes fasten.

I shake my head, still not looking away from her. "It's nothing. You're just beautiful. That's all."

Her cheeks turn a little pink and it's the most adorable thing I've ever seen. It helps override the terror of the affectionate term I just gave her.

"Thanks," Nova says shyly.

I smile. "Come on," I say, pulling her toward the entrance before she can get too embarrassed. "It's much better at the top."

She laughs and lets me guide her up the stairs that lead to the entrance doors, where we pay our way in and take the elevators to the observation area. The wind feels like ice from all the way up here and stings my cheeks. We're so high up it feels like I'm flying and I hold on to Nova while she records the view, staying behind her with my hands on her hips, afraid to let her go as she leans forward and glances at the view below.

"The city looks so small from up here," she notes, then glances over my shoulder with her phone still up in front of her. "I feel like I'm a bird or something."

Smiling, I span my arms out and bring hers along with mine, pretending we have wings. She laughs, turning back around and redirecting her attention to the view and her camera. We stand there silently for the longest time, watching people come and go, the air getting colder and the sky darker. I think about asking her if she's ready to go, but I sense she's having some sort of moment so I remain silent, wondering what she's thinking and if she'll ever share it.

"Landon was afraid of heights," she says unexpectedly, gazing straight ahead as she continues to record. "We couldn't even ride the Ferris wheel when the carnival came to town."

"Lexi was afraid of bugs," I say quietly, resting my chin on top of her head, my fingers delving into her sides because

I have to hold on to something, otherwise I'm pretty sure I'm going to collapse from the adrenaline and emotions barreling through me. "I had to squish one every time she saw it."

"I'm not a fan of them, either," she admits. "But that's not what I fear the most."

"What do you fear the most?" I dare ask, tensing as I wait for her answer.

"Life," she says, looking over her shoulder at me. "And what lies ahead for me. You?"

My scar burns on my chest, feeling like it is splitting open, sending pain all over my body, but despite it, I manage to say, "The past and forgetting it."

She nods, understanding, and I'm glad I don't have to explain it to her. It makes things easier, unlike with my therapist, who wants me to explain everything. Nova gets me without my having to explain everything, and when I do explain things to her, I feel terrified but better. God, it's amazing what she's done for me. How lucky I am that she's here with me.

"Landon said he was tired of life," she whispers. "And that he couldn't find a point of living it anymore, so he just gave up...it always feels like everyone's giving up all the time and I don't understand why."

"Because it's easier," I say. "Than living and fighting to survive."

"But it's worth it?" she asks with so much hope in her eyes it makes me feel the slightest bit of hope, too. "Right?"

"I didn't used to think so…I used to think that the only way to deal with everything was to give up, but now…" I trail off, searching her eyes. "But now it's not so easy anymore."

She turns toward me and slips her fingers through mine. "Good. Because I don't want you to give up. I need you here with me." Then she stands on her tiptoes and kisses me and for a moment everything seems perfect. I'm not sure if I deserve it or not. If it's right or wrong, but regardless I'm selfishly taking it at the moment because I want her, more than anything.

Chapter Fourteen

Nova

We spend the rest of the day exploring the city and I even stop at a few stores to buy a couple of last-minute Christmas presents. We chat while recording every moment, but only because I want to have something to remind me of this day. It's hard, I'll admit, to be walking around when there's such a huge fear looming over my head. Death. It only gets harder when I get a text from Jaxon, one I feared was coming.

Jaxon: Did u seriously play with Lea's band?

"Shit," I curse as I read the text. We're sitting on a park bench watching people go by and Quinton shoots me a puzzled look.

"What's wrong?" he asks, putting his arm on the back of the bench behind me.

I shake my head as I read the text over again. "Jaxon found out I played with Lea's band."

"So? Tell him you did it because she's your friend," he says, the sunlight above shimmering in his eyes.

"I think he's pissed," I say, and then I text Jaxon back.

Me: I'm sorry, but she really needed me. I feel bad for doing it.

Jaxon: You know that's like the ultimate betrayal. Nikko's freakin pissed off as hell. He has this huge grudge against Braxton…says he stole a girlfriend from him a year ago or some shit.

Me: Tell him I'm sorry.

Jaxon: That's not going to do any good at the moment.

I'm about to text back when another text comes through.

Jaxon: He wants to kick u out of the band.

Me: Please don't. Tell him that I'm really sorry and that I'll make it up to him.

"Or how about tell them to get over it," Quinton says, and I realize he's reading my texts over my shoulder. "Don't let them push you around like that, Nova."

"They're not pushing me around. I promise," I say, but it doesn't feel like I'm being truthful to myself. "This is just how bands work."

He brings his foot up on his knee and shakes his head. "Baby, you're too nice sometimes. You need to be more assertive."

We both freeze a few seconds later when we realize that he called me baby. I'm not sure if I like the nickname or not, but at the same time I like that he's given it to me.

"Sorry about the *baby*," he says, his fingers caressing the back of my neck. "I didn't mean for that to come out like that…in fact, I've always thought it was a silly pet name or whatever you want to call it."

My phone is buzzing in my hand, but I don't look down at it. "It's okay," I say. "You can give me a pet name, but maybe just not baby."

He sucks his bottom lip into his mouth. "Then what do you want me to call you? Sweetie?"

I shake my head. "Too sugary. And I'm not sugary."

"I beg to differ," he says musingly. "But if you don't want me to call you that, I won't."

"I've always liked when you call me Nova like the car," I admit, wanting to throw my phone against the ground as it buzzes again. I should be more worried that my band is upset, but being here, and why I came here, have got me distracted.

The corners of his lips quirk. "That's a really long nickname."

"Well, how about this," I say. "How about you just call me Nova, except for special occasions, like my birthday and yours, and then you'll call me Nova like the car."

He wets his lips with his tongue and it makes me want to kiss him again…never stop kissing him. "Sounds good to me," he says, and then he leans in, brushing his lips across mine as if he's read my mind or something.

It's a quick kiss, though, and we end up breaking apart as my phone buzzes for the fourth time.

Jaxon: I told him u were sorry, but he's still pissed.

Jaxon: Nova, I think we might really have to kick u out, at least for a while.

Jaxon: Nova, what the hell. Please respond.

Nikko: I can't believe u played for another band.

I stare at the screen forever, wondering what to type. The more I think about it, the more anxious I get, which isn't what I need at the moment. So in the end I put my phone away and rest my head on Quinton's shoulder.

"Are you okay?" he asks.

I nod. "Yeah, or at least I will be. I just need to relax and breathe for a while."

He doesn't argue, resting his head on mine, and we sit that way for the next hour. It's probably one of the best hours I've had in my entire life, and if I could, I'd just stay this way, frozen in time, but I know I can't. It's part of my problem. Never wanting to let go. Fearing big changes. Fearing what will happen if I alter my life. Take risks.

Finally the sun starts to set and we get up from the bench and make our way home. But we stop at a construction site for Quinton to show me the house he's working on. It's not much at the moment, but I can see why he's so proud. Putting a home together for a family that needs it.

"It's amazing," I say as I make a circle around the first floor, which doesn't have walls. The floor is plywood. There are spotlights set up on the ground to light up the area as people work hard in the dark to get the house finished. "It's like a real house and everything."

He watches me as he grips a beam above our head. "As opposed to a fake one?"

I laugh and then playfully swat his arm. "You know what I mean."

He laughs and the sound is so breathtaking that I have to take out my camera and record it. "Smile for the camera, please," I tell him, lifting my phone up and aiming it at him.

"Are you going to record everything?" he wonders as I zoom in on his face.

I lower the camera, frowning. "Sorry. Is it bothering you?"

He shakes his head, seeming genuine. "No, I just want to know. That's all."

"Oh." I raise the camera back up and he appears on the screen again. "I'll stop in a little while. I just want to remember all this . . . and recording makes me feel better."

"Well, then record away while I give you the grand tour," he says, releasing the beam, then proceeds to lead me around the home, introducing me to people here and there. He smiles so much as he points out everything, telling me which pieces he's put together. He's proud of his accomplishment and he should be. It makes me want to accomplish more myself.

"You look so happy," I dare to say as we head up the stairs to the second floor.

His forehead creases. "I do?"

I nod, tucking a strand of hair behind my ear. "It makes me want to do stuff like this," I say. "Well, not like this, since I can't build, but help people in some way."

"You help people more than you think," he says, trailing off as we arrive on the top floor.

There's a thirtysomething guy with a scruffy jaw, wearing a plaid coat, banging a hammer against a piece of wood. Country music plays on a stereo in the corner and a small light is perched in the center of things, illuminating the darkness night has brought on.

"And this is Wilson," Quinton says as he approaches the guy with a sort of uneasy look on his face.

Wilson glances up at Quinton, seeming startled. "Holy shit, I didn't see you even come in here." His eyes drift to me and he lowers the hammer to his side. "Who's this?" He asks it, but it sounds like he already knows who I am.

"This is Nova," Quinton tells him, stuffing his hands into the pockets of his jeans.

Recognition crosses Wilson's face as he sets the hammer down on the floor, then brushes his hands off on the sides of his pants. "It's nice to meet you," he says, approaching me with his hand extended.

I grasp it and shake it. "It's nice to meet you, too. I've heard a lot about you."

Wilson glances over at Quinton with a cocky look on his face and Quinton rolls his eyes and shakes his head. "Well, I hope good things," Wilson says, returning his attention to me.

I nod, letting go of his hand. "Yes, always good things."

Smiling, Wilson leans over to pick a bottle of water up off the floor. "Okay, so I just have to say that I love your name."

"Thanks," I tell him, glancing over at Quinton, wondering

if he told Wilson the story behind it. "I was named after my father's car."

"I know," Wilson says, taking a drink before setting the bottle back down on the ground beside a blue lunchbox. "Quinton told me, and I have to say that your dad had excellent taste in cars."

He said *had*, which means he knows my father has passed away, which means Quinton's been telling him stuff about me. I like the idea for some reason, that he would take the time to talk about me with Wilson, someone I know he looks up to, even though he hasn't flat-out said it.

After we chat a little bit, Wilson asks if we want to help him for a while. Quinton starts to shake his head, but I say yes, loving the idea of doing something that helps others. Although I don't really help out that much, since I have no idea how to build a house or anything, but I get tools for them when they need them. I start to notice a lot of things as I observe the two of them putting a house together, like how happy Quinton seems to be here. He keeps making jokes and every once in a while he comes over and gives me a kiss on the forehead or cheek, like he's afraid that if he doesn't he'll miss his chance. It feels like we really might be boyfriend and girlfriend or at least close. The last time I was at this place was with Landon and I never thought I'd have that again, but I think I was wrong. I think I want what I had with Landon with Quinton, only better. I want us to be able to talk about stuff no matter what, even if it's difficult.

"What?" Quinton asks at one point, his face masked with curiosity, and I realize that I'm staring at him with a big grin on my face.

I shake my head, unable to erase my smile. "It's nothing. I'm just feeling better. That's all."

"Good. I'm glad." He smiles back and starts hammering a nail while I return to watching him move, because I'm finding it fascinating. After he gets the board nailed into place he glances around confusedly. "Where'd Wilson go?" he asks.

I point at the stairway. "He muttered something about going to check up on the guys below and then wandered in that direction."

"Shit, I didn't even see him walk away."

"That's because you're in the zone."

He smiles at me, then turns to go back to hammering as the song on the radio switches to a slower one.

"It's really pretty up here," I say, looking up at the sky through a small section of the home where the roof isn't up yet. "You can see so many stars."

"You know, I remember the last time you and I looked up at the stars," Quinton says, walking up to me. "In Vegas...we played twenty questions and then we danced."

I look up at him. "Yeah, and you promised me a redo. You know, I've really been dying to see your stellar dancing skills again. The ones your grandma taught you."

"Yeah, I would never have told you that if I hadn't been

high," he says, seeming a little embarrassed. "But anyway." He extends his hand. "You want to dance?"

I glance around at the home with no walls, the sound of power tools filling the air. "Right here?"

He nods as I slip my hand into his and he pulls me toward him. Then he backs to the stereo in the corner and turns up the music so loudly that I can barely hear anything but the beat and lyrics.

"You know, I've never been a fan of country music," I admit as he walks back to me.

"Ha, well, now I know something about music that you don't," he says, placing his hands on my hips. "Because I listen to it all the time."

I wrap my arms around his neck. "Are you a fan?"

He shakes his head. "No, but I know the lyrics to this song."

"I wouldn't be too proud of that," I joke.

"No way," he says as he starts to rock us to the rhythm of the song. "You are so music-superior, but this time I got you."

"Yeah, you totally got me," I say with an underlying meaning that I think he picks up on. But I don't care. He has me right now, in this moment. I'm completely caught up in him and all the bad that was nipping at my heels has dissipated. And it continues to be nonexistent as we dance, laughing when he pushes me away and makes me do a silly little spin. And when he draws me back to him, I can't help but smile as I rest my head on his shoulder.

"Quinton, thank you," I say softly as I hold on to him.

"For what?" he wonders.

"For making me feel better today," I say, his muscles going rigid. "I really needed it."

He pauses and then he pulls me closer, resting his chin on top of my head. "You're welcome, Nova like the car."

We dance for one more song, and then Wilson walks up and catches us. He starts cracking jokes about always knowing Quinton was a softy, something Quinton pretends to be annoyed about, but I don't think it really bothers him.

About an hour later, we leave to go back to Quinton's house. I feel strangely content on the inside, walking under the stars with him. I'm really glad I decided to be impulsive and come out here. It's late, though, and I know that in a few hours I'll have to go to sleep and then when I wake up the magic of this day will be over as I head back home. But I try not to think about it and focus on spending time with him.

When we get back to Quinton's house, his dad is still at work, so he fixes us dinner—grilled cheese and soup. After we're finished, I help him clean up the dishes.

"So what do you want to do?" Quinton asks as he places the last dish into the dishwasher. He's got the sleeves of his shirt rolled up and a bit of dirt on his forehead, which I reach up and wipe away.

I glance down at the dirt on my arms and then sniff myself. "I feel really gross," I say, scrunching my nose. "Can I take a shower?"

"Sure." He shuts the dishwasher door. "Let me show you where it is."

He takes me to the upstairs bathroom, then briefly lingers in the doorway, seeming like he wants to say something, before clearing his throat and leaving me to take a shower. After I pull my shirt off and slip out of my jeans, I turn on the water, then sit down on the edge of the tub, waiting for it to warm up, ready to dive in and wash up. It's been a long day—that's for sure. But it's made me feel better and made me feel like, no matter what happens with Tristan, Delilah, and my band, I can handle it. I hope I'm right. I hope I don't fall apart. I hope I'm strong enough to make it through whatever lies ahead.

I'm about to take my bra off when I hear a knock at the door. "Um, yeah," I say timidly.

"It's me," Quinton utters from the other side of the door. "I brought you some towels."

"Oh." I glance down at my clothes on the floor, wondering if I should put them back on. Then, deciding I don't want to be shy Nova with him anymore, I walk over to the door and crack it open. I stick my head out, ignoring the rush of heat that travels over me just from the sight of him. "Thanks." I take the towels from him and our knuckles graze, causing blinding heat to throb through my veins, and I resist the impulse to shiver.

"No problem." His voice is off pitch and I catch his gaze drifting downward to my exposed leg.

I think about stepping out of his line of sight, but then I

realize that I don't want to. What I want to do is open the door wider and step out into something new, something I've never experienced before, not even with Landon. I don't want to be afraid. I don't want to hide anymore. Life's too short to hide. I just want Quinton. Now. No more waiting, like I've done in the past.

His eyes slowly scroll back up to mine and he blinks like he's forcing thoughts out of his head. "I should go," he whispers, his voice strained.

"Quinton, I…"

I'm not even sure who actually does it. Whether he pushes the door the rest of the way open or I pull it open, but suddenly it's swinging and it bangs against the wall as I step back. I'm standing there in front of him in my bra and panties, feeling as though I should be embarrassed, but I'm not.

"Jesus, you're beautiful." He extends his arm and places his hand on my hip, giving me a gentle tug so our bodies join together.

I moan as his fingertips delve into my skin and the contact is so stimulating I almost collapse to the floor. He seems like he is in pain, torn about what to do next, but then he gives another gentle tug and seconds later our lips collide. I swear to God a year's worth of emotions pour out of us as we grab each other, our tongues entangling, hands grasping each other. All the passion. Heat. Fear. Worry. Longing. Want. Desire. Need. Resistance. It all blazes through my body at once and nearly sends me buckling to the floor. But he holds on to me, his hand slamming against the wall to keep us both on our feet. His body heat is intoxicating, making me feel like I'm melting everywhere he touches me. And all I can think of is how much I want him. How much I've been waiting for this moment.

But then he's pulling away from me, shattering the connection. "Nova, maybe we shouldn't do this." His breathing is ragged, eyes dazed, like he's disoriented. "Not now, when you're so upset."

"I'm not upset anymore." My chest heaves, my hands on his shoulder blades, fingertips digging downward. "And I'm doing this because I want to do this...I want you, Quinton." My cheeks heat as I say it, but I don't want to retract it. I've never said that to a guy before.

He still seems conflicted, but when I slant forward to kiss him he doesn't protest, his tongue willingly entering my mouth. Minutes later the shower is turned off and we've abandoned the bathroom and found our way to his bedroom, having managed not to break the lip lock.

The first thing I notice is the scent of him everywhere, cologne and cigarettes. It reminds me of a different place and time, one where I was lost. The memories are extremely intoxicating, but in a good way because I'm not in that place anymore, and the memories remind me of how far we've come—how far *I've* come.

Then I notice how bare his walls are and I pull away. "You took most of your drawings and photos down?" I ask, noting that there are only three remaining on his wall. One sketch of a girl I think must be Lexi, along with a photo of her, and one of a woman I think is his mom because her eyes resemble Quinton's.

He nods with nervousness in his eyes as he tucks a strand of my hair behind my ear. "Yeah, I was actually doing it this morning right before you called...I woke up and just kind of decided that it was time." He shrugs, like it's no big deal, but it is. It's huge. I know because I've been through something similar with Landon's photos.

Stunned, I return my attention to him. "You should have told me. You just took a huge step."

He grazes my bottom lip with his thumb, a trace of a smile at his lips as he shakes his head. "Stop worrying about me, Nova. I'll be okay...if they were still up, then you'd have to worry." His voice wobbles. "It was good that I took that step even though it was hard."

"I know it had to be hard for you...but I'm proud of you." I slip my arms around his waist. "You're doing so good."

His breathing increases. "I hope I can stay that way."

"You can," I say. "I know you can."

He swallows hard and then he deliberately leans in and presses his lips to mine, stealing my breath away. And just like that all my reservations disappear. Even when he unhooks my bra and slips off my panties, I barely feel my nerves. I only feel him as I help him slide his shirt off his head, then run my fingers across the ridges of his lean muscles, basking in

286

everything about him. His warmth. The way his heart beats in his chest when I press my palm on top of it. The smoothness of his skin. The only thing that pains me is the feel of the scar and the sight of the tattoos and he winces every time I touch them.

"Are you okay?" I ask, withdrawing my hand from his scar.

His eyelids flutter up, terror filling them. "I'm fine... I'm just nervous."

"Good. I'm glad I'm not the only one." I don't mean to say it aloud, it just sort of slips out.

He gives me a crooked smile as my cheeks start to heat, but then he starts kissing me again, slow and sensual, as if he's savoring each second, each brush of his finger, each entanglement of our tongues. When he backs me up toward the bed, I move with him, letting him lay me down and cover my body with his. His fingers roam all over my body, not missing a single part of me, caressing my inner thighs before he slips them inside me and starts moving them. I grasp the blanket, trying to hold on to something as I get lost in a place I didn't think existed. A place where nothing exists, except the two of us. It's the most amazing feeling, one I haven't felt in a very long time. All the stress and worry diminish. All the bad is temporarily gone. And as I cry out, something bursting deep inside me, I want nothing more than to clutch on to this feeling forever. But seconds later, it slowly slips away and I have to return to reality.

Quinton

Feeling her like this...touching her like this...it's more potent and intoxicating than drugs. If I could, I would stay this way forever, tasting her and touching her until my heart stopped beating and I took my last breath. The sight of her, with her head tipped back and her eyes glossed over with pure contentment, has me wishing I could pause the moment so I could stop and draw it.

"Quinton," she moans, letting go of the blanket and holding on to me as if her life depends on it.

It's one of the most terrifying feelings I've ever experienced. Having her want and need me this much and wanting and needing her this much. It's unexpected. Undeserved. But unavoidable. I know this now. Whether I deserve this, if it's wrong, if I'm being selfish because of this, letting Lexi go for a moment to be wholeheartedly with someone else, I can't stop it. Nova owns my heart and I can't get it back from her.

So I keep pushing her to the edge, letting her get lost, until she completely breaks apart in my arms. After she comes down, I dip my lips to hers and kiss her deliberately, my movements calculated as I explore her, memorizing every single inch of her. Her hands start to wander over my body and toward the button of my jeans. With a flick of her finger, she undoes it, then slides her hand down and rubs me hard. Part of me wants to stop her—slow things down—but I'm too far gone to pull back. Before I even realize what I'm doing, I push up from her to get out of my jeans. Then, after grabbing a condom out of my nightstand drawer, I return my body over hers, murmuring something about being sure she wants this. She nods enthusiastically and a few heartbeats later, I'm slipping inside her, with no hesitation. She winces, the pain in her body making her muscles tighten and her legs press firmly against the sides of my hips.

I pause, panting as I gaze down at her. "Are you okay?"

She nods, her hands sliding up my back, her gaze fastened on mine, her brown hair a halo around her head as she lies on my bed, peering up at me. "Yeah, just go slow."

Nodding, I slowly rock inside her again and she grips my back and guides me to her. With each thrust she starts to loosen up and before I know it, she's moving rhythmically with me. Heat builds inside me, my skin dampening with sweat as my heart races madly inside my chest, my attention focused on her and the lost look in her eyes as I push her closer and closer until both of us can barely hold on.

I never thought I'd experience this ever again. Never thought it would be possible to be with someone else like this and not feel pain and anguish, but for the briefest moment they're gone and I am free.

"Quinton." Nova's eyes are wide as she gasps, clinging to me, lifting her hips to meet mine one last time before I lose touch with reality, drifting off into a place of contentment— a place that I've only been able to reach with drugs over the last two years. It breaks me and then puts me back together and for the briefest moment, it feels like everything is going to be okay.

After we both catch our breaths, I slowly slip out of her and then we lie side by side, our fingers laced together as we silently take in what just happened. I feel different. Changed. Confused. Content. Lost. Guilty. Happy. I'm not even sure what to do with the last emotion. I've sort of gotten used to the more complex, darker emotions that I've struggled with in the past. As I lie there struggling to sift through my emotions and trying to figure out how to deal with them, Nova rolls onto her side and faces me. "Tell me what you're thinking?" she asks, propping herself up on her elbow, the blanket resting over her bottom half. She self-consciously pulls it over her chest. "I need to know, otherwise I'm going to sit here worrying that you...that you regret what just happened."

"What?" I gape at her. "Why would you think I regret it?"

"Because you're being so quiet." She bites her bottom lip with apprehension. "And I can't read you right now."

I roll to my side and then sit up, forcing her to drop the blanket from her chest, the sight of her bare chest and big eyes making my heart miss a beat. "I was thinking how amazing that was," I say, tracing a line across her collarbone with my fingers. "And how..." It takes me a second to get enough strength to say it. "And how much I want to draw you right now so I can remember the moment."

"Okay." She's breathless but doesn't hesitate, surprising

me, because I was honestly just talking and not really planning on doing it.

"Okay." I repeat her word, nervously nodding as I realize that this is actually happening—that she and I are really happening. As I reach for my sketchbook, my fingers tremble with my nerves and I wonder, if they keep it up, just how well the sketch is going to turn out.

"Where do you want me?" Nova asks as I sit on the bed with the sketchbook on my lap and a pencil in my hand.

"Right where you are," I tell her, my gaze skimming over her body, half covered by the blanket, her freckled cheeks flushed, her eyes filled with contentment. It's perfect. *She's* perfect.

"Okay," she says timidly, her muscles stiff.

"Try to relax," I say to her as I press the tip of my pencil to the paper, then waver for what seems like forever, because the last time I drew someone like this it was Lexi. It seems like it should feel more wrong than it does, but this feels different, because what's happening between Nova and me feels different from what Lexi and I shared. More intense. More unknown. More unfamiliar.

Releasing the breath I have trapped in my chest, I start moving the pencil across the blank sheet of paper. Stroke by stroke. Line by line. Shading. Recreating her perfection the best I can. The curve of her neck. The fullness of her lips. The freckles on her nose, the ones I've wanted to draw for a while. Her amazing eyes that draw me in every time I look at her, because they carry the pain I can relate to, the life-changing loss, the heartbreak, the guilt, the weight of losing someone you love. We're connected and I try to capture that connection with every stroke of my pencil.

When I'm finally finished, I put the pencil down and crack my aching knuckles, feeling the sting of the moment. It's been a while since I've drawn so intensely and it's almost unbearable to think that I've transferred that moment from Lexi to Nova, but that doesn't mean I regret it.

"Can I see it?" Nova asks, sitting up with her hand out.

I nod, then hand her the drawing, watching as she assesses it. Her eyes light up more the longer she stares at it. "What do you think?" I ask.

She glances up, smiling. "I think it's perfect."

Unable to help myself, I lean down and kiss her, then lie beside her, wrapping my arms around her and pulling her closer as she holds on to the drawing. "What do you want to do for the rest of the night?" I ask.

She angles her head to the side. "I just want to lie here with you, if that's okay? Until I fall asleep."

"That sounds perfect to me." I pull her closer, my chest tightening as I think about the times Lexi and I lay in my bed together. I glance over at the drawing of Lexi, saying a silent apology to her. *I'm sorry I'm letting you go. I hope you can forgive me. I still love you. Always will. But I can't seem to choose death. I'm so sorry.*

Nova and I talk for a little bit until we start to doze. I'm a little afraid to close my eyes, fearing that when I wake up everything will have been a dream and I'll be back in the crack house in Vegas, doped up on methamphetamine. Eventually I do doze off and end up having the most peaceful sleep I've had in the last two years. But it's short-lived, like most peaceful things. That's the one thing about perfection. It never lasts.

Nova

I'm drifting off when I get a phone call. It's not too late, around ten o'clock Seattle time, but I get this bad feeling the moment I hear the phone ring. Maybe it's because I know what's coming; maybe I took off from Idaho so I could be here when I got the call.

"Hello," I answer, Quinton lying to my side, his eyes open, looking tired.

"Nova," my mom says. "Where are you? I called Lea... and she said you just took off—that you were upset."

I rest back down on the pillow. "I was, but I'm feeling better now...I'm actually with Quinton."

"In Seattle?" She's shocked. "Why didn't you let me know you were going?"

"Yeah, it was sort of a spontaneous trip." A much-needed escape from life.

"Well, I hope you're doing okay now," she says. "I've been debating for the last few hours whether or not to call you."

Something clicks. "Mom, why did you call Lea and not me?"

She sighs. "Because I have bad news and I wanted to make sure there was someone there for you. To make sure you were okay."

She doesn't have to tell me what it is. I know before the words leave her mouth. "The body was Delilah's, wasn't it?" I say, and Quinton tenses beside me, his fingers instantly finding mine and holding on.

"I'm so sorry, Nova." She's close to crying.

"How did it happen?" I squeeze Quinton's hand, needing to hold on to something. "How did she die?"

"She was shot," my mom says quietly. "They found her body near a ditch just outside of Vegas . . . they don't know who did it yet, but the police are investigating it."

"It was Dylan," I say as Quinton scoots closer to me, his nerves buzzing off him and suffocating me. It's hard to breathe and I have to concentrate on getting air into my lungs. *Breathe in. Breathe out. You'll survive this.*

"Maybe," she says. "But that's for the police to worry about. Not you." She pauses. "Nova, I don't want you doing anything stupid."

"Like what?" I think I'm in shock. My body numb. My emotions disconnected. And I can't seem to breathe normally. I'm starting to get dizzy, the room is spinning. "Go find Dylan and see if he's the one who did it? I'm not a moron, Mom."

"But you want to fix things you can't always fix," she says, and I glance over at Quinton, his honey-brown eyes watching me with worry. "And you always blame yourself when you aren't able to help people."

"Well, sometimes I deserve to be blamed," I tell her, turning onto my side to face Quinton as the tears finally start to flow from my eyes. Reality sinks in and crashes down on me. Hard. More death. More weight. I can't fix this. What's done is done. Delilah is gone. I can't go back and try to help her. She's gone. I have to accept that. "I have to go, Mom," I say, and as she starts to protest I add, "I'll call you tomorrow." I hang up before she can say anything else.

"Are you going to be okay?" Quinton asks, sitting up and leaning over me.

I nod, not bothering to suck back the tears as they pour out. "I'll be okay eventually, but I need a few moments." Tears stream down my cheeks and drip onto the blanket below me. I don't bother stopping them. It'd make things worse if I did. It's something I've learned over the years, that suppressing the pain will only make it worse in the long run, but letting everything out doesn't make it easier.

Quinton

I remember when I came back from the accident, when they revived me and I woke up. I asked my dad where Lexi was and all he said was, "She's dead." I wished he'd said more—that he were there for me. Like I need to be here for Nova now, if she needs me. But can I? Am I that strong?

More tears pour out of Nova's eyes as her hand finds my arm and she grasps me, her nails piercing my skin. I don't draw back. I let her take out her inner pain on me.

She chokes back a sob, her shoulders heaving as she battles not to lose control. "Quinton, it hurts so bad."

"I know it does," I say as I wrap my arms around her and hug her so tight against me I can feel her heart beating. I want to tell her it'll be okay. That it won't hurt forever. That it'll get easier. But she won't believe me at the moment. If anyone gets that, it's me. There is nothing I can say to take her pain away or make her feel less guilty, so I do the only thing I can do. Something I wish someone had done for me in the beginning and what Nova did for me in the end.

I hold her as she drowns in her pain, making sure she doesn't go completely under.

Nova

I've lost it. I can't breathe. Think. Do anything but sob. I'm letting all the pain out, just like I should, but the ache inside my body feels like it's going to kill me. Another person gone. More tears to shed. More good-byes. Coffins. Flowers. Mourning. It seriously feels like too much, but there's one thing that keeps me from breaking apart completely and that's Quinton. At first I fight it, worry he's not strong enough for me to have a meltdown, but once I let it all out, I can't seem to turn off the tears and emotion pouring out of me. And he lets me sob on his shoulder, allows me to cling to him for hours, smoothing his hand up and down my back and telling me it's going to be okay.

"I should have done something more for her," I whisper through the tears. It's another thing that will haunt me forever. The fact that I should have said more—done more to help her.

"You did all you could," Quinton assures me, kissing the top of my head. "Nova, you can't save everyone...and you've done more good in your life than most people do."

I press my cheek against his chest, feeling his racing heartbeat. "It doesn't feel that way...it doesn't feel like I've done anything."

"Look at me," he begs, and when I don't, he hooks his finger underneath my chin and tips my head back, forcing me to look at him. "It's because of you that I'm here. If it wasn't for you, then I would probably be dead in a ditch somewhere, and you know what?" A pause. An intake of breath. Whatever he's going to say is hard for him. "I'm glad I'm here."

He's admitting he's glad that he's alive. That I saved him. That he got clean. I know that has to be difficult for him. To let go of the pain and guilt enough to admit that he wants to be happy.

"It wasn't just me, Quinton," I say. "Your dad and Tristan helped, too."

He shakes his head, eyes burning with intensity. "Nova, you didn't give up on me no matter what. Do you know how many people would have just let me go? Hell, my fucking dad did until you got involved."

"That was because of my mom," I explain, pushing up on my elbows and looking down at him. "She's the one that called him."

"Yeah, because you made her get ahold of him," he says, his fingers sliding away from my chin, and he cups my cheek in his hand. "It's because of you and your refusal to give up on me that I'm here. And it's because of you that I've stayed in this place and that I want to continue to stay in this place." He brushes his lips across my forehead, before looking back at me. "You give me hope, Nova Reed. Hope that even though life is really, really hard—even if it fucking sucks sometimes—that it's worth living."

Deep down, I know he's right. Life does suck, but it's worth living, especially for moments like the one I just experienced a few hours ago with Quinton. But it's moments like these, the ones when you have to feel the loss of life, that make it so hard to want to keep breathing.

Chapter Fifteen

December 28, the day of the funeral

Quinton

I'm doing everything I can to be there for Nova, not just to pay her back for everything she's done for me, but because I love her. I make sure to give her everything she needs, whether she asks for it or not. I go to Maple Grove for her. I even insist on going to the funeral with her, even though the idea of it terrifies me to my very soul. Part of it is that I knew Delilah and it's always difficult to lose someone you know. But the other part of my fear stems from the fact that it's a funeral and represents death. I haven't actually been to a funeral before, even with how many people I've lost. I was in the hospital when Lexi's and Ryder's took place, but I'm sure I wouldn't have been allowed to go even if I'd been able to. And my grandma took care of me when my mom's went on because they didn't feel like a funeral was a place for a newborn.

So this one will be my first. It doesn't start so well when I lose track of Nova a few hours before. I was hanging out in her room after she said she was going to go finish getting ready. Then she took off from her house without telling anyone and we found her in the car, talking to her camera and crying her eyes out. It nearly killed me, seeing her like that, but I did the only thing I could and let her cry on my shoulder, holding on to her so she wouldn't fall. It's not a lot, but all I can really do for her is be there while she works through her pain, let her know she's not alone.

We don't go to the viewing. I'm glad. It's always freaked me out, the thought of looking at a dead body, preserved to make it look like the person is still alive and just sleeping.

"I completely agree with you," Nova said when I'd reluctantly told her I didn't want to go to the viewing. We were sitting in her car, preparing to go inside the church. "Maybe we should just wait a few more minutes to go inside and then just sit at the back." Her eyes were red and swollen from crying, but she'd managed to pull herself together for the most part.

"If that's what you want," I said, placing my hand on her knee.

She nodded, staring at the church, people wandering up and down the stairs, a lot of them sobbing. "Yeah, I think it's what I want." She finally looked at me after thirty minutes of just staring ahead. "The idea of going in there is freaking me out."

I gave her leg a gentle squeeze. "Just remember, I'm here for you." It felt strange saying it. I'd spent the last couple of years thinking solely of my pain and me. My loss. My inner agony and guilt. And now suddenly all my emotions were centered on Nova and her pain.

After the funeral I leave her with her mom for a while to meet up with Tristan, who drove out here for the funeral with Lea, Nova's friend. I briefly saw him at the church, but he was with his parents and so I couldn't go up to him. But I want to see him before I go back to Seattle, and make sure he's okay. Make sure he's still sober and not going to crack and fall apart like Nova was worried about.

After texting we agreed to meet up at this park we used to spend time at when we were kids. It's within walking distance of Nova's house and so I decide to make the journey on foot, despite how cold it is and that there's three feet of snow on the ground.

When I walk up to the gated area, I find Tristan sitting on a park bench surrounded by piles of snow, smoking a cigarette, with the hood of his coat over his head, a slight flurry of snowflakes drifting down on him. I try to assess the situation as I hike through the snow toward him, pulling my own hood over my head.

"What's up?" I ask, taking my own cigarettes out of my pocket, then lighting one up. "You doing okay?"

"Yeah, I'm fine," he says distractedly as he gazes down at the snow with his arms resting on his knees. "I'm just thinking."

"About Delilah?" I plop down on the bench beside him. It's not like either of us ever really got along with Delilah, but at the same time we lived with her for a while, got to know the cracked part of her, saw the ugly shit that might have eventually led to her death. I remember the time I got into a fight with Dylan over his abuse toward Delilah, when I was high and could barely think straight. It didn't end well. In fact, Delilah got mad at me for intervening. And even though the police haven't found the person who shot her, I think all of us—Tristan, Nova, me—know it was Dylan.

"Yeah, sort of." He glances up from the snow and I'm relieved to see that he's not high. "I was just thinking about how many times we saw Dylan yell at her...we should have done more to stop it."

I take a drag on my cigarette and slowly exhale the smoke. "I tried to intervene a few times, but she wouldn't take my help."

He elevates his eyebrows, returning his attention to the snowy ground as he puts his cigarette into his mouth and takes a drag. "Well, you did better than me. I just got high and overlooked it because I was too involved with myself."

"I overlooked it, too, for the most part," I say, frowning. "And the fact that she died that way...it fucking sucks."

"Then why do you seem so calm?" Tristan asks, glancing up at me. "No offense, but I actually expected you to be a fucking mess over this."

I put the cigarette up to my mouth and inhale. "I'm only calm on the outside and only because Nova needs me to be that way."

"Are you two together, then?" he asks, grazing his thumb across the bottom of his cigarette and scattering ashes all over the snow.

It takes me two more drags before I have enough nicotine in my system to answer. "I don't know... maybe."

He nods, still fascinated with the ground. "Well, if you are, then good for you." There's a small amount of bitterness in his voice that makes me feel guilty, part of which is connected to Ryder's death and the feeling that I owe him for that. It's a gnawing feeling I don't think I'll ever truly be able to get rid of.

I reach up and draw my hood over my head, before inhaling another breath of smoke and exhaling it. "Are you okay if we're together? Or does it... does it bother you?"

He pulls a nah face as he hops off the bench into the snow. "I'll be fine."

"Are you sure?" I get to my feet and trample through the snow after him as he heads for the gate. "Because you can talk to me if it does."

He shakes his head, walking backward so he's facing me, with his hands tucked in the pockets of his coat. "I'm fine with you and Nova being together. You're better for her anyway." He spins on his heels, walking forward and kicking the snow.

I'm baffled as I hurry after him, because I'm not better for her. She just chose to be with me, despite how much I don't deserve her. "I'm not better than you in any way, shape, or form."

"Yeah, you kind of are," he says simply. "And besides, I don't think I'm going to be with anyone for a very long time."

"What do you mean?"

He's quiet for a while, flicking his cigarette ashes into the snow as we reach the gate, where he pauses and faces me. "You know, after I got clean again, I looked at it as a second chance." He opens the gate and then walks through it, turning his back toward me as he continues. "I mean, I fucking nearly died, for Christ's sake, and so I should be grateful I'm alive."

"Aren't you?" I ask, closing the gate behind me.

"I was." He stares out at the icy road as we walk up the side of it. "Until a couple of weeks ago when I found out I have hepatitis C."

I freeze in place, stunned beyond comprehension. "What?"

He shrugs as if he didn't just say something major and life-changing, eyes ahead, refusing to look at me. "Yeah, I feel like it's some kind of cosmic joke. Keep me alive just so I can find out I have some stupid disease that might complicate my life depending on how things go."

I don't know much about the disease, just enough to know that he probably got it from shooting up. It doesn't really matter, though, how he got it. All that matters is his life is changed forever. "Tell me what I can do." I lean forward and catch his eye. "What do you need?"

"There's not much that you can do for me. You and I both know that." He reaches for his pack of cigarettes, thinking. "Just take good care of Nova, if you end up with her." He opens his pack and pops a cigarette into his mouth. "She's one of the good ones—you're fucking lucky to have her." He offers me a cigarette and I take it.

I pull my lighter from my pocket, still stunned beyond words at what he just told me. All that time we spent in the drug world and I was able to walk away from it, while it's going to haunt him forever. It feels so fucked up.

"The roles should be reversed," I mutter, shaking my head. "You should be healthy and with Nova and I should be the one who..." I can't even say it.

"It doesn't really matter," he replies, flicking his lighter and lighting the cigarette. "You're the healthy one. You're the one Nova wants. You're a lucky SOB, so be grateful and take it."

He's right. I am lucky. Lucky to be standing here healthy and sober after everything I've done. Lucky to be alive with all the death in the world, when so many people aren't. Lucky I got to spend the time that I did with someone as amazing as Nova. And I make a silent vow right now to take my second chance and do something good with it. To change my life. Start doing things that matter. Stop being afraid and tell Nova I love her. Stop holding on to the past. It's time to start moving forward.

Nova

The funeral was harder than I thought. I cried more than I wanted. Delilah's mother was a wreck, barely able to walk into the church without falling down. My mom cried, too, and so did Quinton a few times. I hated seeing him so sad and I'd subtly tried to talk him out of coming, even though I wanted him there with me. But he came anyway and I think I might have fallen in love with him a little bit more because I knew how hard it had to be for him.

While I was there, I heard whispers among the people who attended the funeral. There were rumors of Delilah's having been beaten. Raped. Some even said that Delilah's mother was lying about her being shot and that she'd simply OD'd. But Quinton, Tristan, and I have our own theory. We saw how Dylan was with her—they knew he had a gun, which is what we told the police. Whether her death will ever be solved, I don't know. But regardless, it's a tragic story, one that I wish would never happen again.

After it's all over, I can feel that familiar burn inside me, the one that wants to do something instead of sitting around and watching all the bad that surrounds me. I realize I need a change. Need to do the things I want to do in life and stop worrying about the what-ifs. Life's too short to constantly be worrying about everything that could go wrong. And it's time to start chasing my dream of helping people instead of thinking about it so much. But I wonder if I can do it. Give up school. My friends. My band. My job. Quinton.

This is what I'm thinking about as Quinton walks up the path to my house, bundled in his coat, his nose and cheeks reddened from the cold. I've been sitting in the porch swing for about an hour, chilled to the bone, yet I can't seem to bring myself to go inside, frozen in place until I make the decision about which path I'm going to take in life.

"Hey," he says as he reaches the steps. "How are you doing?" He shakes his head as he trots up the stairs, removing his hands from his pockets. "Never mind. Stupid question."

"No, it's not a stupid question," I say as he takes a seat beside me and the swing sways beneath us. "I should talk about how I feel, and I feel like shit."

He places a hand on top of mine as he rocks the swing back and forth. "Tell me what I can do to make you feel better. I want to make you feel better."

"Build me a time machine," I say with a sigh. "So I can go back and pull her out of that house."

"Nova, you can't torture yourself over this," he says in an uneven voice, gripping my hand. "Trust me. It'll ruin you."

"I already feel ruined."

"But this isn't your fault."

"Yes, it is." I shake my head, sliding away from him. "You don't get it. I knew Dylan was wrong for her since they first started dating a few years ago. Knew that he probably was abusive to her, and I didn't do anything to stop it."

"You can't stop everything," he says. "Sometimes things just happen."

"Yeah, but it doesn't make it any easier not to feel guilty." I watch snowflakes swirl down from the sky and dance around us.

"I get that." His voice softens, but I feel him stiffen beside me. There's this long pause when it feels like maybe I should say something, but ultimately he's the one to start talking. "That night…the night of the accident…Lexi was sitting up in the window of the car." He pulls his hand away from my leg and folds his arms, staring straight ahead. "She was kind of crazy like that. Always pushing her limits and being way too adventurous."

I'm not sure what to say. I don't think he's ever talked about this aloud before and I fear that if I speak at all, I might ruin this moment for him as he lets out what's been trapped inside him for years.

"I tried to get her back in…that was actually what I was doing when the other car came around the corner." His brows furrow as if he's confused by the memory. "Whenever I think back to it, I just keep wishing I would have pulled over the car the moment she stuck her head out the window…but we were late and I didn't want to get us into trouble. But we never even made it home…or Ryder and Lexi didn't, anyway."

"Quinton, that's not your fault," I say, putting my arm around him and hugging him close to me. "What happened… that was just a tragic accident."

He looks at me, his eyes glistening with tears, so heart-breakingly beautiful it nearly knocks the wind out of me. "Accident or not, it's something that will always haunt me." He uncrosses his arms and turns to face me, placing his hand on my cheek. "But you make it easier to deal with it…and I want to be there for you like you've been there for me. It's important to me. So please tell me what I can do, because it's killing me seeing you like this."

Shutting my eyes, I rest my head on his shoulder. "I actually do have a favor to ask you," I say.

He wraps his arms around me, alleviating a small amount of pain. "You name it and it's yours."

Snowflakes whisk around us and sting my cheeks. "I need you to tell me you're going to be okay if I decide to take off for a little while."

"Where are you going?" he wonders, confused.

I open my eyes and look up at him. "Remember that project I told you about? The one my professor is working on? Well, I think I want to do it."

He's silent for a while, snowflakes spinning around us so thickly I can't see any of my surroundings but him. "I think you should do it," he finally says. "In fact, I'm going to make you do it."

I laugh for the first time in the last few days. "Oh yeah?"

He kisses my forehead, just a light graze of his lips. "Yeah, and you want to know why?" he asks, and I nod. "Because I think it'll make you happy, and if anyone deserves to be happy, it's you, Nova."

"But what about you and Tristan?" I ask. "Will you be okay?"

"I'll be fine," he says reassuringly. "Wilson has a shit-ton more houses for me to work on and he's even been trying to talk me into going on the road to help build."

I still worry. About him. About Tristan. About everyone in the world who is struggling. "But what about Tristan? I worry that he's going to get into trouble."

"Tristan will be fine," he says, but I detect a slight bit of sadness in his voice. But before I can say anything, he turns us around so we're facing my yard with his arm around my shoulder. "Maybe I'll talk him into joining Habitat for Humanity and hitting the road with me and Wilson. In fact, I think it might be good for him."

"You think he should drop out of school?"

He shrugs. "I don't know…but it's an option, right? To keep him busy and out of trouble."

I want to tell him that it's a great idea. I want to believe that everything will be okay. That we'll go our separate ways and everything will work out in the long run. But I'd be naïve to think that, no matter what, everything will turn out perfect. All I can do is hope and start living my life.

Epilogue

Six months later . . .

Nova

I'm nervous as hell. Not because in just a little bit I'll be watching the documentary I helped out on for four months straight, but because I'll be seeing Quinton for the first time in six months.

It's not like we haven't talked to each other. In fact, we probably talk more than most couples. At least three times a day every day on the phone, plus we text five to six more times on top of that. Being away from him has seriously been hard, but in the end, I think it's been good for us both. Given us time to grow. Heal. Become our own people.

Quinton's helped build so many houses, I've lost track, and listening to him talk about it is really amazing. He always gets really excited, especially when he tells me about the family who's getting the house. He loves every second of it, just like I've loved every second of my journey. Professor McGell, or Dusty as I call him now, decided to put me in charge of the interviews we did with people. He said I had a knack for human compassion and for the most part I think he's right. Quinton completely agrees with him, too, but Quinton thinks highly of me no matter what I say or do, even when I think I'm being mean.

I'm hanging out in my hotel room in Idaho, my clothes scattered across the floor as I decide what to wear to the viewing of the film. I've actually seen it before, a few times, but the fact that it's going out to the world makes it feel brand-new and scary as heck.

I'm wrapped in a towel, my damp hair running down my back, when I hear a knock at the door. Grinning, I step over the pile of dresses I was deciding among and pad over to the door. I peer out the peephole and my grin expands as I open the door.

Quinton smiles back and then his honey-brown eyes widen as soon as he takes in the towel. "Wow, you're getting straight to the point. Aren't ya?"

I laugh, then grab his arm and yank him inside, kicking the door shut behind me. Then I turn around and take him in: his scruffy jaw, his short brown hair, his faded jeans and black T-shirt that look like they've seen a wash or two or twenty-five. He looks like a person who's worked hard, which is good because, he says, the harder he works the better he feels. So he must be feeling pretty damn good right now.

"You look amazing," he says after a minute or two goes

by of us just staring at each other. I've been worried that after six months apart, just talking on the phone, being together is going to be awkward.

I tuck a wet lock of hair behind my ear, chewing nervously on my bottom lip. "So do you . . . you look manly."

He snorts a laugh and then he's moving in to kiss me. "God, I've missed you," he says, and then his lips brush against mine.

It's not a quick kiss. Not at all. In fact, it goes on for so long, my lips are raw and swollen and my body is so hot it feels like it's melting. When we pull away, we're gasping for air, our bodies pressed so tightly against each other, I can feel his chest moving with each intake of breath. Somehow his hands have managed to slip underneath the towel and he's grasping my bare waist.

"I've missed you, too," I whisper, smiling as he leans in to kiss me again.

Then he takes my hand and steers me toward the bed, kicking the clothes out of the way as he sits us down. "As much as I've loved the last six months," he says, his hands wandering from my waist up my sides toward my chest, "I'm really glad it's over. I can't wait to spend time with you and get a break from Tristan and Wilson. As cool as they are, I'd much rather spend my free time with you."

"How is Tristan doing? With everything?" About a month after Quinton and I went our separate ways, he told me that Tristan had found out he had hepatitis C and was struggling with it. He actually relapsed and disappeared for about a week when they were staying in Nebraska. Wilson and Quinton ended up finding him camped out in a hotel room, high on meth. They got him cleaned up, though, and put him back to work, and Quinton's been assuring me that everything's been okay since then—that relapses happen often.

"He's good," he says. "He's actually been really into working long hours lately and doing nothing else."

"Is that good?"

"I think so," he says. "Although it would be nice if he took a break once in a while."

"Maybe I can help with that," I say. We've actually made plans. Not to move in together, although maybe technically that's how it's going to be, since we'll be on the road every waking hour with each other. I'm actually going with him for the next month to make my own documentary about Habitat for Humanity, starring him, Wilson, Tristan, and anyone else fascinating that I come across. "Help him find other things to do."

He's quiet for a moment and I worry that he's taken what I said the wrong way—that he thinks I want to spend extra time with Tristan. But then he smiles and says, "God, I'm so excited you're coming with me."

"Yeah, but the question is, can you deal with me all the time?" I ask in a playful tone. "Like every day—every waking hour."

"Of course, Nova like the car," he says with a wink. "And do you want to know why?"

314

I nod, putting my hands on his shoulders. "Of course."

He smiles. "Because I love you."

I smile back. Every time I hear him say it, it gets to me. Although the first time he said it, three months ago, I panicked and hung up on him. I knew I loved him, but was afraid to say it back, afraid to open my heart up to someone else like that, afraid I'd lose him, afraid I'd never be able to endure the pain of loss all over again. It took me five minutes to get my shit together and call him back.

"I love you, too," I say, putting my hand on his cheek and tracing his cheekbone with my thumb. "I really do."

"Good," he says, then he slants forward to kiss me again, his fingers finding the edge of the towel.

Even though it kills me, I place my hand on top of his and stop him. "Before we do . . . well, that." My cheeks heat and he laughs at me. It's amazing that no matter how many dirty phone conversations we've had, I still manage to get embarrassed every time I talk about things related to sex. "There's something I want to show you first."

He doesn't get angry like most guys probably would, after six months of no sex. Instead he looks concerned.

"Is everything okay?" he asks worriedly.

I nod quickly. "Of course, I just want to show you the video first, before everyone else sees it . . . the dedication especially." It's actually really important to me that he see the film first.

He seems a little anxious about it, but I don't blame him.

The topics of loss, guilt, and pain are captured in every clip. While I was putting it together, it triggered a lot in me, but that wasn't necessarily a bad thing. Just emotional.

But he says, "Of course." Then he sits back on the bed while I get up and grab my computer from the desk. I get it booted up and the video ready, before I go back to the bed and sit down by him. "Are you ready?" I ask, with my fingers hovering over the trackpad. He nods and I lie down beside him and put the laptop between us, clicking play.

The music comes on, but I'm not watching the screen. I'm watching him watch the screen. His jaw is set tight, his eyes a little wide, and his hands are balled into fists as if he's half expecting something horrible to be on there. So I reach over and take his hand, then turn my attention to the screen as it goes black and the dedication pops up.

"For everyone who suffered loss and learned how to live again. Know that you're not alone."

I'm not even sure who starts crying first. It's such a small thing. Two sentences, but they pretty much sum up the helplessness and feeling of being alone that we both felt for years. The pain of it broke us both, shattered us, and will forever scar us, but that doesn't mean that we can't heal. Yeah, we're not the same people, but we're still alive and we're not alone anymore.

I want to ask Quinton what he thinks when his grip on my hand tightens. I clutch him and then suddenly he's pulling me closer to him, needing me to be beside him.

"What do you think?" I ask as his arms fasten tightly around me, our bodies aligned together.

He presses a kiss to my forehead, each of my cheeks, and then ultimately my lips. When he leans away, his tearstained eyes search mine. "I think it's perfect."

Nova Reed used to have dreams—of becoming a famous drummer, of marrying her true love. But all of that was taken away in an instant. Now every day blends into the next... until she meets Quinton Carter.

Please see the next page for a preview of

Breaking Nova

Chapter One

Fifteen months later...

May 19, Day 1 of Summer Break

Nova

I have the web camera set up perfectly angled straight at my face. The green light on the screen is flickering insanely, like it can't wait for me to start recording. But I'm not sure what I'll say or what the point of all this is, other than my film professor suggested it.

He'd actually suggested to the entire class—and probably all of his classes—telling us that if we really wanted to get into filming, we should practice over the summer, even if we weren't enrolled in any summer classes. He said, "A true videographer loves looking at the world through an alternative eye, and he loves to record how he sees things in a different light." He was quoting straight out of a textbook, like most of my professors do, but for some reason something about what he said struck a nerve.

Maybe it was because of the video Landon made right before the last seconds of his life. I've never actually watched his video, though. I never really wanted to and I can't, anyway. I'm too afraid of what I'll see or what I won't see. Or maybe it's because seeing him like that means finally accepting that he's gone. Forever.

I originally signed up for the film class because I waited too long to enroll for classes and I needed one more elective. I'm a general major and don't really have a determined interest path, and the only classes that weren't full were Intro to Video Design or Intro to Theater. At least with the video class I'd be behind a lens instead of standing up in front of everyone where they could strip me down and evaluate me. With video, I get to do the evaluating. Turns out, though, that I liked the class, and I found out that there's something fascinating about seeing the world through a lens, like I could be looking at it from anyone's point of view and maybe see things at a different angle, like Landon did during his last few moments alive. So I decided that I would try to make some videos this summer, to get some insight on myself, Landon, and maybe life.

I turn on "Jesus Christ" by Brand New and let it play in the background. I shove the stack of psychology books off the computer chair and onto the floor, clearing off a place for me to sit. I've been collecting the books for the last year, trying to learn about the human psyche—Landon's psyche—but books hold just words on pages, not thoughts in *his* head.

I sit down on the swivel chair and clear my throat. I have no makeup on. The sun is descending behind the mountains, but I refuse to turn the bedroom light on. Without the light the screen is dark, and I look like a shadow on a backdrop. But it's perfect. Just how I want it. I tap the cursor and the green light shifts to red. I open my mouth, ready to speak, but then I freeze up. I've never been one for being on camera or in pictures. I'd liked being behind the scenes, and now I'm purposely throwing myself into the spotlight.

"People say that time heals all wounds, and maybe they're right." I keep my eyes on the computer screen, watching my lips move. "But what if the wounds don't heal correctly, like when cuts leave behind nasty scars, or when broken bones mend together, but aren't as smooth anymore?" I glance at my arm, my brows furrowing as I touch a scar with my fingertip. "Does it mean they're really healed? Or is it that the body did what it could to fix what broke…" I trail off, counting backward from ten, gathering my thoughts. "But what exactly broke…with me…with him…I'm not sure, but it feels like I need to find out…somehow…about him…about myself…but how the fuck do I find out about him when the only person that truly knew what was real is…gone?" I blink and then click the screen off, and it goes black.

❧

May 27, Day 9 of Summer Break

I started this ritual when I got to college. I wake up and count the seconds it takes for the sun to rise over the hill. It's my way of preparing for another day I don't want to prepare for, knowing that it's another day to add to my list of days I've lived without Landon.

This morning worked a little differently, though. I'm home for my first summer break of college, and instead of the hills that surround Idaho, the sun advances over the immense Wyoming mountains that enclose Maple Grove, the small town I grew up in. The change makes it difficult to get out of bed, because it's unfamiliar and breaks the routine I set up over the last eight months. And that routine was what kept me intact. Before it, I was a mess, unstable, out of control. I had no control. And I need control, otherwise I end up on the bathroom floor with a razor in my hand with the need to understand why he did it—what pushed him to that point. But the only way to do that is to make my veins run dry, and it turned out that I didn't have it in me. I was too weak, or maybe it was too strong. I honestly don't know anymore, what's considered weak and what's considered strong. What's right and what's wrong. Who I was and who I should be.

I've been home for a week, and my mom and stepfather are watching me like hawks, like they expect me to break down again, after almost a year. But I'm in control now. *In control.*

After I get out of bed and take a shower, I sit for exactly five minutes in front of my computer, staring at the file folder that holds the video clip Landon made before he died. I always give myself five minutes to look at it, not because I'm planning on opening it, but because it recorded his last few minutes, captured him, his thoughts, his words, his face. It feels like the last piece of him that I have left. I wonder if one day, somehow, I'll finally be able to open it. But at this moment, in the state of mind I'm stuck in, it just doesn't seem possible. Not much does.

Once the five minutes are over, I put on my swimsuit, then pull on a floral sundress over it and strap some leather bands onto my wrists. Then I pull the curtains shut, so Landon's house will be out of sight and out of mind, before heading back to my computer desk to record a short clip.

I click Record and stare at the screen as I take a few collected breaths. "So I was thinking about my last recording—my first—and I was trying to figure out what the point of this is—or if there even had to be a point." I rest my arms on the desk and lean closer to the screen, assessing my blue eyes. "I guess if there is a point, it would be for me to discover something. About myself or maybe about...him, because it feels like there's still so much stuff I'm missing...so many unanswered questions and all the lack of answers leaves me feeling lost, not just about why the hell he did it, but about what kind of person I am that he could leave so easily...Who was I then? Who am I now? I really don't know...But maybe when I look back and watch these one day far, far down the road, I'll realize what I really think about life and I'll finally get some answers to what leaves me confused every single day, because right now I'm about as lost as a damn bottle floating in gross, murky water."

I pause, contemplating as I tap my fingers on the desk. "Or maybe I'll be able to backtrack through my thoughts and figure out why he did it." I inhale and then exhale loudly as my pulse begins to thrash. "And if you're not me and you're watching these, then you're probably wondering who *he* is, but I'm not sure if I'm ready to say his name yet. Hopefully I'll get there. One day—someday, but who knows…maybe I'll always be as clueless and as lost as I am now."

I leave it at that and turn the computer off, wondering how long I'm going to continue this pointless charade, this time filler, because right now that's how it feels. I shove the chair away and head out of my room. It takes fifteen steps to reach the end of the hall, then another ten to get me to the table. They're each taken at a consistent pace and with even lengths. If I were filming right now, my steps would be smooth and perfect, steady as a rock.

"Good morning, my beautiful girl," my mother singsongs as she whisks around the kitchen, moving from the stove to the fridge, then to the cupboard. She's making cookies, and the air smells like cinnamon and nutmeg, and it reminds me of my childhood when my dad and I would sit at the table, waiting to stuff our mouths with sugar. But he's not here anymore and instead Daniel, my stepfather, is sitting at the table. He's not waiting for the cookies. In fact he hates sugar and loves healthy food, mostly eating stuff that looks like rabbit food.

"Good morning, Nova. It's so good to have you back." He has on a suit and tie, and he's drinking grapefruit juice and eating dry toast. They've been married for three years, and he's not a bad guy. He's always taken care of my mom and me, but he's very plain, orderly, and somewhat boring. He could never replace my dad's spontaneous, adventurous, down-to-earth personality.

I plop down in the chair and rest my arms on the kitchen table. "Good morning."

My mom takes a bowl out of the cupboard and turns to me with a worried look on her face. "Nova, sweetie, I want to make sure you're okay... with being home. We can get you into therapy here, if you need it, and you're still taking your medication, right?"

"Yes, Mom, I'm still taking my medication," I reply with a sigh and lower my head onto my arms and shut my eyes. I've been on antianxiety medication for a while now. I'm not sure if it really does anything or not, but the therapist prescribed it to me so I take it. "I take them every morning, but I stopped going to therapy back in December, because it doesn't do anything but waste time." Because no matter what, they always want me to talk about what I saw that morning—what I did and why I did it—and I can't even think about it, let alone talk about it.

"Yeah, I know, honey, but things are different when you're here," she says quietly.

I remember the hell I put her through before I left. The lack of sleep, the crying... cutting my wrist open. But that's in the past now. I don't cry as much, and my wrist has healed.

"I'm fine, Mom." I open my eyes, sit back up, and over-lap my fingers in front of me. "So please, pretty please, with a cherry on top and icing and candy corn, would you please stop asking?"

"You sound just like your father...everything had to be referenced to sugar," she remarks with a frown as she sets the bowl down on the counter. In a lot of ways she looks like me: long brown hair, a thin frame, and a sprinkle of freckles on her nose. But her blue eyes are a lot brighter than mine, to the point where they almost sparkle. "Honey, I know you keep saying that you're fine, but you look so sad...and I know you were doing okay at school, but you're back here now, and everything that happened is right across the street." She opens a drawer and selects a large wooden spoon, before bumping the drawer shut with her hip. "I just don't want the memories to get to you now that you're home and so close to... everything."

I stare at my reflection in the stainless-steel microwave. It's not the clearest. In fact, my face looks a little distorted and warped, like I'm looking into a funhouse mirror, my own face nearly a stranger. But if I tilt sideways just a little, I almost look normal, like my old self. "I'm fine," I repeat, observing how blank my expression looks when I say it. "Memories are just memories." Really, it doesn't matter what they are, because I can't see the parts that I know will rip my heart back open: the last few steps leading up to Landon's finality and the soundless moments afterward, before I cracked apart. I worked hard to

328

stitch my heart back up after it was torn open, even if I didn't do it neatly.

"Nova." She sighs as she starts mixing the cookie batter. "You can't just try to forget without dealing with it first. It's unhealthy."

"Forgetting *is* dealing with it." I grab an apple from a basket on the table, no longer wanting to talk about it because it's in the past, where it belongs.

"Nova, honey," she says sadly. She's always tried to get me to talk about that day. But what she doesn't get is that I can't remember, even if I really tried, which I never will. It's like my brain's developed its own brain and it won't allow those thoughts out, because once they're out, they're real. And I don't want them to be real—I don't want to remember *him* like that. Or me.

I push up from the chair, cutting her off. "I think I'm going to hang out next to the pool today, and Delilah will probably be over in a bit."

"If that's what you want." My mom smiles halfheartedly at me, wanting to say more, but fearing what it'll do to me. I don't blame her, either. She's the one who found me on the bathroom floor, but she thinks it's more than it was. I was just trying to find out what he felt like—what was going on inside of him when he decided to go through with it.

I nod, grab a can of soda out of the fridge, and give her a hug before I head for the sliding glass door. "That's what I want."

She swallows hard, looking like she might cry because she thinks she's lost her daughter. "Well, if you need me, I'm here." She turns back to her bowl.

She's been saying that to me since I was thirteen, ever since I watched my dad die. I've never taken her up on the offer, even though we've always had a good relationship. Talking about death with her—at all—doesn't work for me. At this point in my life, I couldn't talk to her about it even if I wanted to. I have my silence now, which is my healing, my escape, my sanctuary. Without it, I'd hear the noises of that morning, see the bleeding images, and feel the crushing pain connected to them. If I saw them, then I'd finally have to accept that Landon's gone.

∼

I don't like unknown places. They make me anxious and I have trouble thinking—breathing. One of the first therapists I saw diagnosed me with obsessive-compulsive disorder. I'm not sure if he was right, though, because he moved out of town not too long after. I was left with a therapist in training, so to speak, and he decided that I was just depressed and had anxiety, hence the antianxiety medication for the last year and three months.

The unfamiliarity of the backyard disrupts my counting, and it takes me forever to get to the pool. By the time I arrive at the lawn chair, I know how many steps it took me to get here, how many seconds it took me to sit down, and how many more seconds it took for Delilah to arrive and then for her to take a seat beside me. I know how many rocks are on the path leading to the porch—twenty-two—how many branches are on the tree shielding the sunlight from us—seventy-eight. The only thing I don't know is how many seconds, hours, years, decades, it will take before I can let go of the goddamn self-induced numbness. Until then I'll count, focus on numbers instead of the feelings always floating inside me, the ones linked to images immersed just beneath the surface.

Delilah and I lie in lawn chairs in the middle of my back-yard with the pool behind us and the sun bearing down on us as we tan in our swimsuits. She's been my best friend for the past year or so. Our sudden friendship was strange, because we'd gone to high school together but never really talked. She and I were in different social circles and I had Landon. But after it happened…after he died…I had no one, and the last few weeks of high school were torture. Then I met her, and she was nice and she didn't look at me like I was about to shatter. We hit it off, and honestly, I have no idea what I'd do without her now. She's been there for me, she shows me how to have fun, and she reminds me that life still exists in the world, even if it's brief.

"Good God, has it always been this hot here?" Delilah fans her face with her hand as she yawns. "I remember it being colder."

"I think so." I pick up a cup of iced tea on the table between us and prop up on my elbow to take a sip. "We could go in," I suggest, setting my glass down. I turn it in a circle until it's perfectly in place on the condensation ring it left behind, and then I wipe the moisture from my lips with the back of my hand and rest my head back against the chair. "We do have air-conditioning."

Delilah laughs sardonically as she reaches for the sparkly pink flask in her bag. "Yeah, right. Are you kidding me?" She pauses, examining her fiery red nails, then unscrews the lid off the flask. "No offense. I didn't mean for that to sound rude, but your mom and dad are a little overwhelming." She takes a swig from the flask and holds it out in my direction.

"Stepdad," I correct absentmindedly. I wrap my lips around the top of the flask and take a tiny swallow, then hand it back to her and close my eyes. "And they're just lonely. I'm the only child and I've been gone for almost a year."

She laughs again, but it's breezier than before. "They're seriously the most overbearing parents I know. They call you every day at school and text you a thousand times." She puts the flask back into her bag.

"They just worry about me." They didn't used to. My mom was really carefree before my dad died, and then she got concerned about how his death and seeing it affected me. Then Landon died, and now all she does is constantly worry.

"*I* worry about you, too," Delilah mumbles. She waits for me to say something, but I don't—I can't. Delilah knows about what happened with Landon, but we never *really* talk about what I saw. And that's one of the things I like about her—that she doesn't ask questions.

One ... two ... three ... four ... five ... breathe ... six ... seven ... eight ... breathe ... Balling my hands into fists, I fight to calm myself down, but the darkness is ascending inside me, and it will take me over if I let it and drag me down into the memory I won't remember; my last memory of Landon.

"I have a brilliant idea," she says as she interrupts my counting. "We could go check out Dylan and Tristan's new place."

My eyes open and I slant my head to the side. My hands are on my stomach, and I can feel my pulse beating through my fingertips, inconsistent. Tracking the beats is difficult, but I try anyway. "You want to go see your ex-boyfriend's place. *Seriously?*"

Swinging her legs over the edge of the chair, Delilah sits up and slips her sunglasses up to the top of her head. "What? I'm totally curious what he ended up like." She presses her fingertips to the corners of her eyes, plucking out gobs of kohl eyeliner.

"Yeah, but isn't it kind of weird to show up randomly after not talking to him in, like, forever, especially after how bad your guys' breakup was," I say. "I mean, if Tristan hadn't stepped in, you would have probably hit Dylan."

"Yeah, probably, but that's all in the past." She chews on her thumbnail and gives me a guilt-ridden look as she smears the tanning-spray grease off her bare stomach. "Besides, that's not technically accurate. We kind of talked yesterday."

Frowning, I sit up and refasten the elastic around my long, wavy brown hair, securing it in a ponytail. "Are you serious?"

I ask, and when she doesn't respond, I add, "Nine months ago, when he cheated on you, you swore up and down that you'd never talk to that"—I make air quotes—"'fucking, lying, cheating bastard' again. In fact, if I remember right, it was the main reason you decided to go to college with me—because you needed a break."

"Did I say that really?" She feigns forgetfulness as she taps her finger on her chin. "Well, like everything else in my life, I've decided to have a change of heart." She reaches for the tanning spray on the table between us. "And besides, I did need a break, not just from him, but from my mom and this town, but now we're back and I figure I might as well have some fun while I'm here. College wore me out."

Delilah is the most indecisive person I've ever met. During our freshman year, she changed majors three times, dyed her hair from red, to black, then back to red again, and went through about half a dozen boyfriends. I secretly love it, despite how much I pretend that I don't. It was what kind of drew me to her; her uncaring, nonchalant attitude, and the way she could forget things in the snap of a finger. I wish I could be the same way sometimes, and if I hang around her a lot, there are a few moments when I can get my mind on the same carefree level as hers.

"What have you two been talking about?" I wonder, plucking a piece of grass off my leg. "And please don't tell me it's getting back together, because I don't want to see you get crushed like that again."

Her smile shines as she tucks strands of her red hair behind her heavily studded ears, then she removes the lid from the tanning spray. "What is with you and Dylan? He's always put you on edge."

"Because he's sketchy. *And* he cheated on you."

"He's not sketchy...he's mysterious. And he was drunk when he cheated."

"Delilah, you deserve better than that."

She narrows her eyes at me as she spritzes her legs with tanning spray. "I'm not better than him, Nova. I've done supercrappy things, hurt people. I've made mistakes—we all have."

I stab my nails into the palms of my hands, thinking of all the mistakes I made and their consequences. "Yes, you are better. All he's ever done is cheat on you and deal drugs."

She slaps her hand on her knee. "Hey, he doesn't deal anymore. He stopped dealing a year ago." She clicks the cap back onto the tanning spray and tosses it into her bag.

I sigh, push my sunglasses up over my head, and massage my temples. "So what has he been up to for a year?" I lower my hands and blink against the sunlight.

She shrugs, and then her lips expand to a grin as she grabs my hand and stands, tugging me to my feet. "How about we go change out of our swimsuits, head over to his place, and find out?" When I open my mouth to protest, she adds, "It'd be a good distraction for the day."

"I'm not really looking for a distraction, though."

"Well, then you could go over and see Tristan." She bites back an amused smirk. "Maybe reheat things."

I glare at her. "We hooked up one time and that's because I was drunk and…" *Vulnerable.* I'd actually been really drunk, and my thoughts had been all over the place because of an unexpected visit from Landon's parents that morning. They'd wanted to give me some of his sketchings, which they'd found in a trunk upstairs—sketchings of me. I'd barely been able to take them without crying, and then I'd run off, looking to get drunk and forget about the drawings, Landon, and the pain of him leaving. Tristan, Dylan's best friend—and roommate—was the first guy I came across after way, way too many Coronas and shots. I started making out with him without even saying hello.

He was the first guy I'd made out with since Landon, and I spent the entire night afterward crying and rocking on the bathroom floor, counting the cracks in the tile and trying to get myself to calm down and stop feeling guilty for kissing someone else, because Landon was gone and he took a part of me with him—at least that was what it feels like. What's left of me is a hollow shell full of denial and tangled with confusion. I have no idea who I am anymore. I really don't. And I'm not sure if I want to know or not.

"Oh come on, Nova." She releases my hand and claps her hands in front of her. "Please, can we just go and try to have some fun?"

I sigh, defeated, and nod, knowing that the true feelings of why I don't want to go over there lie more in the fact that I hate new places than anything else. Unfamiliar situations put me on edge, because I hate the unknown. It reminds me just how much the unknown controls everything, and my counting can sometimes get a little out of hand. But I don't want to argue anymore with Delilah, either, because then my anxiety will get me worked up and the counting will, too. Either way, I know I'm going to have a head full of numbers. At least if I go with Delilah, then I can keep an eye on her and maybe she'll end up happy. And really, that's all I can ask for. For everyone to be happy. But as I all too painfully know, you can't force someone to be happy, no matter how much you wish you could.

Chapter Two

Quinton

I ask myself the same question every day: *Why me? Why did I survive?* And every day I get the same response: *I don't know.* Deep down, I know there really isn't an answer, yet I keep asking the same question, hoping that maybe one day someone will give me a hand and give me a clear answer. But my head is always foggy, and answers always come to me in harsh, jagged responses: regardless of why I survived, it was my fault, and I should be the one buried under the ground, locked in a box, below a marked stone. Two people died because of me that day. Two people I cared about. And even though the guy I barely know miraculously lived, he could have very easily died, and his death would have been my fault, too.

All my fault.

"Thanks for letting me stay here, man," I say for the thousandth time. I can tell my cousin Tristan is getting a little irritated by how many times I've said it, but I can't seem to stop. I'm sure it wasn't easy for him to help out the most hated member of our family. The one who destroyed lives and split apart a family. But I needed to leave, despite how much I didn't want to; something that became clear when my dad finally spoke to me after over a year of near silence.

"I think it's time for you to move out," he'd said, eyeing my lazy ass sprawled out on the bed as music played in the background. I was sketching something that looked like an owl in a tree, but my vision was a little blurred, so I couldn't quite tell for sure. "You're nineteen years old and getting too old to live at home."

I was high out of my mind, and I had a hard time focusing on anything except how slow his lips were moving. "Okay."

He studied me from the doorway and I could tell he was disappointed in what he saw. I was no longer his son, but a washed-up druggie who lay around all day wasting his life, ruining everything he'd worked so hard to achieve. All that time spent in high school, getting good grades, winning art fairs, working hard to get scholarships, was exchanged for a new goal: getting high. He didn't try to understand why I needed drugs—that without them, I'd be worse off—and I never wanted him to. It wasn't like we'd had a good relationship before the accident. My mom had died in childbirth, and even though he never said it, I sometimes wonder if he blamed me for killing her when she brought me into this world.

Finally, he'd left, and the conversation was over. The next morning, when my head had cleared a little, I realized I actually had to find a place to live in order to move out. I didn't have a job at the moment, due to the fact I failed a random drug test at the last job, and I had a bad track record of getting fired. Not knowing what else to do, I'd called up Tristan. We used to be friends when we were younger... before everything happened... before I killed Ryder, his sister. I felt like a dick for calling him, but I remembered him being nice, and he even talked to me after the funeral, even though his parents no longer would. He seemed reluctant, but he agreed, and a couple of days later I packed up my shit, bought a ticket, and headed for my temporary new home.

"Dude, for the millionth time, you're good, so stop thanking me." Tristan picks up the last box out of the trunk of his car.

"Are you sure, though?" I ask again, because it never really seems like I can ask enough. "I mean, with me staying here, especially after... everything."

"I told you on the phone that I was." He shifts his weight, moving the box to his free arm, and then scratches the back of his neck uncomfortably. "Look, I'm good, okay? You can stay here until you can get your feet on the ground or whatever... I'm not going to just let you live out on the streets. Ryder wouldn't have wanted that, either." He almost chokes on her name and then clears his throat a thousand times.

I'm not sure I agree with him. Ryder and I were never that close, but I'm not going to bring that up, considering things have already gotten really awkward and I've only been here for, like, five minutes.

"Yeah, but what about your parents?" I ask. His parents insist that the accident was my fault and that I should have been driving more safely. They told me that I ruined their family, killed their daughter.

"What about them?" His voice is a little tight.

"Won't they be pissed when they find out I'm living with you?"

He slams the trunk down. "How are they going to find out? They never talk to me. In fact they've pretty much disowned me and my lifestyle." I start to protest, but he cuts me off. "Look, you're good. They never stop by. I barely talk to them. So can you please just chill out and enjoy your new home?" He heads for the gate and I follow. "I do have to say, though, that it probably would have been better if you drove out here. Now you're stranded if you want to go anywhere."

"It's better that way." I adjust the handle of the bag over my shoulder and we walk toward a single-wide trailer. The siding is falling off, one of the windows is covered with a piece of plywood, and the lawn is nonexistent; instead there's a layer of gravel, then a fence, followed by more gravel. It's a total crack house, but that's okay. This is the kind of place where I belong, in a place no one wants to admit exists, just like they don't want to admit I exist.

"You know there's no bus here, right?" He steps onto the stairway, and it wobbles underneath his feet. "It's a freaking small-ass town."

"That's okay." I follow him with my thumb hitched under the handle of my bag. "I'll just walk everywhere."

He laughs, shifting the box to one arm so he can open the screen door. "Okay, if you say so." He steps inside the house, and I catch the screen door with my foot, grab the handle, and hold the door open as I maneuver my way inside.

The first thing I notice is the smell; smoky but with a seasoned kick to it that burns the back of my throat. It's familiar, and suddenly I feel right at home. My eyes sweep the room and I spot the joint burning in the ashtray on a cracked coffee table.

Tristan drops the box on the floor, steps over it, and strides up to the ashtray. "You good with this?" He picks up the joint and pinches it in between his fingers. "I can't remember if you're cool or not."

It's not really a question. It's more of a warning that I have to be cool with it if I'm going to live here. I let the handle of the bag slide down my arm and it falls to the floor. "I used to not be." I used to care about things—I used to think that doing the right thing would make me a good person. "But now I'm good."

His eyebrows knit at my vague answer and I reach for the joint. As soon as it's in my hand and the poisonous yet intoxicating smoke starts to snake up to my face, I instantly feel at ease again. The calm only amplifies as I put it to my lips and take a deep drag. I trap it in my chest, allowing the smoke to burn at the back of my throat, saturate my lungs, and singe my heart away. It's what I want—what I need—because I don't deserve anything more. I part my lips and release the smoke into the already tainted air, feeling lighter than I have since I got on that goddamn plane.

"Holy fucking shit, look what the dog drug in." Dylan, Tristan's roommate, walks out from behind a curtain at the back of the room, laughing, and a blond girl trails at his heels. I've only met him a couple of times during the few visits my dad and I made to Maple Grove to visit Tristan's parents. He looks different—rougher—a shaved head, multiple tattoos on his arms, and he used to be a lot stockier, but I'm guessing the weight loss is from the drugs.

"Hi, Quinton." The blonde waves her hand, then winds around Dylan and moves toward me. She keeps her arms tight to her side, pressing them against her chest, so her tits nearly pop out of her top. She seems to know me, yet I have no fucking clue who she is. "It's been a long time."

I'm racking my brain for some sort of memory that has her in it, but the weed has totally put a haze in my head, putting me right where I want to be—numb and obliviously stupid.

When she reaches me, she glides her palm up my chest and leans in, pressing her tits against me. "The last time I saw you, you were a scrawny twelve-year-old with braces and glasses, but good God you've changed." She traces a path from my chest to my stomach. "You're totally smoking hot now."

"Oh, it's Nikki, right?" I'm remembering something about her...a time when we were kids and the whole neighborhood decided to play baseball. But it's nothing more than a distant memory I'd rather forget. It reminds me too much of what was and what will never be again. "You've..." I scroll up her body, which I can pretty much see all of. "Changed."

She takes it as a compliment, even though I didn't mean it that way. "Thanks." She smiles and shimmies her hips. "I always try to look my best."

I still have the joint in my hand and I take another hit, trapping it in until my lungs feel like they're going to explode, then I free the smoke from my mouth and ash the joint on the already singed brown carpet. I hand it to Tristan, allowing the numbness to leach into my body. "Where should I put my stuff?" I ask him.

Dylan hitches a finger over at the hallway. "There's a room at the back of the hall. It's a little small, but it's got a bed and shit."

I collect my bag and move around Nikki, heading for the hall. "I'll take whatever's easiest on everyone."

Dylan nods his head at the hallway and then says to Nikki, "Nikki, why don't you show Quinton where the room is?"

"Absolutely." She flashes an exaggerated smile at me and snatches the joint from Tristan's hand. She wraps her lips around the end, inhales, and then lets it out. She hands it back to him and then saunters in front of me so I can watch her ass as she struts down the hallway.

"Are you two dating?" I ask, glancing back and forth between Nikki and Dylan.

Nikki rolls her eyes. "Um, no."

Dylan departs for the small, cluttered kitchen in the corner of the house. "I don't really date," he points out with a nonchalant shrug as he stuffs his hands in the pockets of his jeans. "Besides, I have an old girlfriend of mine coming over tonight."

"Delilah?" Tristan asks as he flops down on the couch, and Dylan nods. "Is Nova back, too? Is she coming over with her?"

"Nova?" I question. "Is that like her car?"

Tristan shakes his head and laughs. "No, it's a girl, you dipshit."

"Interesting name," I say, curious what a girl who's named after my favorite car would be like, but it doesn't really matter. None of it does. I'll never date again, never feel for anyone.

"Would you get over her?" Dylan scoops up a plastic cup that's by the kitchen sink and throws it at Tristan, who ducks as it zips above his head. "You made out with her one time, and she was fucking trashed."

"So what?" Tristan retorts as he leans over the arm of the chair to pick up the cup. When he sits up, he throws the cup back at Dylan, but it lands on the floor a few inches away from him. "You're still hung up on Delilah after eight months of her being gone, and I can still have a thing for Nova if I want to. And it's not really even a thing, so much as I'm curious about what she's like now after a year."

"You're such a fucking liar." Dylan kicks the cup across the

345

floor and jerks the fridge door open. "And besides, Nova's got more baggage than you can handle."

"You don't know how much I can handle," he mutters, staring down at the brownish orange carpet. He rubs his hand across his face and then blows out a breath, his gaze flicking up to me. There's a hint of anger transpiring in his eyes, directed toward me and what I represent, but beneath the anger there's also pain. Lots and lots of pain masked over by weed.

It's my cue to leave. I put some of Tristan's baggage there, since I'm the one solely responsible for the death of his sister. I follow Nikki down the hallway, feeling like shit again as my past catches up with me. But I focus on the few steps ahead of me, knowing what's going to happen when I reach the room. It's obvious what Nikki wants, and honestly, I need the distraction. Today's been a rough day, especially after my father dropped me off at the airport. I could tell he didn't want to be there, but I think he felt obligated because I'm his son.

"See you later," was all he said, and then he left me at the entrance doors.

I shouldn't have cared that he didn't give me a hug or anything, but I haven't been hugged in a year and sometimes I miss it, the connection, the contact, knowing that someone loves you.

"So the bed's supersoft." Nikki plops down on the twin bed and gives a little bounce, crossing her legs.

I drop the bag on the floor of the closet-sized room and

stand in front of her, staring down at the filthy mattress. "Oh yeah?"

She seductively grins at me. "Definitely." Then she reaches up and snatches the front of my shirt, tugging me down to her mouth.

Her lips are dry and taste like weed, but I close my eyes and kiss her back, shutting myself down as I lean over her and we collapse against the bed. I know it's wrong. Neither of us really gives a shit about the other. There's no meaning to it. It's as pointless as existing and equally as insignificant. But that's exactly what I deserve, and the moment that I do feel meaning—the moment I feel the slightest bit of contentment and happiness with another woman—is the moment I break my promise to Lexi.